Recent Titles by Sally Spencer from Severn House

Writing as Alan Rustage

BLACKSTONE AND THE GOLDEN EGG

BLACKSTONE AND THE GOLDEN EGG

Sally Spencer

writing as

Alan Rustage

This first world edition published in Great Britain 2004 by
SEVERN HOUSE PUBLISHERS LTD of
9–15 High Street, Sutton, Surrey SM1 1DF.
This first world edition published in the USA 2005 by
SEVERN HOUSE PUBLISHERS INC of
595 Madison Avenue, New York, N.Y. 10022.

British Library Cataloguing in Publication Data

Rustage, Alan, 1949-
   Blackstone and the golden egg
   1.   Blackstone, Sam (Fictitious character) - Fiction
   2.   Police - Great Britain - Fiction
   3.   Detective and mystery stories
   I.   Title II. Spencer, Sally, 1949-
   823.9'14 [F]

   ISBN 0-7278-6161-1

Typeset by Palimpsest Book Production Ltd.,
Polmont, Stirlingshire, Scotland.
Printed and bound in Great Britain by
MPG Books Ltd., Bodmin, Cornwall.

For Vicky, and baby Michael

Prologue

Central Russia – Late Summer 1899

Count Rachinsky's country estate was justly famed for its hunting and shooting, and the royal party had had a glorious and bloody day, in the course of which several score of feathered creatures had met the violent fate they had been bred solely to fulfil. The shoot had been followed by a twelve-course meal – relatively modest by Russian standards – and once that had been dispensed with, the company had ambled through to the smaller of the two ballrooms, where there had been more drinking and some dancing.

The Prince of Wales had enjoyed himself tremendously, but he was quite ready to retire to his bed by the time the party finally showed signs of breaking up in the early hours of the morning. He had been drinking himself, but he was not drunk – food, women and gambling rated much higher than alcohol on his scale of indulgences – and so those who were later told of what had happened were quite prepared to accept his account of events.

That account ran as follows: he had been asleep for some time when he heard a scuttling sound in the corner of the room. He had thought at first that it might be a rat, for however many servants his Russian hosts employed to keep their rodents down, this was the countryside, where vermin roamed free in the barns and outhouses. The intrusion of the furry alien annoyed the Prince, but did not alarm him, for – despite his increasing girth and shortness of wind – he still considered himself to be a manly man who could

1

well look after himself. Thus, instead of calling for the burly Russian peasant who had been deputed to stand guard outside his door, he turned his mind to what weapon he could use against the intruder.

There was his hairbrush – solid silver, a gift from his sister, the Dowager Empress of Germany – but it would be a pity to use such a magnificent piece of workmanship to douse the life of such a lowly creature as a rat.

There were his boots, but his valet would surely have taken them away, to shine them to perfection for the next morning's shoot.

What, then, could he employ for his violent purpose? Perhaps, on reflection, it would be best to call for the help of the burly muzhik on the other side of the door after all.

It was while he was still musing on the problem that he heard a slightly grating sound, which at first he found hard to place. Then, as if to shed light on the matter, an *actual* light appeared – or rather the *evidence* of light, since the naked flame itself was shielded from his eyes by the bulky frame which was bending over his dressing table.

Not a rat, then!

A man!

A man who had had the temerity to enter the royal bedchamber – to soil the royal possessions with his common touch.

It was outrage, rather than fear, which flooded through the Prince's corpulent frame, and it would have been outrage which was expressed through the royal mouth, had not a foul rag, smelling of some noxious chemical, been thrust down hard on the lower half of his face.

For several seconds he struggled against this further violation of his royal personage, then his brain gave in to the fumes and he fell into a troubled unconsciousness.

It seemed like only moments later – though in fact several hours had passed – that the Prince felt something damp being pressed against his forehead. With an effort, he opened his eyes. His vision was cloudy at first, but when it cleared he found himself looking up at the concerned face of his host, Count Rachinsky.

'Oh, Your Royal Highness,' wailed the Count, his voice thick with anguish and concern. 'What can I say? To think that this should have happened to you under my roof. The shame of it! The humiliation!'

Even in his confused state, it seemed to the Prince of Wales that the Count was more concerned with soliciting sympathy for himself than in bestowing it on his guest.

'What happened?' he demanded roughly.

'A terrible thing!' the Count said, stating the obvious. 'At some time in the night the muzhik I left to guard you must have fallen asleep. I would order the man to be severely punished, but unfortunately, while he was in dereliction of his duty, an intruder seems to have cut his throat.'

'*Two* intruders!' said the Prince.

'Two?'

Yes, it had to be two, the Prince was sure of that. There had been the one at the other side of the room who had struck the match, and the second who had stuffed the foul rag over his royal mouth.

'I swear to you, on my honour as a gentleman, that I will find them,' the Count promised. 'And that once I do have them in my power, their lives will not be worth a kopek.' He paused for a moment. 'But what did these intruders do to you, Your Royal Highness? Did they harm you?' Another pause, even longer and more portentous this time. 'Do you think that these villains might perhaps have stolen something?'

'One of them was over by my dressing table,' the Prince said.

And though the words had left his mouth, they also stayed inside his head, echoing around in every corner of his brain.

One of them was over by my dressing table! One of them was over by my dressing table!

'Oh God!' he moaned. 'Oh merciful God, no!'

Fresh alarm spread around the room.

'Look at him! He has gone so pale,' said an unidentified voice to the Prince's left.

'Is he having an attack, do you think?' asked a second concerned voice to his right.

'Your Royal Highness . . .' the Count said worriedly.

'They can't have taken it,' the Prince moaned.

'Taken what?'

'They . . . simply . . . *can't* . . . have . . . taken . . . it,' the Prince repeated, his voice sounding increasingly desperate.

'What is it that you think might be missing?' the Count asked. 'Is it something of particular value to you? Would you like me to check to see if it is still there?'

'No!' the Prince gasped, with what little calm and majesty he could summon at that particular moment.

'Are you sure?' the Count pressed. 'It would not take me a second.'

'*Please* do not look,' the Prince said, almost begging now. 'It's of no immediate importance. I will search myself, when I'm feeling a little stronger.'

One

The prison was quiet that early September morning, Inspector Sam Blackstone thought as he strode down the long stark corridor.

Unnaturally quiet.

Often, during the course of his career, he had walked these corridors and heard the moaning of prisoners wrapped up in their troubled sleep – a moaning *so* disturbed that it had managed to penetrate even the thick iron doors. Sometimes he had sensed the slight reverberation of tin plates being tapped against pipes, as the solitary prisoners had attempted – despite the severe punishments they knew they would suffer if they were caught at it – to communicate with their fellow inmates.

But not that day. That day, he had only the clicking of his own heels on the stone floor to keep him company and mark out his progress.

The silence did not surprise him. In this most desperate of desperate places, there was always an extra air of despondency on the morning of an execution, and though no one had told any of those incarcerated that such thing was about to happen, they knew. They *always* knew.

Blackstone reached the condemned cell, and tapped on the door. The spy-hole cover slid back, then the door itself creaked reluctantly open on its heavy hinges to admit him.

There were three men in the cell – two warders and the condemned man. The prisoner, Jappee Sloane, had been sitting on his bed, but as Blackstone entered the cell he stood up.

Alarm crossed the two warders' faces. Then they relaxed.

The condemned man was not seeking trouble, they realized. He wanted to do no more than look the policeman squarely in the eye.

'I didn't think you'd come,' Sloane said.

Blackstone shrugged. 'Didn't you, Jappee? Why ever not? You invited me, didn't you?'

'Oh, I invited you, all right,' Sloane agreed. 'But I still didn't think you'd have the stomach for it.'

'The stomach for it?' Blackstone repeated. 'What can you mean by that?'

'I just didn't think you'd be brave enough to confront the man whose life you're taking from him,' the prisoner explained.

'If anybody's responsible for what's about to happen, it's you yourself, Jappee,' Blackstone said evenly. 'You're the one who poisoned your mother for her pitiful savings.'

'She was old. She wouldn't have lasted much longer anyway,' Sloane protested.

'Then it's a pity you couldn't have waited.'

'I never thought I'd be caught.'

'You'd be surprised how many men have gone to the gallows thinking just that.'

There was the sound of several fresh pairs of footsteps in the corridor – the priest, the governor, the warders who would lead Sloane to the gallows, and the hangman himself.

'Don't you feel no remorse about sending a young man like me to his death?' Sloane asked.

'None at all,' Blackstone answered him.

'I just wonder how you'll sleep tonight,' Sloane said belligerently.

'I'll tell you,' Blackstone replied. 'I shall sleep like a baby.'

The footsteps were drawing ever closer. The execution party entered the cell, led by the governor.

'Can Blackstone be there when I drop?' Sloane asked.

The request seemed to trouble the governor and he thought about it for quite a while. 'If that is both your wish and his, then Inspector Blackstone may be there,' he said finally.

'But it's *not* your wish, is it, Inspector?' Jappee Sloane asked tauntingly. 'Visiting me in the condemned cell is one thing. But standing there and watching me drop? Well, that's something else entirely. That's something you *haven't* got the stomach for!'

Blackstone smiled. 'You always did underestimate me, Jappee, lad,' he said. 'To tell you the truth, underestimating me was one of the main reasons you got caught.'

'I don't believe it,' Sloane said, as he felt the one consolation he had left in the remaining few minutes of his life – the one thing he had been holding on to – crumble beneath him.

'Don't believe what?' Blackstone asked. 'Don't believe that's why you got caught?'

'Don't believe you'll come to the gallows with me.'

Blackstone leant forward, so that his mouth was almost touching Sloane's ear. 'I'll tell you what, Jappee,' he said softly. 'If you think it'll make me suffer to watch you die, why not make it even worse for me?'

'What do you mean?'

'Why not ask if I can pull the pin that opens the trapdoor? Because I'll do it if they let me, Jappee! I'll do it with pleasure!'

It was five minutes after eight when the prison door opened and Blackstone stepped out into the street. Jappee Sloane would still be hanging from the gibbet, he thought as he stopped to light a cigarette. He'd still be hanging there because, though he would be deeply unconscious – and would have been from the moment he dropped – he wouldn't be *medically* dead for at least another fifteen minutes. That was the way that hanging worked.

Some said the rope was barbaric, but Blackstone didn't think so. He'd seen his own mother slowly die from overwork, when he'd been no more than a nipper, and there'd been nothing he could do about it. Jappee, on the other hand, had stood there and watched as his mother had writhed in an agony that he'd been the direct and only cause of. In

7

Blackstone's book, hanging had been a mild punishment for that.

It was as he took his first drag on the cigarette that Blackstone noticed the carriage. It was parked a little way up the road. It wasn't a truly splendid carriage, like those the aristocracy swanned around in, but it was affluent enough, and looked out of place in the shadow of this grim, forbidding prison.

He walked towards it, more out of curiosity than because it was on his route. As he drew level, the carriage door opened, and a voice from its interior said, 'Climb in, Inspector Blackstone.'

Blackstone recognized the man who had invited him into this unaccustomed splendour. His name was Sir Roderick Todd. He'd been some kind of diplomat for most of his career, but for the previous six months he had been Assistant Commissioner of the Metropolitan Police.

'You are probably wondering why I have arranged for us to meet in such clandestine circumstances, Mr Blackstone,' Sir Roderick said, after he'd bade the Inspector sit opposite him.

'Yes, sir,' Blackstone replied dutifully, because he knew that was what was expected of him, and while he had no scruples about antagonizing the Scotland Yard top brass when it proved to be necessary for his investigation, he was not quite reckless enough to do it purely for his own pleasure.

Sir Roderick tapped on the roof of the carriage with his cane, and the coachman urged the horses forward in a slow trot.

'I have within my gift a case which most officers in the Yard would give their right arms for,' Sir Roderick said portentously, as the coach began to leave the prison behind. 'And you, my dear Inspector, are the lucky blighter who will actually be given the assignment.'

The word 'blighter' did not fall easily from his lips, Blackstone noted. Nor should it have done. It was not at home in this man's natural vocabulary. Rather it was an effort on his part to speak the language of the lower ranks.

Blackstone coughed slightly. 'I am honoured, sir,' he said.

'I rather thought you might be.'

'But with the greatest possible respect, I feel I should point out that I already have six cases pending, and it would be very difficult – if not impossible – for me to handle any more.'

The Assistant Commissioner frowned. When a man offers a dog a bone, his expression seemed to say, he has the right to expect that the dog will wag its tail, rather than stick its arse in his face.

'So you consider yourself to be overworked, do you, Inspector?' he said coldly.

'We're all overworked, sir,' Blackstone replied.

'And why is that?' the Assistant Commissioner asked, as if suspecting that the Inspector was guilty of levelling unreasonable criticism against those in charge of the Metropolitan Police Force. 'Is it because there are not enough policemen available?'

'No, sir,' Blackstone replied. 'Not at all.'

'Well, then?'

'It's because there are too many criminals.'

Todd laughed, though he did not seem particularly amused. 'You may well be right about that, Inspector,' he said. 'But while all crime is a serious matter, some crimes are more serious than others. And this crime is just such a case. Shall I tell you about it?'

'There'd really be no point, sir,' Blackstone said stubbornly. 'As I've just told you, I've got my hands full at the moment.'

'And yet you can find the time to travel to this grim place and witness an execution.'

'That was different.'

'In what way?'

'I was challenged to come by the man who was due to die. I find it very hard to turn down that kind of challenge.'

9

'Then this is just the case for you. A real challenge. Would you like to hear the details?'

Blackstone suppressed a sigh.

'If I must, sir,' he said, just as the coach ran over a set of uneven cobblestones and rattled loudly.

'What was that you said?' the Assistant Commissioner demanded sharply, when the coach had stopped rocking.

'I said, why don't you give me the details, sir?' Blackstone lied.

The AC nodded. 'Very well. But before I go any further I must caution you that you will not discuss what I tell you with anyone else. And that includes that rather portly young man who is your assistant – Sergeant . . . Sergeant . . .?'

'Sergeant Patterson, sir,' Blackstone supplied.

'Just so. Sergeant Patterson,' the AC agreed.

'I tell Patterson everything,' Blackstone pointed out. 'He's my sounding board.'

'A mute needs no sounding board,' the AC said, and laughed, as if he had been incredibly witty. 'But to return to the matter in hand. His Royal Highness, the Prince of Wales, has recently paid an unofficial visit to Russia. Whilst there, he graciously consented to spend a few days on the country estate of a certain Count Rachinsky.'

Graciously consented to eat him out of house and home, from what I've heard, Blackstone thought.

But he wisely kept silent.

'On the third night of his visit to the estate,' Sir Roderick continued, 'an intruder broke into his room, and not only severely manhandled the Prince himself, but also stole a Fabergé golden egg.'

'A what?' Blackstone asked.

Sir Roderick looked at him in amazement. 'Have you never heard of the famous Fabergé eggs?'

'No, sir, I can't say that I have.'

'But everyone knows about them.'

'Perhaps in your social circle, sir,' Blackstone said, 'but certainly not in mine.'

10

The AC sighed, as if he were finding all this much harder work than he'd anticipated.

'Pierre Fabergé is a St Petersburg jeweller,' he explained patiently. 'There are those who say that he is the finest jeweller in the entire world. And his speciality – the pieces of work which have attracted the most acclaim – are his eggs.'

'Eggs?' Blackstone repeated.

'Eggs,' Sir Roderick confirmed. 'Eggs which are made of gold or platinum, and encrusted with precious stones.'

There were people slowly starving to death not more than a few dozen yards from this coach, Blackstone thought. And there were probably folk in exactly the same condition in St Petersburg. So what business did this Fabergé bloke have making golden eggs encrusted with diamonds? And what business did people like the Prince have buying them?

'So this egg was stolen somewhere in Russia,' he said. 'What's that got to do with us?'

'It was stolen from the man who will soon be your king,' the AC said severely.

Not *my* king, thought Blackstone, who had republican leanings. But aloud, all he said was, 'Even so, it's a matter for the Russian police.'

'The police in Russia are more concerned with watching political dissidents than they are with apprehending criminals,' Sir Roderick said. 'Besides, they are not to be told of the matter.'

'Why aren't they?' Blackstone asked, in a tone which came close to being a demand.

'The egg in question was a gift to the Prince from His Majesty, the Tsar of Russia,' Sir Roderick explained.

'And presumably, the man who stole it was a *subject* of the Tsar, so it's still a Russian matter,' Blackstone countered.

'That is not the way our masters in government see it, and thus it is not the way we see it, either,' Sir Roderick said. 'It has been agreed that we will investigate the robbery

11

ourselves. To which end, you and I will sail to St Petersburg tomorrow, and travel from there to the Count's estate in the country.'

Blackstone considered what to say next. Outright refusal was clearly out of the question, so he was going to have to be sneaky.

'I'm an orphan,' he said. 'I was brought up in Dr Barnardo's home for orphans.'

'I fail to see what that can possibly have to do with the matter in hand,' the AC said frostily.

'After I left the orphanage I joined the Army and served in the ranks,' Blackstone continued. 'And since then I've been a policeman.'

'We're both policemen, Inspector.'

'But not the same *kind* of policemen, sir. I don't deal with cabinet ministers and mandarins in the civil service. My work involves me with what people like to call the dregs of society.'

'I'm a patient man by nature,' Sir Roderick said, in a voice which revealed quite the contrary inclination. 'But even my patience has its limits. So tell me, Inspector, exactly what point are you trying to make?'

'I'm not used to dealing with members of the aristocracy,' Blackstone said. 'Not even members of the *Russian* aristocracy. You'd be far better off taking someone else with you.'

'Two years ago, you had a case which involved not just the aristocracy but the very monarchy itself,' Sir Roderick said.

'Oh, you've heard about that, have you?' Blackstone asked disappointedly. 'I thought it was supposed to be a secret.'

'It *is* a secret,' Sir Roderick agreed. 'But I am a member of the charmed circle which has been told about your exploits.' He laughed, genuinely amused this time. 'Don't look so down in the mouth, Inspector. Even if you do find it difficult to deal with your betters, there'll be no need for you to have much contact with them on this particular case.'

'Won't there?' Blackstone asked.

'Of course not! You'll be investigating a *robbery*, Inspector Blackstone. And when you do apprehend the criminal, you'll probably find that he differs very little – apart from his nationality – from the scum who you're normally forced to rub shoulders with.'

'In other words, you've already ruled out the idea that any of the other guests at the house could have been the robber,' Blackstone said.

'Naturally,' Sir Roderick replied, clearly astonished. 'The other guests will all have been people of quality. And people of quality do not act like common criminals.'

No, they don't, Blackstone thought. Sometimes they can act one hell of a lot worse.

But, again, he kept the thought to himself.

Two

The man by the window was going under the name of Sasha for the moment, though that would – almost inevitably – change soon. He was looking down on to Nevsky Prospekt, the widest and most fashionable street in all St Petersburg. He could see the carriages which carried the rich ladies single-mindedly intent on shopping for luxuries until exhaustion overtook them, and the trams which rattled along at some speed as they transported the city's army of bureaucrats from one ministry to another.

But there was more to the Prospekt than mere silk ribbons and red tape, he thought.

It was on this street that the imposing Kazan Cathedral and the Passage Theatre were located, both institutions serving – in their own ways – as soup kitchens for the perpetual hunger of the Russian soul.

And just beyond the Prospekt stood perhaps the most impressive building in an altogether impressive city. The Winter Palace!

Once a year, in early spring, the Tsar would emerge from this symbol of his imperial power in great state, and walk with due solemnity over the few hundred yards to the frozen River Neva.

Except it wasn't called the Neva on that special day, thought 'Sasha', who, in one of his many other incarnations, had witnessed the event himself. No, for that day alone, it was re-christened the River Jordan.

The Tsar would come to a halt at a hole cut in the ice, and accept a cup of Neva water – of *Jordan* water – from the Archbishop. And he would drink it! This man – on whose inadequate shoulders the mighty Russian Empire rested – would actually *drink* the polluted water of the Neva. It hadn't killed him yet – though it might well have done. It hadn't even seemed to make him ill. So perhaps there really was something behind the mumbo-jumbo after all.

'Sasha' brushed aside such fanciful thoughts. His job was not to examine the mystical foundations on which tsarism rested, but to attend to the nuts and bolts which truly held it in place – to concentrate on the immediate problems, rather than the larger sweep of history.

'Have all the necessary arrangements been made?' a voice behind him asked.

The speaker was a man approaching sixty. He was sitting in a chair near the door – he always liked to keep his escape route open, 'Sasha' thought – and was dressed in an expensive and elaborate uniform which identified him as an important official rather than a high-ranking soldier.

'Sasha' turned to face him. 'Yes, everything is in place, sir,' he said.

'You're absolutely sure about that? We would not like there to be any mistakes made.'

Always so precise, 'Sasha' thought. Always getting ready to apportion blame before anything had even gone wrong.

'The soldiers have their instructions, the officials have been informed of what is involved,' he said aloud.

'And the newspapers?'

'The newspapers have been warned that if they step out of line, then what will happen to them will make what they have suffered previously seem like a mushroom hunt in the woods.'

'And what about the arrangements from the London end?' asked the man in the chair, who was never satisfied.

'They, too, are well underway.'

'Who can we expect to be arriving?'

'Sir Roderick Todd, who knows something of the nature of Russia – though considerably less than he imagines he does – and an Inspector Blackstone, who knows nothing at all.'

'Are you happy with the choice?'

'I am as happy as I could be, given that the circumstances under which they will be used are not of my making. I have considerable confidence in one of our visitors, and some hopes for the other.'

'There are those who will not want these Englishmen to succeed,' warned the man in the chair.

'I know,' 'Sasha' said. And he was thinking: Well, of course there are those who will not want them to succeed! There are *hundreds* of such people. Perhaps even *thousands*!

'They – these people to whom I refer – may not be content merely to *hope* that Todd and Blackstone meet with failure,' the man in the chair said. 'They may take positive steps to *ensure* that failure.'

'I am aware that there are inherent dangers in the plan as it stands.'

'Good. It is always wisest to be aware of that.'

'And I have marshalled every resource available to me in an effort to ensure that nothing goes wrong.'

'There were other options to this plan of yours,' the man in the chair reminded him.

Yes, there were, 'Sasha' thought.

But they would all have failed! Because you do not – you *cannot* – adjust the workings of a sensitive and exquisite timepiece with a hammer. It calls for a much lighter touch

15

– for the employment of much more delicate instruments.

'Yes, indeed, there were *several* other options,' the man in the chair said, underlining his point. 'Options which were put forward by wiser and more experienced heads than yours. But you *would* have your own way. You would insist on using the Englishmen as your agents.'

'They are *not* my agents,' 'Sasha' said.

The man in the chair raised a heavy, sceptical eyebrow. 'Are they not?' he asked.

'At least, they do not *know* they are my agents,' 'Sasha' amended. 'They do not know that they are working for purposes other than their own.'

'They may find out,' the man in the chair cautioned.

'They *will* find out,' 'Sasha' countered. 'But by then it will be too late, because they will already have fulfilled their purpose.'

'And once they have "fulfilled their purpose", as you put it, will they be allowed to live?'

'Sasha' shrugged. 'Sir Roderick Todd is not without some influence in certain important English circles. It might prove difficult to explain why he had suddenly disappeared.'

'And the other man? The inspector?'

'He is part of what the English call "the poor bloody infantry". He has no influence of any sort.'

'So you *will* kill him?'

'Sasha' shrugged again. 'At this stage of the operation, who can say anything for certain?' he asked.

Three

Blackstone and Sir Roderick Todd had been met at the docks in St Petersburg by a closed carriage. With the blinds firmly down, they had been whisked across the city to a railway station, the name of which – since he did not read Russian script – Blackstone still did not know. Once there, they immediately boarded the train. They had now been on it – travelling south – for more than thirty-six hours.

It was, Sir Roderick informed the Inspector, the express train, a term which seemed to indicate – in Russian terms – that it was almost always quicker to take it than to walk. It stopped at countless small wooden stations, where it disgorged peasants in filthy sheepskin jackets, and minor officials in top hats and frock coats. It delivered parcels from St Petersburg – a place which was surely no more than a distant rumour to those who received the packages – and took on further bundles to be delivered to Kiev, which was the end of the line.

None of the frantic activity induced by the arrival of the train in these decaying hamlets – the pushing and shoving, the shouting and cursing, the chasing after escaped piglets and bartered transactions involving sacks of turnips and pieces of cloth – touched Blackstone and Sir Roderick Todd in any way. Even at points where the rest of the train was full to bursting, no peasant attempted to enter their carriage. And even the top-hatted bureaucrats would do no more than give it a look – a mixture of envy and resentment – before moving on.

In the carriage itself, there were two sleeping compartments – one for each of them – and a small, but well-equipped bathroom which they were expected to share. The rest of the space was taken up by a simple kitchen and an extensive lounge with space in it for two armchairs, a chaise longue, a dining table and a cast-iron, pot-bellied stove, the flue of which disappeared through the carriage roof. A blank-faced, tight-lipped attendant in a white braided jacket was always on hand to serve them drinks and cook their meals on a small spirit stove, but otherwise contrived to make himself invisible. For an orphanage boy like Blackstone, who had never left the East End of London before he joined the Army, travelling in this manner was something of a revelation.

Sir Roderick seemed perfectly at ease in his surroundings, though not with the company he was forced to keep. He had, in fact, said no more than a few dozen words since the two of them had set sail from Tilbury.

Perhaps it was snobbery, Blackstone thought – the gentleman policeman in all his finery not wishing to waste his time making small talk with the working-class policeman in thick boots and a second-hand suit. Perhaps, more charitably, it was awkwardness – Sir Roderick might *wish* to talk, but simply did not know what to *say* to someone so much further down the social ladder than he was.

But the Inspector did not actually think it was either of these things.

Sir Roderick was more guarded than aloof. It was as if he had a secret locked tightly away inside him, and he was afraid that if he opened his mouth too often it might just spill out. Thus he stayed hidden behind his opened newspaper, which he bought as they left England and by now must have read in its entirety at least a dozen times.

To occupy his own mind, Blackstone gazed at the countryside which moved past the open window at the speed of a lethargic snail.

So this was Russia, he told himself. This was the place where the only woman he had ever loved had once lived.

He had served in India, a country sixteen or seventeen times larger than the one in which he had been born. He had marched across Afghanistan – a state which could have conveniently hidden little England in the middle of one of its high mountain ranges. But nothing – *nothing* – had prepared him for this. Russia was vast. It was unremitting. As he gazed at the flat, unrelenting land which stretched from horizon to horizon, it seemed almost impossible to believe that there was space left on the planet for anything else. And though he remembered the mountains and valleys, hills and dales, they now all seemed to him like nothing more than a dream. For how could waterfalls and seashores truly exist, he asked himself, when everything was Russia – and Russia was everything?

The meal on the second evening included small black specks which looked to Blackstone like frog spawn, but were – according to Sir Roderick – the finest and most expensive Caspian Sea caviar. Blackstone took a tentative taste, then – deciding that the caviar's greatest quality was its outrageous cost – pushed the rest to the edge of his plate.

The meal over, the attendant withdrew to some other part of the train, and Sir Roderick folded his now-well-worn newspaper and announced that he intended to retire for the night.

Blackstone himself did not feel so much tired as drained from lack of activity, and instead of going to his sleeping compartment, he lit a fresh cigarette and gazed out of the window. Occasionally, he caught sight of the flickering lights of some hamlet that the train chugged past, but for most of the time there was nothing to see but the unrelenting darkness.

He was being kept in the dark himself, he thought. In fact, the more he considered the matter, the less he understood why he was in Russia at all. In the grand scale of things, the robbery of a golden egg seemed insignificant. And even if it were valuable – even if it were worth a king's ransom – there seemed little point in arriving at the scene so long after the robbery itself. Whoever had stolen the egg would probably be long gone by the time he and Todd got there, and even if the thief had remained, the egg itself would by then undoubtedly be in Antwerp or Paris – places where it was likely to fetch the best price.

An even bigger question was why, given that it had been decided someone *had* to be sent on this fruitless quest, he should be the one selected. There were other officers in Scotland Yard who knew more about jewels, and had at least a passing familiarity with Russia. There were other officers who were better at dealing with the aristocracy, too. In fact, he couldn't think, off-hand, of a single one who was worse at dealing with the upper classes than he was himself. There had been complaints about his antagonism towards his 'betters' – complaints which were on his record for all to see – and he rightly suspected that if he hadn't been such a good thief-taker, he would have been out of the Force long ago.

So why him? Why was he there at all?

The wheels of the train had kept up a constant rattling against the rails since the train had pulled out of the station in St Petersburg, but now Blackstone's sharp ears detected a new source of rattling – one which was even more insistent and perhaps more urgent.

He glanced across the carriage. Someone was at the door which connected it to the next carriage!

It could be the attendant, he told himself.

But there was no reason at all why *he* should have returned. Besides, the attendant would expect the door to be locked – since he was the one who had locked it when he left – and would have opened it with his key.

Blackstone's instincts beginning to override his thought processes – and his heart already beating at a gallop – he looked around the carriage for a suitable weapon. The heavy poker, resting against the stove, seemed his best bet – and, springing out of his chair, he had almost reached it when the lock broke, and the men burst into the room.

There were two of them, big brutes with heavy beards. One carried a vicious-looking club, and the other held a length of twine with the ends wrapped around his hands. Blackstone hoped they would both rush him at the same time, but instead – like the professionals they were – they separated, in order to come at him from different sides.

Blackstone thought of screaming for help, but he knew that screaming would take energy he could not afford to waste, and that even if his cries were heard, it would be all over by the time anyone else got there.

The two men were only a few feet from him now. The one with the cord made a lunge forward.

Blackstone was not fooled. The cord was for later, when he was less able to resist, and the job of weakening him was in the hands of the man with the club. He stepped to the side and lashed out with the fire poker at the spot he expected the club-swinger to be occupying a split second later.

His arm jarred as the poker struck muscle and bone. The club-swinger grunted, but there was no time to assess how badly he was hurt, because though the strangler had been planning to hold back, he would undoubtedly now be on the offensive.

Blackstone swivelled round to regain his original position, but he was too late. Far too late!

The strangler, having moved with astounding speed, was now behind him, and even as his mind was registering the fact, the Inspector felt the cord tightening around his neck.

The cord bit into his skin, and though Blackstone struggled he could sense that – already – there was not enough air getting through to his brain.

The poker had caught the man with the club on his arm, and instinct had made him drop his weapon, but now he was coming to terms with the pain, and it would not be long before he picked the club up again. And all the time, the pressure around Blackstone's throat was getting harder, his brain was screaming for relief, and he was getting black spots before his eyes.

He had, at the maximum, half a minute – and at the minimum a few seconds – to take some kind of counter-action. Despite the agony it cost him, he twisted round and pushed, so that the strangler's right hand was sandwiched between his head and the stove pipe.

The effect on the strangler was instantaneous. The Russian screamed – loudly and deeply.

For his part, Blackstone felt as if his head had been thrust into a furnace, but it would be even worse for the Russian, whose hand was being cooked.

The cord around his neck went suddenly slack, and Blackstone pulled away. The strangler was gazing down at his burnt hand in disbelief, but the club-wielder was ready for action again and, rather than stop to pick up his weapon, he lashed out with his leg and caught Blackstone a heavy blow on the knee.

The pain was indescribable, and though he knew it would be fatal to allow it to happen, Blackstone felt his leg buckle beneath him.

The moment he hit the floor he started to wriggle out of the way, which meant that the club-wielder's foot slammed into his chest, instead of its intended target, which was his head.

But even that was enough, he thought, as he felt the air rush from his lungs. Even a kick to the diaphragm was sufficient to put him out of action long enough for them to do what they wanted to do.

He braced himself for a fresh assault. Knowing that it was a pointless exercise. Knowing he was only prolonging his own agony, while only slightly delaying the inevitable.

The promised attack never came. Instead, the club-wielder grunted again, and slumped to the floor beside him.

Blackstone forced himself to look up. Two new men had entered the carriage. They were as big as his attackers, and had rags hiding the lower halves of their faces. One of these men, it became plain to him, had knocked the clubman out, while the other had dealt with the strangler, and now there were three men lying on the floor of the carriage.

One of his rescuers walked over to the side of carriage and opened the door which would let out on to the platform when the train was standing at the station. That task completed, he dragged the club-wielder over to it, and flung him out into the darkness. His companion did the same with the strangler. Then, still not having said a word, either to each other or to Blackstone, the two men exited through the broken door into the next carriage.

Blackstone, still gasping for air, lay where he was for perhaps another two minutes, then, slowly and painfully, dragged himself over to the chaise longue. He would rest for a short while, he promised himself, and then he would follow his rescuers and demand to know what was going on.

He was still thinking that when he fell into a deep and troubled sleep.

Four

Ker-clank . . . ker-clank . . . ker-clank . . .
For his first few semi-conscious moments, Blackstone tried to rationalize the mechanical noise that seemed to be entering his head through his right ear, which was pressing down on some sort of soft, yielding surface.

Ker-clank . . . ker-clank . . . ker-clank . . .

Wheels! Rails! Train! Russia! his brain informed him, delivering each thought in the same rhythm as the sound it was attempting to explain.

It was all coming back to him now. The murderous intruders. His rescuers. The ruthless and efficient dispatch of the former by the latter.

How long ago had that all been? Some considerable time, obviously, since the brightness – which managed to penetrate even his closed eyelids – told him it must be morning.

He opened his left eye cautiously, then closed it again, and opened his right. He was where he'd thought he'd be – lying on the chaise longue in a railway carriage somewhere in Central Russia.

Both eyes now open, he swung his legs off the seat and twisted his body round. It hurt – Jesus, it hurt! – but he supposed, given the circumstances, that it could have been a devil of a lot worse.

Still cautious, he turned slowly towards the carriage's kitchen area. The Russian in the braided white jacket was standing with his back to him, next to the steaming samovar.

'Any chance of a cup of tea?' Blackstone asked, noting as he spoke that though his voice came out as loud as he intended it to, there was a cracked and unnatural quality to it which he could have done without.

'Tea!' he repeated.

The Russian grunted a response. Perhaps he understood the words and perhaps he didn't – given his blank-faced approach to life it was difficult to tell – but he had clearly divined the intention, since he reached across with one of his slab-like hands and picked up a cup.

Blackstone looked around the carriage. Any number of things must have been disturbed during the course of the fight, but there was certainly no evidence of that now. Even the poker was back where it should have been.

He rose to his feet, walked tentatively over to the door which led through to the next carriage, and forced his eyes to focus on the lock. It had been smashed the night before, but now, apart from a few scratches on the woodwork, there was no evidence of that damage, either.

The attendant handed him his cup of tea, and Blackstone took it over to one of the armchairs. He took a sip or two of the hot, sweet liquid and started to feel better. He would be bruised, he was sure of that, but as far as he could tell, he'd had no bones broken.

The door to Sir Roderick's sleeping compartment swung open, and the Assistant Commissioner – as spruce as ever – stepped into the main carriage. Then he glanced across at Blackstone – and a look of disdain came instantly to his face.

'Just because we're far away from home, that's no reason to let your standards slip, Inspector,' he said severely. 'You look as though you've been to bed in that suit.'

'I'll smarten myself up before we meet the Russian bigwigs,' Blackstone promised.

But he was thinking: How could you possibly have slept through the disturbance last night?

'I'm going to have some breakfast,' Sir Roderick said, the tone of censure still evident in his voice. 'I suggest, as part of pulling yourself together again, that you do the same.'

Blackstone joined him at the table. The moment he looked

at Sir Roderick's dilated eyes, he knew he had an answer to the question he had posed to himself only moments earlier. Todd had slept so soundly because his sleep had been induced by some kind of drug – most probably opium.

The Inspector wondered if the high-ups back in the Home Office – or any of the men who dined with Sir Roderick regularly at the exclusive club they were all members of – had even the slightest suspicion that the Assistant Commissioner was in the grip of an unfortunate and debilitating habit.

The table had already been laid with bread, butter and jam. To these, the stolid attendant added two plates of fried eggs, delivered with all the finesse of a pile-driving hammer. Then, without a word, he took his leave.

I need more information, Blackstone thought. Much, much more information.

He looked down at the fried eggs – swimming in a sea of butter – and wondered whether his poor stomach would regard their arrival as a reward or as a punishment.

He didn't like the idea that someone was trying to kill him, he told himself. But it was made all the worse by the fact that he had no idea *why* they should want him dead. And though he was grateful that he also had two guardian angels who seemed intent on him staying alive, he would dearly have liked to know what *they* hoped to get out of it.

A younger – less experienced – Blackstone would probably have put the question directly to the Assistant Commissioner. This Blackstone, who had seen much – and would like to have forgotten a great deal of it – decided to approach the subject with more caution.

If Sir Roderick didn't know what was going on, he argued, then news of the murder attempt might throw him into a panic.

If, on the other hand, Sir Roderick knew *exactly* what was happening – and had chosen not to confide in Blackstone, despite the obvious danger to the other man – then he was not likely to open up now, just because a mere inspector had very nearly been killed.

It was wiser then – more prudent – to go about things indirectly.

'The best way to make a pig squeal is to poke it with a sharpened stick,' a red-faced country boy who'd served with Blackstone in India had once said.

It had made sense to Blackstone back then. It still did. And there had never been a better time than now to produce that stick.

Blackstone took his initial jab with his sharpened stick as the train slowly rolled out of yet another drab country station.

'So I am right in assuming that the Tsar doesn't know that the golden egg has been stolen, sir?' he said, giving the Assistant Commissioner no more than a gentle prod.

'Of course the Tsar does not know,' Sir Roderick replied curtly, then made a show of spreading Golden Syrup on his bread.

'*Why* doesn't he know?' Blackstone persisted.

'Because he simply would not understand.'

'Wouldn't understand? Has he led such a sheltered life that he's never heard of robbery?'

Despite having announced his intention to eat a hearty breakfast, Sir Roderick had so far shown very little enthusiasm for his food – that'll be the drugs, taking away his appetite, Blackstone thought – but now he abandoned all pretence of interest, and laid his knife down.

'Of course His Imperial Majesty has *heard of* robberies,' the Assistant Commissioner said, almost wearily. 'Even coming from the privileged background from which he *does* come, he is naturally aware that such unfortunate occurrences as robberies *do* exist ...'

'I'm relieved to hear that,' Blackstone said, almost to himself.

'. . . but that is not at all what I meant when I said His Imperial Majesty wouldn't understand.'

'Then what *did* you mean?'

'I meant that it would be inconceivable to him that any of his subjects would dare to steal something which he had personally bestowed as a gift on his uncle, His Royal Highness, the Prince of Wales.'

'Then maybe, in the interest of his education, it's time he learned that somebody *has* dared,' Blackstone suggested.

'Even if one of his courtiers were brave enough to tell him the truth about what has occurred – and that, in itself, is highly unlikely – he would see it in a very different light to the way that you or I might see it.'

'Would he now?'

'Indeed he would! Rather than accept that even *one* of his subjects does not grant him the respect he feels he deserves, he would be inclined to believe that His Royal Highness placed so little value on the gift bestowed upon him that he was careless enough to lose it.'

'If *I* had an uncle, I suppose I might get annoyed with him from time to time,' Blackstone said. 'Families *do* fall out once in a while. It's only human nature. But does that really matter to anybody else?'

Sir Roderick laughed condescendingly. 'Of course it matters. *Everything* the Tsar does or thinks matters.'

'And why is that?' Blackstone asked, now feeling so much like a country bumpkin pig-prodder that he almost wished he had a straw to suck on.

Sir Roderick sighed the sigh of a man who finds himself dealing with a lower and less subtle intelligence.

'Our own dear Queen may *guide* her government – and do so superbly, as we all freely acknowledge – but she certainly does not *command* it,' he explained. 'The Tsar knows of no such restrictions. His title says he is the "absolute autocrat" and that is no more than a statement of the truth. If he chooses to, he can make a family disagreement spill over into a wider world. To put it another way, he can completely sour British–Russian relations on a political level.'

'But it wouldn't work the other way round?'

'What do you mean by that?'

'If, say, the Prince of Wales was annoyed with the Tsar?'

'Naturally not.'

27

'In other words, the Prince doesn't really matter a toss, but if the Tsar breaks wind, we all have to pretend he's letting off perfume.'

Sir Roderick glared at Blackstone. 'That is both a crude and an unpatriotic way to phrase the matter,' he said. 'And I cannot help but note that it is some considerable time since you have addressed me as "sir".'

'Sorry, sir,' Blackstone said, *almost* sounding sincere. 'But I'm right, aren't I? That is how things are.'

'In a manner of speaking,' Sir Roderick agreed reluctantly.

'There's something else that's been bothering me,' Blackstone said, risking another prod.

'And what might that be?'

'Are all visitors to Russia given their own personal railway carriages to travel around in?'

'I know nothing of the transport arrangements in this country,' Sir Roderick replied. Then, observing that his answer had failed to satisfy the Inspector, he felt obliged to add, 'I did not say that *no one* in the Russian government knew of the fate of the egg.'

'Didn't you, sir? Given that you've kindly taken the time to explain to me that the Tsar *is* the government, I rather thought you'd said *just* that.'

Sir Roderick's eyes narrowed. 'Are you trying to be witty, Blackstone?' he demanded. 'Or are you really as naive as you seem?'

Blackstone met his gaze. 'I'm a simple copper, sir,' he said. 'That's why I didn't feel I was the right man for this case from the start. I believe I may have mentioned that at the time.'

Todd sighed again, from pure exasperation this time. 'The Commissioner controls the Metropolitan Police Force,' he said slowly, 'but that is not to say that he dictates every action of every policeman on every beat. You can surely appreciate that, can't you?'

The Commissioner has no idea what it's like to even *be* on a beat, Blackstone thought.

But aloud, he contented himself with saying, 'Yes, sir, I think I can appreciate that.'

'Very well, then. In the same way as the Commissioner is not aware of the day-to-day running of the Metropolitan Police Force, the Tsar knows nothing about the theft, nor about us. But there are people within his government who have sanctioned what we are doing.'

'In other words, we *are* travelling under the patronage of the Tsar's government,' Blackstone persisted.

'There is a certain Russian minister – his name is of absolutely no interest to you – who feels that it might be better for all concerned if the egg were recovered as soon as possible,' Sir Roderick conceded. 'Indeed, this whole expedition would not be practicable without his co-operation. But you need not let his invisible presence inhibit you. I have been assured that he is quite content this should be a Scotland Yard investigation.'

He'd prodded as much as he dared for the moment, Blackstone thought, but he still hadn't got his pig to squeal anything he could really make sense of.

Sir Roderick's explanation of why they were in Russia would have sounded very plausible the day before – or at least, plausible enough not to have been dismissed completely out of hand. But after what had happened overnight, it had lost all credibility.

Assassins were not sent out to kill policemen whose only job was to investigate the theft of a golden egg. So while the egg might possibly figure in the investigation, it was not what the investigation was *about*.

Then what *did* it concern? What was its *purpose*? Sir Roderick knew, but Sir Roderick was saying nothing.

Unless, Blackstone thought with a shudder . . .

Unless Todd was as much in the dark as he was himself. Unless they were *both* being used as dupes!

Sir Roderick, having pushed his uneaten food to one side, made a show of consulting his pocket watch.

'If we're running on schedule then we should be almost there,' he said.

'At the Count's estate?' Blackstone asked.

Sir Roderick laughed. 'The Count's estate? Oh no, Inspector. This isn't little England, you know, with a railway station within walking distance of every country house. When we get off the train, we'll still have at least thirty or forty more miles to travel.'

The train slowed and then pulled into the station. It was, in most details, like a dozen or so other stations they'd stopped at – a wooden structure which looked more like a cattle shed than an office of a serious-minded railway network. But in one major way, it was very different. At this station there were no peasants holding sacks which they were taking to the nearest market. At this station there were no top-hatted local officials standing around, trying to look important. The platform was empty save for half a dozen common soldiers and the elaborately uniformed officer commanding them.

Our escort, Blackstone thought. Laid on, no doubt, by the minister back in St Petersburg.

What was it Sir Roderick had called him?

An 'invisible presence'.

Interesting choice of words, that.

Blackstone had a feeling which he couldn't quite justify – even after what had happened already – that there would be a fair number of invisible presences waiting for him at the Count's estate.

Five

The six soldiers lined up on the platform had adopted the approved military stance – eyes forward, the butts of their rifles resting on the ground, the ends of their rifle barrels cupped in both hands. Their uniforms were the workaday sort that Blackstone had worn often enough in his time, but their officer – who was standing apart from them – sported a splendid scarlet uniform which would not have looked out of place at a regimental ball.

Sir Roderick saw the officer at the same time Blackstone did, and whistled softly to himself.

'My goodness, we are honoured indeed,' he told the Inspector.

'Honoured?' Blackstone repeated. 'It's an honour when they bother to send us an escort, is it?'

'No, it is an honour because of the *calibre* of the escort they have chosen to send us. That captain is in the uniform of the Hussar Guards. It's one of Russia's truly elite regiments. The Tsar himself has served in it.'

'Actually *served* in it,' Blackstone said. 'How did he manage that? Start at the bottom and work his way up?'

'Your lack of respect for your betters is becoming rather tiresome,' Sir Roderick said.

'I keep telling you I'm the wrong man for the job,' Blackstone replied, risking another jab with his pointed mental stick.

'You do not have to convince me of that,' Sir Roderick told him. 'And I note that you have fallen out of the habit of calling me "sir" again.'

'Sorry, sir,' Blackstone said.

'No, you're not,' Sir Roderick said sharply.

You're right, Blackstone agreed silently. I'm not.

The two Englishmen stepped down from the train. The escort snapped to attention, bringing up their rifles and resting the barrels on their shoulders. Or at least, five of them did. The sixth misjudged the manoeuvre, so that his rifle slipped from his hands and clattered noisily on to the platform. The unfortunate man was on the point of retrieving his weapon when the officer screamed something at him. The soldier looked confused at first, then adopted the same stance as his comrades – though without his rifle he looked awkward, rather than smart.

31

The officer strode furiously across the platform and came to a halt in front of the hapless soldier. For several moments he stood perfectly still, then he raised his arm and slapped the soldier hard across the face. To his credit, the man hardly moved, but when a second slap followed the first, and a third came after that, he began to wobble, and on the fourth he lost his balance and staggered backwards against the station wall.

'Now you couldn't get away with that kind of thing in *our* army,' Sir Roderick said.

'No, you couldn't,' Blackstone agreed.

'More's the pity,' Sir Roderick added.

The officer, finally satisfied with his handiwork, turned smartly on his heel and walked towards the new arrivals. He was in his early thirties, Blackstone guessed. He had a high forehead, a cruel mouth and black eyes, but he did not look unintelligent.

The Captain came to halt in front of the Englishmen, and favoured Sir Roderick with a slight bow.

'I am Captain Dobroskok,' he said. 'You must forgive what you have just witnessed.'

'Must I?' Blackstone asked.

The Captain did not notice the irony. 'Our sergeants do all they can with the men during their training,' he explained, 'but even they can never make a peasant truly worthy of the officer he serves under.'

'It's the same in Britain,' Sir Roderick said diplomatically. 'Whatever you threaten them with – whatever punishing paces you put them through – you'll never make a silk purse out of a sow's ear.'

The soldier had retrieved his rifle and was now standing in line with the other men, Blackstone noted – which was no mean feat considering the battering he had endured.

'You are Sir Roderick Todd?' the Captain asked.

'I am.'

'I have a coach waiting for you outside. Will your man here . . .?'

'He'll ride with me,' Sir Roderick said.

The Captain gave a puzzled nod, which as much as said that, yes, he'd heard they did things very strangely in England. Then he turned towards the exit and gestured that Blackstone and Sir Roderick should follow him.

The carriage which awaited them had all the elegance of an English aristocrat's coach, right down to the elaborate crest in the door, but was, Blackstone noted, considerably more robustly built.

'Our Russian roads require sturdy vehicles,' Captain Dobroskok said, reading Blackstone's mind. 'This country is demanding, but that is what makes us strong.'

They climbed into the carriage – the Captain positioning himself as far from Blackstone as the limited space allowed. Flanking the coach, Dobroskok's men mounted their horses. The unfortunate soldier whom the Captain had beaten was still somewhat groggy, Blackstone observed, and had to be helped on to his mount by his comrades.

Dobroskok tapped on the roof of the coach with his stick, and the party pulled away from the rickety station.

Once they had cleared the few shacks which surrounded the railway, they were once again absorbed by the vastness of the land.

'I am told the North American prairies are somewhat like this,' Dobroskok said to Sir Roderick. 'Though, of course, they are much smaller,' he added with quiet pride.

'You speak very good English,' Blackstone commented.

The remark seemed to puzzle – perhaps even *offend* – the Captain. 'Why shouldn't I?' he asked.

'Because you're Russian?' Blackstone suggested.

Dobroskok laughed at Blackstone's ignorance. 'I am a gentleman,' he said. 'I was brought up speaking English and French. Russian is a language I only use when talking to enlisted men and servants.'

'The ordinary people,' Blackstone elucidated.

'Enlisted men and servants,' the Captain repeated. 'I do not know any other *ordinary* people.'

Well, you've met one now, Blackstone thought.

'I notice there were no passengers waiting to get on the train when we arrived,' he said aloud.

'That is correct,' the Captain agreed.

'And why was that?'

'Because until you have finished your work here – and I must quickly add, Sir Roderick, that I myself have no idea what the nature of that work is – no one is *allowed* to leave.'

'Do you mean by that they're not allowed to leave by train?' Blackstone asked.

'I mean that they are not allowed to leave *at all*.'

'So you sealed off the whole area?'

'Yes.'

Blackstone looked out of the carriage at the unending steppe. 'It's a big job,' he commented.

'Fortunately, I have sufficient men at my command to adequately enforce the restriction.'

'But to seal off an area like this would take several hundred soldiers,' Blackstone protested.

The Captain nodded appreciatively, and the new expression on his face said that perhaps he had been a little hasty in judging Blackstone solely on his rather inelegant appearance. 'You have obviously been a military man yourself, at one time,' he said.

'Yes, I have.'

'What rank did you hold?'

'Blackstone was an officer, naturally, though now he is in the police force we do not refer to his previous rank,' Sir Roderick said.

He's trying to build me up in Dobroskok's eyes, Blackstone thought. He probably even thinks he's doing me a favour – but favours based on lies are no favour at all.

'Sir Roderick has obviously been misinformed about my military career,' he said. 'The truth of the matter is that I started out as a private and was eventually promoted to sergeant.'

The look of disdain returned to the Captain's eyes, and he sniffed as if he had suddenly noticed the overpowering odour of the lower classes.

'I see,' he said loftily.

'And now I'm an inspector in the Metropolitan Police, which certainly counts for something in England,' Blackstone continued. 'And not only that, but I'm *the* inspector who Her Majesty's Government has entrusted with investigating this case.' He paused and looked at Sir Roderick. 'Entrusted me with it whether I wanted to be or not.'

A superior smile came to the Captain's face. 'So you think it is your government which wants you here, do you?'

'Isn't it?'

The Captain's supercilious smile widened further. 'Perhaps it is. What would I know? I am just a soldier, who obeys the orders of his commanding officer without question.'

Oh no, you're much more than that, Blackstone thought. For a start, you're a pretty smug bastard, even by the standards of smugness displayed by the English officer class.

'I'm sure you know your job, Captain,' he said, 'but are you *quite* sure that no one has left the area since the "incident" – which, of course, you know nothing about – occurred?'

Dobroskok glared at him. 'No one at all has left.'

'The Prince of Wales left,' Blackstone pointed out.

'I naturally did not include him in my statement,' Dobroskok said. 'Nor did I include—' He stopped abruptly, as if his throat had suddenly frozen.

'Nor did you include *who*?' Blackstone prompted.

The Captain's face blackened. He hates being questioned by a man like me – someone only a step up from a peasant – Blackstone thought. He *really* hates it. But he has no choice – because the 'invisible presence' who set all this up has ordered him to co-operate.

'Nor did you include *who*?' the Inspector repeated.

'Nor did I include the Prince of Wales's entourage,' the Captain said, unconvincingly.

'So all the other guests who were attending the house party are still there, several days after the robbery?'

'Naturally.'

'Don't they mind?'

The Captain shrugged, obviously feeling on safer ground again – elevated ground from which he could look down on Blackstone.

'A Russian house party is not to be confused with the common drinking session you will have experienced in the sergeants' mess,' he said cuttingly. 'It is altogether a more leisurely affair. Guests sometimes have to travel for many days, under very difficult conditions, to reach it. Once they have arrived, it is natural that they should stay for quite some time. Besides . . .'

'Besides what?'

'Their own wishes in the matter are of very little importance. What we are dealing with here is an affair of state.'

'I thought you said you didn't know *what* it was about,' Blackstone said sharply.

'Nor do I,' the Captain agreed, deflecting this particular parry with ease. 'But I do know on whose orders I am acting, and that is enough to convince me of the gravity of the matter.'

Blackstone tried to imagine the same situation in England – tried to picture what would happen if the inhabitants of, say, Hampshire, were suddenly told that they could not leave the area, however important their particular reasons for travelling. There would be strong protests at the very least, he decided. And at worst, there would be a riot.

But then this was not England, where neither the Queen nor the Prime Minister aspired to the title of 'absolute autocrat'.

'Of course, it must have taken you and your men some time to get here,' Blackstone said, appearing to be thinking aloud, 'and it's always possible that any number of people slipped away *before* you arrived.'

'No, it is not possible,' the Captain said definitely.

'How can you be so sure?'

'Because we were already here when the incident – whatever it was – occurred.'

Blackstone looked out again at the wide steppe. 'You were *here*?' he repeated.

'That is correct.'

'But why, in God's name? I know from my own experience – even if the experience was that of a mere *sergeant* – that it's a complicated matter moving large numbers of soldiers around. Expensive, too. They've got to have transportation, and they need forage. It's hardly ever done without a purpose. So what was the purpose here? You can't have been expecting an invasion – not unless the invading army was planning to land by hot-air balloon!'

Captain Dobroskok's mouth opened, then closed again, as if to shut off the words he'd been about to speak. He turned to Sir Roderick, and the look in his eyes said he needed rescuing.

'Perhaps the soldiers were here to protect His Royal Highness, the Prince of Wales,' Sir Roderick said, providing the requested lifeline.

'Several *hundred* of them?' Blackstone asked.

'This is, in some ways, a dangerous country,' Sir Roderick explained. 'It is, of course, quite as civilized as England in so many important ways,' he added, in order not to injure the Captain's sense of national pride, 'but out in open countryside, the like of which we simply do not have in England, there are still plenty of bandits and brigands. Given that situation, His Imperial Majesty, the Tsar, will have been at pains to ensure that His Royal Highness – who is not only the son of a fellow monarch, but also his uncle – should have been well protected.'

A look of enlightenment came to Blackstone's face, followed by an abashed expression which might have been taken to indicate that he considered himself stupid for not working all that out on his own. Sir Roderick Todd noted the process, and visibly relaxed.

'But apparently, he only needed the protection when he was *coming* here,' Blackstone mused.

'I don't understand,' Sir Roderick said.

'I should have thought it was obvious, sir,' Blackstone

countered. 'This area is so unsafe that the Prince needs a small army to escort him here. But later – after the worst fears are confirmed, and he has not only been robbed but assaulted – he leaves the place without that escort. And how do we know that? We know it because we have Captain Dobroskok's word for it that the escort is still here!'

'The Prince may well have been shaken by the experience and wanted to get away from here as quickly as possible,' Sir Roderick said, clearly improvising as he went along. 'Under those circumstances, he will naturally not have wanted to wait for the whole troop to be mobilized, and no doubt he instead decided to leave under an escort of a few of Captain Dobroskok's most trusted men. Isn't that what happened, Captain?'

'Yes,' Dobroskok said, in a flat – almost dead – voice. 'Yes, that is what happened.'

Blackstone put his clenched hands behind his head and stretched out his legs. 'Well, I'm certainly glad all that's been cleared up,' he said, almost lazily. 'But there's still just one small point I haven't got straight in my head. Well, I suppose there are two, really.'

'And what "two small points" might they be?' the Captain asked, with a considerable show of reluctance.

'You say you cordoned off the area straight after the incident?'

'That is correct.'

'And that you did so on orders from St Petersburg?'

'Again, that is correct.'

'But how did you get your orders so *quickly*?'

'What do you mean?'

Blackstone looked out of the window again. 'It's a very bare landscape,' he said reflectively. 'True, we've seen the odd village and the odd clump of trees in the distance, but what we haven't seen is any *poles*.'

'Poles?' the Captain repeated, mystified. 'There are no Poles any more. What was once Poland is now the Vistula Province, under the benevolent rule of His Imperial Majesty.'

'I meant *wooden* poles. Poles to carry the telegraph and telephone wires. There aren't any. So from that, I assume this part of the country is very backward in terms of modern communication.'

'Backward!' Dobroskok repeated hotly. 'How dare you insult my fatherland in such a way! Certainly, we do not have telephones connected to every tiny hamlet as you do in your country, but that is because we live in a magnificent sweeping land – a land that has depth and breadth – not in a stinking little cabbage patch of an island like yours.'

'I say, steady on there, old chap!' Sir Roderick protested. 'Doesn't do to go insulting each other's countries, you know.'

'It's my fault,' Blackstone apologized. 'I never meant to insult Russia, Captain Dobroskok, and if I did so inadvertently, then I'm truly sorry. All I was doing was asking whether or not there was a telephone or telegraph line to the Count's estate.'

'There will be, in time,' the Captain said, somewhat mollified.

'But there isn't now?'

'No.'

'In fact it's probably several hours ride to the nearest telegraph office? And several hours ride back?'

'It is certainly not close,' the Captain admitted grudgingly.

'So how were you able to receive orders from St Petersburg almost as soon as the incident occurred?'

The Captain stared at Blackstone for fully half a minute, and when it became plain that the Inspector had no intention of flinching, he said, 'You told me you had two questions. What was the second one?'

'You said earlier that you knew nothing of the incident we were sent here to investigate, didn't you?'

'I did. And are you now calling me a liar?' the Captain demanded angrily. 'Because if you are, I will overlook the fact that you are no gentleman and demand satisfaction. Swords or pistols. You shall have the choice.'

Blackstone laughed. 'Good heavens, Captain, you do get

worked up about nothing, don't you?' he said. 'I wasn't calling you a liar at all.'

'It certainly seemed that you did,' Dobroskok said sullenly.

'Not at all,' Blackstone assured him. 'I accept that as an officer and a gentleman you are a man of your word. Which makes it even more surprising that when Sir Roderick and I were discussing the fact that the Prince of Wales had been robbed and assaulted – which is the incident you know nothing about – you didn't even bat an eyelid.'

The Captain turned his head, and looked out of the window. 'We are approaching the village,' he said. 'Soon, we will reach the Count's estate.'

Six

The coach had been keeping up a fair pace to that point, but now slowed down to almost a crawl.

'We are approaching the cordon I have thrown up around the Count's chateau and the village,' Captain Dobroskok said. 'Now you will see for yourself, Sir Roderick, just how effectively I have sealed off the area.'

Blackstone stuck his head out of the window. Ahead of the coach was a line of mounted soldiers – spaced no more than twenty yards apart – which only started to curve inwards in the middle distance.

'Well, *Sergeant*, what do you think?' Dobroskok asked complacently. 'Would it come up to the standards that you – as a *non-commissioned* officer – would regard as acceptable?'

'It's very impressive,' Blackstone said.

And it was! He had heard officers boast of their own efficiency more times than he cared to remember – give a man a smart uniform, shiny leather boots and a charger to ride, and he is already halfway to believing that he is God Almighty – but this particular boast was far from empty. Dobroskok had the area in an iron grip. No one could get anywhere near the cordon without being noticed. Even under the cover of darkness, it would be all but impossible to break through.

Blackstone did a rapid mental calculation. Dobroskok had claimed he had hundreds of men at his command, but based on the deployment he had seen so far, the Inspector was willing to wager that was an underestimate – that there had to be a thousand or more. If he'd ever had any doubts about the affair being concerned with more than the disappearance of a golden egg, those doubts were now completely quashed.

The carriage came to a halt. Captain Dobroskok opened the carriage door, rose from his seat, and stepped down to the ground.

'No doubt we will meet again at the Count's chateau, Sir Roderick,' he said through the open door.

'No doubt,' Sir Roderick agreed.

Blackstone watched the Captain mount his horse, then said with a frivolity he was far from actually feeling, 'You don't think it was my questions which drove him away, do you?'

'Does your ignorance know no bounds, Blackstone?' Sir Roderick demanded. 'Captain Dobroskok is an officer in the Hussar Guards. A true commander of his men. An inspiration to all those who serve under him.'

'Yes, I saw how he "inspired" the soldier who dropped his rifle at the railway station,' Blackstone said dryly.

'A true commander of men, who leads from the front,' Sir Roderick continued, ignoring the comment. 'It is not seemly that he should ride in a carriage while his men are on horseback.'

'Really?' Blackstone said. 'That's funny, because I got the distinct impression that, ever since we left the railway

41

station, riding in a carriage had been exactly what he was doing.'

'He rode with us as a matter of courtesy – but you would know nothing about such things, would you?'

Sir Roderick was angry, Blackstone thought.

But then that came as no surprise. The anger had been building ever since he himself had had the temerity to question Dobroskok, and was bound to come to eruption point sooner or later.

'You were extremely rude to the Captain,' the Assistant Commissioner said. 'More than rude. You were downright insolent!'

'I was questioning him about the "incident". Isn't that standard police procedure, sir?'

'And you used *me*,' Sir Roderick continued, his fury mounting. 'Me! Your acknowledged superior! An assistant commissioner! Let me tell you, Blackstone, I didn't come all the way to Russia just to have a mere inspector like yourself make me into his dupe.'

Then whose dupe *did* you come all this way to be? Blackstone wondered.

But he settled for saying no more than, 'I'm afraid I don't know what you're talking about, sir.'

'Don't know what I'm talking about!' Sir Roderick repeated contemptuously. 'That . . . that . . .' He paused, to take a deep breath. 'You let me explain away the fact that there were so many soldiers already here – which I only did out of politeness, to save Captain Dobroskok from embarrassment – and then you took my argument to pieces before my very eyes, making me look a complete fool.'

You *were* a complete fool, Blackstone thought.

'Wouldn't it have been better to let the Captain's embarrassment run its full course, sir?' he suggested. 'That way, we might have found out the *real* reason the soldiers were here.'

'There are certain . . . certain *forms* . . . which have to be observed whatever the situation,' Sir Roderick said, waving his hands in the air in front of him. 'When one asks questions,

42

one must always remember the status of the person one is questioning.'

'That's not the way things happen during a criminal investigation,' Blackstone said.

'Your approach simply won't do,' Sir Roderick told him. 'It won't do at all. I am your superior, in case you've forgotten, and I will dictate the lines on which this investigation travels.'

'Then we'll never catch our man,' Blackstone said simply.

'So now Captain Dobroskok has gone, you're turning your insolence on me, are you, Inspector?' Sir Roderick blustered.

'I'm merely stating the facts as I see them,' Blackstone replied. 'You have no experience of investigations, sir, whereas I have a large number of cases already to my credit. If we use your methods, we'll fail. If we use mine, we'll have at least some chance of success.'

'Your methods, as you choose to call them, have already enraged an officer in His Imperial Majesty's cavalry,' Sir Roderick pointed out.

'And I'll probably get right up a few more important noses before I've finished, sir,' Blackstone countered. 'But it's the only way that we have any chance of getting a result.'

The procession of coach and escort entered the village, if village was what it could be properly called. It had no centre, as did villages in England. Instead, it was spread out along a dirt road which was passable enough at that moment, but must have been nothing less than a sea of mud when the rains fell or the winter snow melted.

The small square houses which made up the village were constructed of roughly hewn logs, and squatted close to the ground like malevolent and poisonous toads. Beside each one of the hovels there was a patch of land on which the villagers grew the vegetables they used to supplement their otherwise meagre diet. One of the huts, no less cramped and squalid than the rest, had a crude onion-shaped dome atop of it to signify that it was the church.

The peasants themselves stood by the side of the road. The men, dressed in loose blouses and baggy trousers, were barefoot and had long hair and bushy beards. They were short, but heavily built, with muscles made hard by countless hours of back-breaking labour in the fields. The women, of similar build to their husbands, wore drab long skirts and had their heads covered with kerchiefs. All had their eyes fixed firmly on the ground, and could not strictly have been said to be watching the procession pass at all, but there was no doubt that they were well aware of what was going on. Only the small children – too young as yet to know any better – gazed up with frank and startled curiosity.

Not a word had been spoken by these peasants, not an angry gesture made in the direction of the coach or the soldiers, yet Blackstone sensed an animosity as great as any he had felt when patrolling through the hostile villages of Northern India in his army days.

'Of course, if you refuse to conduct yourself in a manner that I consider appropriate, I could always send you packing back to London, you know,' said Sir Roderick, who had obviously been turning their previous heated exchange over in his mind ever since it had come to a close. 'And if I do that – if I do send you back – your career will be in ruins.'

'I've only ever met two Russians before,' Blackstone said, almost reflectively. 'Both of those encounters took place in London, a couple of years ago now.'

It was not quite true. He had, in fact, met *three* Russians. But one of them had been Hannah, his one true love who was lost to him for ever – and he was not prepared to bring her into the conversation with this bureaucratic stuffed-shirt who liked to pretend he was a policeman.

'I don't see how the number of Russians who you've met – or haven't met – has anything at all to do with the matter we are currently discussing,' Sir Roderick said.

'One of them was a Count Turgenev,' Blackstone said, ignoring the comment. 'He offered me ten thousand pounds to help in his murderous endeavours. I turned him down.'

'Ten thousand pounds!' Sir Roderick repeated incredulously. 'But that's . . . that's a fortune.'

'Yes, it is,' Blackstone agreed. 'I could work for a hundred years and never earn anything like that.' He paused for a moment, as if reflecting on the kind of the life the money could have bought him. 'The other Russian said he was called Vladimir,' he continued, 'but I don't think that was his real name. He was a member of the Russian secret police – the *Okhrana*. He offered me another ten thousand pounds, on behalf of the Tsar. I didn't have to do anything for it. The money was simply a reward for *not* helping Count Turgenev. I turned him down as well. You don't have to believe me, of course, but, looking at the expression on your face, I think you do.'

'What's the point of all this?' Sir Roderick Todd asked, intrigued, despite himself.

'I can't be bribed, and I can't be threatened,' Blackstone said. 'You might be able to get me kicked off the Force—'

'There is no *might* about it!'

' . . . but I'll find some kind of work – even if it's only as a labourer on the docks – and I'll survive as I always have.'

'Good God, hearing you talk like that, it's almost as if you were driven by some notion of . . . of honour,' Sir Roderick said, disbelieving. 'Is that how you see it, Blackstone?'

'No, sir, I certainly wouldn't put it as strongly as that,' the Inspector replied. 'Honour's something that's been pretty much reserved for gentlemen like yourself, so I'd prefer to think of it as preserving my *integrity*.'

Sir Roderick took a handkerchief out of his pocket, and mopped his brow. 'Look here, Blackstone, it is very important that we solve this case. There are people back in London who are watching both of us, you know.'

He realized he'd made a mistake the second the words were out of his mouth, but for a moment he looked as if he thought he'd got away with it.

45

Then Blackstone said, '*Both* of us?'

'You have a rather patchy record, you know,' Sir Roderick said weakly. 'Some brilliant successes, I'll grant you, but there have been occasions when you've crossed the wrong person. And that's always a mistake.'

'And what about you?' Blackstone asked.

Despite a relative chill in the carriage, sweat was pouring from Sir Roderick. He mopped his brow again. 'No one in authority questions my ability,' he said shakily, 'but there have been certain concerns raised about my health. I need to prove that I am robust enough to carry out my duties effectively.'

So they *do* know about your drug-taking, do they? Blackstone thought.

And was shocked to discover that his main feeling for Sir Roderick at that moment was one of *pity*.

'Some of the things I'll do during the course of the investigation, I'll do because I have no choice in the matter,' he was surprised to hear himself say. 'I'll do them because, as far as I know, there's no other way.'

'But . . .' Sir Roderick protested.

'But, on the other hand, it's true that I do tend to go after my targets like a dog that's scented a bitch on heat,' Blackstone continued. 'And maybe that's not always appropriate in this particular kind of situation. So perhaps when you think I'm going too far, you'll warn me, and I'll pull back – if I can.'

What was this? Blackstone asked himself. Why was he feeling sorry for a man who, in his entire life, had never had to struggle for anything?

Because, he supposed, Sir Roderick never *had* had to struggle.

A bloke brought up in an orphanage – like he'd been – was used to taking knocks, and sprang back easily. But for someone like Sir Roderick – whose path had always been made smooth for him – it must be quite devastating to learn that things didn't *automatically* go as he might wish them to.

'I think we got off on the wrong footing,' Sir Roderick said. 'You're quite right that you can be like a dog that's scented . . . like a bull in a china shop. But perhaps I . . . perhaps I haven't always been as understanding of our different backgrounds as I might have been.'

It must be a big step for a man like Todd to admit to a man like him that he'd been wrong, Blackstone thought.

And for a moment he almost found himself quite liking the Assistant Commissioner.

'I think we're almost there,' Sir Roderick said.

They were. The coach passed through a pair of large ornate iron gates, and in doing so left one world behind it and entered another quite different one. It was no longer running along a rough track, but over a road which was so smooth that the coach frame hardly rattled at all. Nor was the view of drab peasant huts any longer. On either side of the road were carefully manicured lawns and flower beds of such richness and profusion of colour that it must have taken a team of full-time gardeners to keep it like that.

Blackstone pulled down the window and stuck his head out of the coach. Ahead of him, he could see the Count's house. A *chateau*, Captain Dobroskok had called it, and though he had never seen one himself, Blackstone could quite believe that was exactly what it was.

The main building was three storeys high, and appeared to have been faced with the finest white marble. A terrace ran the entire length of the middle floor, and was supported by carved columns which would have looked a little osten-tatious in even a largish Greek temple. There were two more wings, running at right angles to the main building, and equally as long as it. Blackstone could not even begin to guess how many rooms the 'chateau' contained.

To the right of the house was a large artificial lake with a fountain in the middle of it. Beyond the lake were six or seven massive greenhouses. Swans glided on the water, and peacocks strutted on the lawns, both of them enjoying a life of luxury such as the peasants in the village they had just left behind them could only ever dream of.

'Impressive, isn't it?' said Sir Roderick's voice behind him.

Blackstone pulled his head back into the carriage. Sir Roderick seemed not have changed his position since they entered the grounds, and from where he was sitting, he could not possibly have seen the house.

'You been here before, have you, sir?' Blackstone asked.

'To this particular estate?' Sir Roderick replied. 'No, I have not. But I have visited enough Russian stately homes in my time to know exactly what to expect from it. For you, I imagine, it is something of a revelation. A place like this is something your undernourished imagination could never have properly envisaged in a million years.'

He was getting some of his confidence back, Blackstone thought – and with it, some of his arrogance.

'I hope you see now that you need me just as much as I need you – if not more so,' the Assistant Commissioner continued. 'Houses like this one are as familiar to me as the slums of the East End must be to someone of your background. I have spent a great deal of my time attending civilized house parties like the one at which the Prince was robbed.'

'Civilized?' Blackstone repeated. 'What happened to the Prince doesn't seem very civilized.'

Sir Roderick gave him a small smile, a further indication – if one were needed – that he felt very much back in control of the situation, and was not about to be rattled again by a comment from a mere inspector.

'Only the robbery itself was unpleasant,' he said. 'I'm sure the party which preceded it was most urbane.' He paused for an instant. 'You do take my point, don't you, Blackstone? You're on totally unfamiliar territory, and without a guide, you'll soon be hopelessly lost.'

That would be true if the guide *really* knew his way around, Blackstone thought. But if the guide was like Sir Roderick – a man who knew how things seemed, rather than how they were; who could observe events happening but not know *why* they had happened – then he might well

48

be better off striking off on his own and trusting to chance.

The carriage had come to a halt in front of the house. Immediately – and apparently from nowhere – half a dozen servants in impeccable livery appeared by the door.

One to open the carriage door, one to greet us, one to take our baggage, Blackstone thought.

And what about the rest? There was probably even one there ready to scratch their arses, should they start to itch.

'A different world, Blackstone,' Sir Roderick said, making no attempt to keep the amusement out of his voice.

Yes, it was, wasn't it? Blackstone silently agreed.

Seven

The Count was a tall broad man, with greying hair and an aquiline aristocratic nose. Like Captain Dobroskok, he was dressed in the uniform of the Hussar Guards, though his uniform was that of a colonel. He welcomed Sir Roderick graciously – and even gave Blackstone an acknowledging nod – but it was plain from his demeanour that he was not pleased to have them in his house.

The reason for his ill-humour was made clear the moment he had taken them into his study on the second floor.

'I could have cleared this whole matter up days ago, without any help from the outside,' he said, without preamble.

'How would you have done that, sir?' Blackstone asked.

'The Fabergé egg must be somewhere in the village,' the Count replied, speaking slowly, as if addressing a simpleton. 'Finding it involves no more than searching all the filthy hovels in which the muzhiks live.'

'Even assuming one of the peasants *did* take it,' Blackstone

49

said, 'there's no reason he should have hidden it in the village itself. Knowing that the village would be searched, he might have concealed it elsewhere. For instance, he could have buried it in one of the fields, or in the common pasture.'

'Perhaps you're right,' the Count agreed. 'It would be unlike the muzhiks to think far enough ahead to come up with such a plan, but I suppose it is just possible that they did.'

'And there's a lot of ground to search,' Blackstone pointed out. 'Even with all the men at your command, you'd be very lucky to find it.'

The Count favoured him with a supercilious sneer. 'Do you take me for a complete fool?' he asked. 'Do you think I'd set my men digging before I knew *where* to dig?'

'But how *could* you know?'

'I would know because I would have already extracted the necessary information.'

'Extracted it?' Sir Roderick said. 'How?'

'His Majesty's grandfather might, in his wisdom, have freed the muzhiks from servitude, but they are still serfs at heart,' the Count explained. 'They expect to be whipped by their betters as a matter of course, and there isn't a muzhik yet born who will not tell me what I want to know after a good thrashing.'

'How would you know which one to whip?' Sir Roderick asked, in a tone which seemed to Blackstone to be more curious than outraged.

'Any one of them would do,' the Count replied indifferently. 'They are like animals – and rather unpleasant ones, at that. They huddle together for protection against the hostile world, and they have no secrets from one another such as *we* might have from our friends. Thus, it does not really matter whom I choose to whip. He will have the answers I require, and when I have had enough skin flayed off his back, he will give them to me.'

'I would have thought that if they knew the name of the murderer, they would have revealed it already, especially since he killed one of their own,' Blackstone suggested.

50

'Murderer?' the Count repeated, mystified. 'What murderer? I was not aware that anyone had been murdered.'

'The robber had to kill one of your servants in order to gain access to the Prince's room,' Blackstone reminded him.

'Oh that,' said the Count airily. 'The servant in question – I cannot recall his name, if I ever knew it – was probably drunk, in which case he more than deserved what he got.'

'Did you smell his breath, to see if he *had* actually been drinking?' Blackstone asked.

'One does not get close enough to one's lower servants to smell *anything* about them,' the Count said haughtily.

'Who was in the house at the time of the murder?'

'Naturally, I was here, and so was my wife.'

'But not your children?'

'My children were away visiting friends, with their governess. In addition to my wife and myself, my normal complement of servants was here, but you need have no suspicions about them.'

'How can you be so sure?'

The Count glared at Blackstone, as if he suspected his judgement was being called into question.

'I know how to pick my staff. They understand their duty, and they are fiercely loyal to me.'

Except the one who, *according to you*, had so little sense of duty that he got drunk and allowed his throat to be cut, Blackstone thought.

'What about the guests?' Sir Roderick said, asking an uncharacteristically policeman-like question.

'The Prince was here with his attendants,' the Count said.

'That much is obvious,' Sir Roderick said. 'But what about the others? Who are they, and where are they now?'

'They are all dining in the grounds,' the Count said. He walked over to the French door which led on to the balcony, and opened it. 'You may observe them from here, if you wish.'

'I would very much like to do that, Count,' Sir Roderick

51

replied, at the same time shooting a look across at Blackstone which said: You see now how easy it is to get co-operation from people of quality when you approach things in the proper manner?

The company below was seated around a large, and obviously expensive, table. There were twenty of them, Blackstone found, doing a quick head count – twelve men and eight women. The women were all wearing elegant, elaborate and totally impractical dresses and huge hats with wide brims. The majority of the men were in some kind of military uniform or other. Hovering in the background were at least a score of servants, eager to satisfy their slightest whim.

'You perhaps already know some of the distinguished company personally, Sir Roderick,' the Count said, 'but for the sake of simplicity I will name them all for you.'

'That would be most kind of you,' Sir Roderick replied.

'Sitting at the head of the table, as befits his position in society, is Grand Duke Ivan,' the Count began, pointing to a corpulent man with a bald head and huge white whiskers. 'He is, as I am sure you are aware, His Highness's uncle.'

'Indeed,' Sir Roderick chimed. 'I once had the honour to be entertained at his magnificent palace on the Neva.'

Which means you've already got your head halfway up his backside, even before we talk to him, Blackstone thought.

The Count continued to list the guests, supplying not only their names and titles but also their family connections.

'And that is the Duc de Saint-Cast,' he said, pointing at a bald man with an elaborately waxed moustache.

'A Frenchie, eh?' Sir Roderick said. 'I trust he's not one of those *nouveau* aristocrats that bounder Napoleon created.'

The Count winced, as only a man whose own ancestry is not entirely illustrious could.

'No, indeed,' he said through clenched teeth. 'The Duc can trace his line back several hundred years – and never tires of doing so.'

The Frenchman seemed to have other interests, besides his own family tree, Blackstone thought. Even from a distance, it was possible to guess from his extravagant, almost-theatrical gestures that he was flirting with every woman at the table in turn.

'Who's that stunning creature?' asked Sir Roderick, pointing to a woman sitting several seats away from the Duc.

'That is Mademoiselle Durant, the Duc's "companion",' the Count replied, with some disgust.

'Well, you have to say the man's got good taste in his doxies,' Sir Roderick said enthusiastically.

Blackstone knew exactly what he meant. The other women at the table undoubtedly took great care of their appearance, but Mademoiselle Durant could have dressed in sacking and still been the centre of all the male attention, save that of the Duc. There was a femininity about her that the other women there lacked. She gave off an air of being fragile, but also extremely energetic. And she probably left no man she met in any doubt that, should she choose to grant him her favours, he would be spoiled for other women for ever.

The Count's finger had moved on, and was now pointing at a young British officer with heavy side-whiskers. 'I expect you know who that young man is, don't you?' he asked.

'It's not . . . it can't be . . . by God, it is. It's young Georgie Carlton,' Sir Roderick exclaimed.

'He mentioned that you were acquainted,' the Count said.

'More than just acquainted,' Sir Roderick said. 'His father used to be my dearest friend. He was Sir *Horatio* Carlton, you know. Did you ever happen to meet him?'

'Yes, I did, as a matter of fact,' the Count said.

And so did I, Blackstone thought, as he felt an involuntary shudder run through him.

He'd known Colonel Sir Horatio Carlton well – though in a vastly different world to the one in which Sir Roderick would have known him. As *Sergeant* Blackstone, he'd been part of Carlton's command during the Afghan Campaign – on the long, bloody march to Kandahar. They'd said Carlton was mad – and maybe he had been – but he was still one

53

of the finest soldiers Blackstone had ever been privileged to serve under.

'So that's little Georgie Carlton, is it?' Sir Roderick said wonderingly. 'Not so little now, is he? Fine strapping figure of a man.' He sighed. 'The years do fly by, don't they?'

'Indeed they do,' the Count concurred. 'Now, concerning the matter of your quarters – I have issued instructions that a room in the West Wing be prepared for you. As for your man, here, I assume you would have no objection to him bedding down with the other servants.'

'I . . . er . . . I'm not entirely sure,' Sir Roderick said. 'What would that entail, exactly?'

'He'd be found some sort of mattress in the male servants' dormitory, I expect,' the Count said.

The look that crossed Todd's face suggested he was momentarily tempted to take revenge on Blackstone for his earlier behaviour, and agree that 'some sort of mattress' in the men's dormitory would suit him fine. Then, with just a show of reluctance, he shook his head.

'I'm afraid that really won't do at all, my dear Count. Inspector Blackstone is a ranking officer in the Metropolitan Police. We must think not of his own dignity, necessarily, but of the dignity of the Force. And with that in mind, I rather think he should be given a private room.'

The idea seemed novel – and perhaps a little dangerous – to the Count, but Sir Roderick was his guest, and, as such, his wishes were paramount.

'In a house the size of this one, I'm sure we can find your man a room of some kind,' he agreed. 'Now, about your investigation?'

'Yes?' Sir Roderick said.

'You probably would like to take a hot bath and have a rest after such a long journey. But when you're fully refreshed, I assume the first thing you'll want to do is to take a contingent of soldiers into the village and start interrogating the muzhiks. I am more than willing to accompany you, should you wish it, but it will not really be necessary. Just tell the sergeant in charge which of the filthy

54

creatures you want whipped, and he'll see to it that it's done.'

Blackstone coughed discreetly. 'The first thing we'd like to do is to visit the scene of the crime,' he said.

'You'd like to do *what*?' the Count asked, astounded.

'Visit the scene of the crime,' Blackstone repeated.

The Count looked at him as if he were an idiot. 'But the thief won't be there, you know,' he said. 'He'll have gone scurrying back to the village as soon as he got his hands on the egg.'

'Visiting the scene of the crime is standard British police procedure,' Sir Roderick said. 'It may seem strange to you with your own way of going about things. Indeed,' he continued, diplomatically, 'it sometimes seems strange even to me. But those are the rules that are laid down for us, and you know what sticklers we British are for following the rules.'

The Count nodded, as if to indicate that he had long since learned to accept – if not understand – that the British were the oddest race on earth.

'Well, if that is your standard procedure, you must certainly follow it here,' he said graciously.

'Could you tell us who was occupying the rooms close to that of the Prince?' Blackstone asked.

'Could I do *what*?' the Count asked.

'Do you think your butler will have a record of who was sleeping in which room on the night of the robbery?' Sir Roderick interceded.

'He may have,' the Count said. 'I wouldn't know about that. It is not a gentleman's place to be familiar with the mundane running arrangements of his household.'

'Indeed it is not,' Sir Roderick agreed, giving Blackstone another significant glance. 'Do you think that my man might talk to your butler to ascertain whether such records exist?'

'Certainly,' the Count agreed. 'If nothing else, it will serve to keep the idle devil fully occupied while you take your well-earned rest.'

'True,' Sir Roderick replied, not quite able to hide his smile.

Eight

The corridor on the first floor of the West Wing was roughly the same width as many of the streets in Blackstone's normal stamping ground. But there the resemblance ended. The streets of the East End of London were made up of crudely cut, badly laid cobblestones, whereas the corridor was floored with precision-cut marble tiles. The streets were full of stinking rubbish; the corridor was as clean and sparkling as the best-run hospital. In the overcrowded slums, personal space was something to be prized above all things. Here, it was in such abundance that it could be squandered at will.

'You were assigned a room after all, were you, Inspector?' Sir Roderick asked, as they walked along the corridor.

'Yes, if that's what you want to call it, sir.'

'And what would you call it?'

'I'd call it a cupboard,' Blackstone said. 'An airless hole in the wall with no window.'

'Still, when one considers what the Count *wanted* to give you, I suppose you should be grateful.'

'My cup runneth over,' Blackstone said dryly.

There were no numbers on the doors – 'It's not a *hotel*, you know,' Sir Roderick had said snootily, when Blackstone had commented on the fact – but the rooms were numbered on the butler's list, and Blackstone was counting them off as he passed them. He came to a halt about half-way down the corridor.

'This is it,' he announced. He glanced back over his shoulder. 'It's a long way back to the staircase.'

'Am I supposed to draw some special significance from that?' Sir Roderick asked.

'The guard on the door would have had ample warning that the intruder was approaching,' Blackstone pointed out.

'Unless, as the Count suggested to us, he was inebriated. If that were the case, he probably wouldn't have noticed a herd of wild elephants rampaging down the corridor.'

'And once he'd committed the robbery, the thief had a long way to go until he was safe again,' Blackstone said.

'True, but thieves do tend to be rather reckless, don't you think?' Sir Roderick said.

'Not in my experience, no,' Blackstone told him. 'A good thief's a skilled craftsman. He doesn't cut corners, and he doesn't take any more chances than he has to.'

'Well, you obviously have more experience in these matters than I do,' Sir Roderick said, making it seem as if experience was a positive disadvantage for a policeman investigating a crime.

'According to the list, there was no one in the rooms on either side of the Prince,' Blackstone said.

'Well, of course there wouldn't be,' Sir Roderick agreed. 'The Prince is a man who both values and *expects* his privacy.'

Blackstone consulted the list again. 'His private secretary was two doors down to the left, and his equerry two doors down to the right. What about his personal servants?'

'Expect they were sleeping at the foot of his bed like a pack of faithful hounds,' Sir Roderick said. He laughed. 'Only joking, of course. They will have been quartered in a more appropriate part of the house, far away from the Quality. The Prince probably wouldn't have needed them in the night, but if he had suddenly felt such a need, he'd only to ring a bell by his bedside to have them come running, hadn't he?'

Blackstone crouched down and examined the lock. 'No signs of forced entry,' he said. 'But then, that's only to be expected.'

'Is it? Why?'

'This is a substantial door. The noise which the intruder would have had to make forcing it open would have woken the Prince. And probably his secretary and equerry, for that matter.'

'So the lock was picked,' Sir Roderick concluded.

'Don't think that, either. This is an Underwood 37.'

'And what the devil is that supposed to mean?'

'It means that it was made by one of the finest locksmiths in London. There's not more than a couple of dozen thieves in the whole of the Smoke who could pick it. Outside London, they're even fewer. The chances that anyone in this Godforsaken hole could manipulate it are next to nothing.'

'So perhaps the door wasn't locked at all,' Sir Roderick suggested.

'I would have thought that if there was reason enough to post a guard on the door, then there was reason enough to lock the door as well.'

'So you think the intruder had a key?'

'Yes.'

'Which he had clearly stolen?'

'Which was clearly used by a person not authorized to use it, given the Prince had a right to expect that only he and his people would have access,' Blackstone said enigmatically.

'Then the solution to the crime is obvious,' Sir Roderick said. 'All you have to do is find out which of the servants have access to the keys, and you have your man.'

'Some servants steal,' Blackstone admitted. 'Some servants are stupid. But it would be a very dishonest and very stupid servant indeed who'd risk this kind of thing, knowing, as he would have done, that the finger of suspicion would point directly at him.'

'The lower orders are not famed for the size of their brains,' Sir Roderick said.

'Perhaps not,' Blackstone said, biting back the comment that small brains were not the exclusive prerogative of the working class. 'But most of them have a very strong instinct for self-preservation. And it would have taken a very fool-hardy servant to run a risk like this one.'

'Would it, indeed?' Sir Roderick asked sceptically.

'Yes, it would. We no longer hang people for theft in England – and, for all I know, they don't here, either – but I wouldn't give this robber much of a chance of survival once the Count got his hands on him.'

'So you're saying that it *wasn't* one of the servants?'

'Yes.'

'Then the Count is right, and it was one of the peasants from the village who committed the crime.'

Blackstone shook his head, almost despairing of getting through to Sir Roderick.

'How would a peasant get his hands on the key?' he asked. 'Come to that, how would he gain access to the house? Why would he want to steal the golden egg rather than the hundreds of other valuable things which are lying round just asking to be stolen? And if he had set his heart on the egg, how would he have known which of the dozens of bedrooms he'd find it in?'

'Perhaps one of the servants . . .'

Blackstone drew the shape of a circle in the air. 'If it can't be the servants, according to you, it must be the peasants, and if it can't be the peasants, it must be the servants,' he said wearily. 'We're chasing our own tails here. And the *reason* we're doing that is because you won't recognize the obvious truth, even when it's right under your nose.'

'From the very beginning, you've been determined to prove that it was one of your betters who was responsible for this terrible crime,' Sir Roderick said. 'I regret to say it, Blackstone, but I'm afraid you're prejudiced.'

'So you're saying they couldn't *possibly* have done it?'

'You must understand that these are all extremely honourable people,' Sir Roderick exploded. 'Besides,' he added, after a moment's thought, 'I doubt if any of them need the money.'

'Doubt?' Blackstone asked, pouncing on the word.

Sir Roderick looked uncomfortable. 'Men of breeding are not always as rich as they like to appear,' he admitted. 'And

I do remember once, when a certain Lord X . . . but I'm sure that was the exception, rather than the rule.'

'In other words, you think they're honourable men – but only as long as they can afford to be,' Blackstone summed up.

'I didn't say that.'

'But it's what you meant. If you really want to get the Fabergé golden egg back—'

'But of course I do.' Sir Roderick shuddered. 'It would be simply unthinkable not to.'

'. . . then you're going to have to cast all *your* prejudices aside, and start looking at the facts.'

For an instant, it looked as if Sir Roderick would strike him, then the Assistant Commissioner sighed and said, 'How do *you* suggest I conduct the investigation?'

'We'll have to question all the guests.'

'That's unthinkable.'

'It is if we admit we're questioning them because we suspect them,' Blackstone agreed. 'If, on the other hand, we make it seem – *you* make it seem – that we're only asking for their help in finding the guilty party, they'll find it very difficult to refuse. And there's something else you could do.'

'What?' Sir Roderick asked, suspiciously.

'You'll be with them at times when I'm excluded from their company,' Blackstone said. 'Over meals, and in the smoking room, for example. You'll be able to listen to them when they're relaxed – perhaps when they're drunk. If you pay particular attention, you might be able to pick up some clues.'

'You're asking me to *spy* on my fellow guests?' Sir Roderick asked, outraged.

'You may be being *treated* like a guest, sir, but you're not one,' Blackstone reminded him. 'You're here to do a job. And you'll only be spying on the guilty party. As far as the rest of them go – the ones who haven't committed any crime – you'll be doing no more than taking a polite interest in their conversation.'

60

Sir Roderick laughed with what seemed, for once, like genuine amusement. 'You certainly have a persuasive manner and a way with words about you, Blackstone,' he admitted. 'Do you suppose that – given time – I might actually grow to like you?'

'Do *you*, sir?'

Sir Roderick thought about it for a while. 'No,' he said finally. 'I might come to respect you – in some ways that's already started to happen – but I'll never like you.'

'Well, respect's certainly a good enough basis for us to be able to work together on the case,' Blackstone said.

'Work *together*!' Sir Roderick repeated. 'You seem to have got hold of the wrong end of the stick entirely, Blackstone. We will certainly not work *together*, as you put it, but if you continue to make suggestions, I will consider them carefully, and may sometimes see the merit in them.'

'That's all I ask,' Blackstone said.

That's all I *can* bloody ask! he thought.

'For instance, I have now considered your suggestion that I ask the other guests if they would be willing to answer a few questions. I can see no harm in it at all, though, to be honest with you, I can't believe that anyone as important as the Grand Duke Ivan would submit to the process. And as far as the Count's concerned, I think he probably feels that he's answered enough of your questions already.'

'Perhaps you can start with someone who's likely to be agreeable,' Blackstone suggested.

'Have you got anyone specific in mind?'

'Major Carlton. He's British. Besides, since you know him, he's likely to want to do anything he can to help you.'

'Good point,' Sir Roderick agreed. 'I'll talk to young Georgie first, and see how it goes from there.'

Blackstone took a deep breath. 'It will, of course, be necessary for me to attend the interrogations.'

'Now that *is* quite out of the question,' Sir Roderick said. 'Even an amenable chap like young Georgie would object to the presence of a . . . of a . . .'

'Of a peasant?' Blackstone suggested.

'We have no peasants in England,' Sir Roderick replied pedantically. 'I was going to say, "In the presence of an obvious social inferior".'

'I need to be there,' Blackstone said stubbornly. 'I need to be there – and you need to find a way to make sure that I am.'

'Perhaps if we could contrive some reason for your being in the room – find some way to make you blend into the background – it might just be possible,' Sir Roderick conceded.

'Maybe I could be polishing your boots for you,' Blackstone suggested facetiously.

Sir Roderick shook his head, missing the point completely. 'No, that would never do,' he said. 'Boots, as far as I know, are polished somewhere in the servants' part of the house.'

'Or maybe, if I got down on my hands and knees, you could use me as a footrest,' Blackstone suggested.

'Is that meant to be funny, Inspector?' Sir Roderick demanded. 'Because if it was, I fail to see the joke.'

'Sorry, sir,' Blackstone said.

And he meant it. He had got more from Sir Roderick than he'd ever dared hope – he'd be a fool to lose all that just for the sake of letting the Assistant Commissioner know what he really thought of him.

'Perhaps you could be there to serve the drinks,' Sir Roderick said. 'Yes, the guests would probably accept that. Never having had to deal with policemen before, they'd probably see you as some kind of butler. Would that sort of arrangement suit your purposes?'

'It would suit them perfectly,' Blackstone said. He swallowed hard, as he knew would be necessary if he were ever to force the next words out of his mouth. 'Thank you, sir.'

Nine

The Count had referred to the room he'd graciously set aside for the interviews as the 'small' library, which, Blackstone assumed, meant that somewhere else in the vast house there was also a 'big' library. If such a thing did indeed exist, he thought, it must be a breathtaking sight, since even in the 'small' library, there were more books than he – a fair frequenter of libraries himself – had ever seen before. Yet despite all the volumes it housed, the room had no aura of scholarship about it. In fact, given the precise and regimented way in which the books had been placed, the Inspector had the distinct impression that they were there more to fill up shelf space than actually to be read.

Sir Roderick surveyed the library. 'Don't see any sort of drinks cabinet,' he complained. 'Strange, don't you think?'

'I certainly do,' Blackstone agreed. 'What's the point of a library if you can't have a drink in it?'

'Well, exactly!' Sir Roderick said, taking the statement at face value. 'But it does leave us with a bit of a problem, doesn't it? We need to come up with some sort of excuse for you to be in the room when I'm talking to these people, and we can't have you serving drinks if there are no drinks to serve.'

'That would seem logical,' Blackstone said.

Sir Roderick walked over to a large mahogany table which was situated close to the door, and sat down.

'We'll just have to improvise, won't we?' he said. 'Used to be quite good at this sort of thing.' He furrowed his brow, as people of limited imagination often do when they're supposed to be thinking. 'Got it!' he continued. He waited for a moment for Blackstone to ask what exactly it was he'd got, and when it became plain that the Inspector was about to do no such thing, he added sulkily, 'Don't you want to know what my idea is?'

'Of course, sir,' Blackstone said, deadpan.

'When people arrive, you go to answer the door as if you were some kind of major-domo. You show them in, then you just hang around on the fringes, and see what you can pick up from the conversations.' Sir Roderick beamed. 'Not a bad plan for the spur of the moment, eh?'

Brilliant! Blackstone thought sarcastically. It makes the man who planned the Charge of the Light Brigade seem like an amateur. But he contented himself with saying, 'Yes, that would probably work.'

There was a knock on the door, and Blackstone opened it to admit Major George Carlton. The Major bounced, rather than walked, into the room – a little like a happy puppy eager to greet its owner. Sir Roderick stood up and offered the Major his hand, but Carlton was having none of that, and instead threw a bear hug round the reluctant Assistant Commissioner.

'Wonderful to see you again, Uncle Roderick,' George Carlton said enthusiastically.

Uncle Roderick? Blackstone echoed silently.

The Major broke away from Todd, and turned to face Blackstone. 'He's not my real uncle,' he said, as if he could read the Inspector's mind. 'As a matter of fact, he's my dear old godfather.'

'I'm sure Blackstone's not interested in details of such a personal nature,' Todd mumbled, clearly embarrassed by his godson's exuberance. 'Why don't you take a seat, Georgie?'

'Right-ho,' the Major said, turning the chair opposite Todd's around, and straddling it. 'What would you like to know, Uncle Roderick?'

'Perhaps the first thing I should ask you is why you're still here?' Sir Roderick said, doing his best to sound professional with the man who had just embraced him so heartily.

'Why shouldn't I still be here?' Carlton asked, clearly puzzled.

'Well, according to the reports I've had so far, His Royal Highness's whole party left the morning after the robbery.'

'Oh, I see what you're getting at,' Carlton said, as enlightenment dawned. 'You're wondering why I didn't leave, too.'

'Precisely.'

'I didn't leave because I wasn't with the Prince's party.'

'You weren't? Then what *are* you doing here?'

'You remember my mother's sister, my Aunt Sarah, don't you?' Carlton asked.

'I can't say that I do,' Sir Roderick replied.

'No, thinking about it, you probably wouldn't,' Carlton said. 'Fact is, she married the Count's father some time back in the Stone Age. That makes the Count my cousin, so you could say that my visit is of a family nature.' He turned to Blackstone again. 'I should explain,' he said.

'I'd very much appreciate it if you would,' Blackstone replied, finding it almost surprising that, unlike most of the people he'd met in the house so far, Carlton was not treating him as if he were invisible.

'I was with General Kitchener in the Sudan, last year,' Carlton said. 'Got myself caught up in a cavalry charge just before the main Battle at Omdurman. The whole business was a terrific blunder, though I suppose, in a few years' time, they'll be calling it a *glorious* charge, and writing all kinds of bombastic poems about it.' The boyish glow drained from his face as thoughts of the charge returned to him. 'We lost seventy cavalrymen in under two minutes. I knew most of them. They were good men. Solid men.' He sighed, and some of his colour slowly returned. 'Anyway, the upshot was that I was wounded myself. Only a scratch really, not worth bothering about, but the doctors insisted that I recuperate before I rejoined my regiment. So that's what I'm doing here. Recuperating!'

'And you had no idea that His Royal Highness was planning to visit this estate?' Sir Roderick asked.

'Good heavens, no. Could have knocked me over with a

65

feather when I was told – one of the Prince of Wales's feathers!' Carlton chortled at his own joke. 'Fact is, from what I've heard about Tum-Tum, he's a pretty impulsive fellow, and he's likely to turn up anywhere at any time.'

Sir Roderick scowled. No doubt he disliked the idea of his godson referring to the Prince of Wales in such a disrespectful manner, Blackstone thought – especially in front of one of the 'other ranks'.

'The reason I've asked you to come and talk to me before I speak to any of the other guests, Georgie, my boy,' Todd said, 'is that I thought I'd get a sight more sense out of a solid British chap such as yourself than I ever would out of these Russkies.'

Carlton looked thoughtful, rather than flattered. 'You should not underestimate any of the guests at this house party, sir, nor indeed, the Count and his family. I've found them all to be damned intelligent – and damned good company, to boot.'

'Yes, I'm sure you have,' Sir Roderick said hastily. 'Certainly never meant to disparage anyone here, especially since . . .'

He said no more, but his eyes – as they glanced at Blackstone – confirmed that he'd just committed the same cardinal sin as his godson had, and while it was all right to run down the foreign aristocracy in front of people of quality, it was certainly *not* proper to so when one of the underclass was present.

'Tell me about the night of the robbery,' Sir Roderick said.

'There was quite a party,' Carlton said. 'Must have been at least fourteen courses at dinner. There was dancing afterwards – the French lady, Mademoiselle Durant, is an absolute wizard on the pianoforte. His Royal Highness seemed to be enjoying himself, though, of course – given his tremendous girth – he hasn't personally danced for years. The party broke up around three o'clock, I would estimate, and then we all went to bed.'

'Was the Prince drunk?' Blackstone asked.

'Damn you, Blackstone, how dare you be so imperti-
nent!' Sir Roderick growled.

'We need to know,' the Inspector said levelly.

Sir Roderick was turning purple. 'It's none of your damn
business whether or not—'

'The Prince was not drunk,' Major Carlton interrupted.
'From what I've heard, he very rarely is.'

'And the rest of the party?' Blackstone asked, pressing
his advantage while he had one.

'It's jolly hard to tell with the Russians,' Carlton admitted.
'They have cast-iron stomachs and rarely show the effect,
however much they drink. The Duc de Saint-Cast was obviously a little worse for wear, though, and to tell you the
truth, I was a little squiffy myself.'

'Where did you spend the night?' Blackstone asked. 'On
the same floor of the house as the Prince?'

Major Carlton laughed. 'Good heavens, no! I'm
nowhere near important enough to be placed close to the
Royal presence. I had quarters in the other wing of the
house.'

'So you heard nothing?'

'No. Apart from the cavalry charge in my head, brought
on, I must admit, by over-indulgence on my part, I didn't
hear a bally thing.'

'So what's the next thing you do remember?'

'Waking up with a hangover in the middle of complete
bloody pandemonium,' Carlton said. 'The servants were all
running around like headless chickens, the Count was
bellowing at the top of his voice – he can be very excitable
when roused – and the Hussar Guards had already formed
a tight cordon around the house.'

Blackstone was thinking back to what he and Captain
Dobroskok had said when they'd been together in the coach.

*'Are you quite sure that no one has left the area since
the "incident" occurred?'* Blackstone had asked.

'No one at all has left,' Dobroskok had replied, glaring
at him.

'The Prince of Wales left.'

'I naturally did not include him in my statement. Nor did I include—'

'Nor did you include who?'

'Nor did I include the Prince of Wales's entourage.'

'I quite understand that you were feeling a little the worse for wear,' Blackstone said to Carlton, 'but were you up and about in time to see both coaches leave?'

'Yes, as a matter of fact, I *was* up for that, and I have to say they were going at a hell of a rate when they . . .' The Major paused, then frowned. 'I'm sorry, did you say *both* coaches?'

'Yes.'

'Then I'm afraid you're in error, old chap. There was only one coach which left that morning.'

'Yet you just said that "*they* were going at a hell of a rate",' Blackstone pointed out.

'Ah, yes,' Carlton said, looking around the room as if desperately searching for an answer. 'Yes, I . . . er . . . can see how that might have seemed confusing, but there's a perfectly simple explanation.'

'And what is it?'

'When I said they were going at a hell of a rate, what I should have said was that both the coach and the *baggage wagon* were going at a hell of a rate.'

'So the coach and the baggage wagon *did* leave together?'

'Spot on! That's exactly what happened.'

If I were leaving in a hurry – as the Prince apparently was – I wouldn't let myself be slowed down by a baggage cart, Blackstone thought. I'd get away as quickly as I could, and have the baggage sent on. But then I'm not a prince of the Blood Royal, so what do I know?

'Thank you, Georgie, you've been very helpful,' Sir Roderick said, without much conviction.

'Does that mean I can go?' Major Carlton asked, and Blackstone thought he could detect a note of relief in the Major's voice.

'Of course, you may go,' Sir Roderick said, expansively. 'Didn't *have* to come in the first place, if you know what I mean. After all, it's not as if you're a suspect or anything.'

'Quite so,' Carlton agreed, rising from his seat with just a little unseemly haste. He walked over to the door. 'You won't be working on your investigation all the time, will you, Uncle Roderick?' he asked, as his hand reached for the door handle. 'We will get a few minutes together for a chin-wag about my pater and the good old days, won't we?'

Sir Roderick smiled benevolently. 'I'm sure we will.'

'There is just one more question I'd like to ask Major Carlton,' Blackstone said.

'Well, what is it?' Sir Roderick asked snappishly.

'You do know why we're here? What it is exactly that we're investigating?' the Inspector asked.

'I should jolly well hope I do, given all the incessant chattering that's been going on about it since the blasted thing happened,' Major Carlton said.

'So you wouldn't mind telling me in your own words?'

'No harm in that. As I understand it, some bounder broke into Tum-Tum's room and stole a golden egg which the Tsar had given him as a present. That's about the long and short of it, isn't it?'

'Yes,' Blackstone agreed. 'That's about the long and short of it.'

'Well, there you are, then,' Major Carlton said.

For a few seconds he stood clumsily in the doorway, then he stepped out into the corridor and closed the door behind him.

'Would you do me the courtesy of telling me what that was all about, Blackstone?' Sir Roderick said, as the sound of Carlton's footsteps gradually got fainter.

'What *what* was all about?' Blackstone asked.

'You know very well what I'm talking about,' Sir Roderick countered. 'Why did you ask my godson that last question of yours?'

'Because, as I understand it, the Tsar must never learn that the egg was stolen, as he's likely to interpret it as an act of carelessness by his uncle.'

'That's perfectly correct. But I still fail to see the point you're attempting to make.'

'If you want to keep a secret *truly* secret, then the first thing you do is make sure that as few a number of people know about it as possible,' Blackstone explained. 'So why is it that everyone in this house – from the servants upwards – knows that the egg was stolen? Why didn't they come up with some other story?'

'Such as?'

'They could have said the Prince had his purse stolen, for example.'

The look of contempt, which was becoming a feature of their conversations, came to Sir Roderick's lips.

'The Prince doesn't carry money,' he said. 'He spends it – like water sometimes – but he doesn't actually keep it about his person. He has flunkeys to do that.'

'Then his watch,' Blackstone said. 'Unless he has flunkeys to tell him the time, too.'

'He does.'

'Or his rings, for God's sake!' Blackstone said exasperatedly. 'His diamond cravat pin! The silver buckles on his shoes! He must have had something else about his person which they could claim had been stolen, so why did they tell the truth and admit it was the egg that had gone?'

'It's very easy to say that – with hindsight,' Sir Roderick answered. 'But just put yourself in their place for a moment, Blackstone. Young Georgie told you how the whole house was thrown into a panic by what happened, and no doubt someone – perhaps even the Count himself – inadvertently let the secret out. Or perhaps they didn't even see the significance of the robbery until they'd had time to think about it. At any rate, I think you're making a mountain out of a molehill.'

You would, Blackstone thought. You bloody well would!

'Who will we be seeing next?' he asked aloud.

Sir Roderick – having no flunkey himself to tell him the time – reached into his waistcoat pocket and took out his watch.

'I'm afraid we'll have to leave it there, for the moment,' he said. 'I've been invited to afternoon tea with the Count.'

'You've *what*?' Blackstone asked.

'There's no point in you taking that attitude,' Sir Roderick said – mildly for him. 'I could have refused the invitation, I suppose – though it would have been considered very bad form – but there would simply have been no point.'

'Wouldn't there?'

'No, because all the people who you insist we need to talk to would have been attending the tea party anyway, and we'd have been left here all alone, twiddling our thumbs.'

'We're investigating a murder!' Blackstone said, only just able to keep his outrage under control.

'Hardly that,' Sir Roderick replied. 'We're here – and I shouldn't need to remind you of this – to investigate the theft of the golden egg. The death of one of the Count's servants is not really our concern.'

'And you don't think they might be, in some way, connected?' Blackstone asked.

Sir Roderick stood up. 'Oscar Wilde can use sarcasm to its full effect in his witty plays, Blackstone,' he said. 'Coming from your mouth, it merely sounds clumsy and inept. I would reflect on that, if I were you, while I'm taking tea with the Count and his guests.'

'Is that all you'd like me to do?' Blackstone said. '*Reflect?*'

'That will do for a start,' Sir Roderick said urbanely, as he walked over to the door. 'And if you still have time on your hands when you've finished that, you might just think of doing a little investigating. After all, that is what you're here for.'

Ten

Whatever Blackstone might have said in anger to Sir Roderick, and whatever Sir Roderick may have said in retaliation to him, they both knew the reality of the situation. And that reality was that without the Assistant Commissioner by his side to give him some small measure of importance of his own, there was nothing the Inspector could really do to further his investigation.

And that being the case, Blackstone told himself, I might as well go out for a walk.

It was still a relief to get out of the rarefied atmosphere of the house, and breathe in the cool, pure, Russian air – which even the Count had not yet worked out a way to deny to anyone who could not claim an impressive family tree.

Blackstone's legs took him to the stables, and for some minutes he simply stood in front of them, watching what was going on inside. The horses were magnificent. The grooms who worked on them were easily skilful enough to have been employed by a crack cavalry regiment.

It did not take him long to realize that his attentions were unwelcome. The grooms did not actually tell him to leave, but neither did they attempt to draw him into their enthusiasm for their horses – as grooms in England would probably have done – and when he gave them a friendly smile they merely looked away.

He circled the hothouses, wherein were grown flowers he had never seen before, and fruits he had never eaten. The gardeners, like the grooms before them, seemed to regard him not as an interested spectator, but more as a malevolent presence.

But it wasn't the stables nor the greenhouses which were destined to be the most intriguing sight he came across on his short walk. That honour was reserved for the bed of flowering plants in front of the house.

The beauty of what lay before him was not what attracted him, though it was still perhaps the most splendid display he had ever seen, with each plant at its moment of perfection – a moment which was far from frozen in time, and would start to fade even as the sun set. No, his interest lay more in the arrangement – the governing intelligence behind the display.

The flowers had not been planted at random, he decided, and neither did they seem to be following any rigid geometric master-plan – yet there was undoubtedly a definite purpose in the way they had been placed, if only he could work out what it was.

He followed the sweeps and curves with his eyes, and realized that the rows of plants formed numbers and letters, and that while they could be more clearly seen from the upstairs terrace than from where he was standing, it was perfectly possible to make sense of them from ground level.

LE 7, he read.

LE 7? Was that some kind of code?

S . . . E . . . P . . . T . . .

It was the date, Blackstone thought. It was the bloody date!

He read the rest of it, just to confirm his suspicions.

E . . . M . . . B . . . R . . . E.

And after the letters came more figures – *1 . . . 8 . . . 9 . . . 9.*

The 7th of September, 1899.

This was monstrous! The Prince of Wales had a flunkey on hand should he wish to know the time. But the Count . . .

The peasants in the village faced a constant struggle to survive, but the Count had his servants devote thousands of man-hours – and God alone knew how many resources – to a task which ensured that, should he happen to want to know the date when he was standing on his balcony, he had only to look down.

'There's not much meat on you, but you make up for that with length,' a voice with a slight Scottish burr said from somewhere behind him.

Blackstone turned around. The woman who had spoken was in her late twenties or early thirties, he guessed, and dressed in tweed skirt and a silk blouse. She was of medium height, with cheeks as round as small apples, and dark eyes which, even from a distance, seemed to sparkle with amusement.

'Russians tend to grow outwards rather than up, so it's nice to see a tall man for a change,' the woman continued unabashed. 'You'll be one of those policemen from London – and, from the way you're dressed, I'd say you're the one who's expected to do all the work.'

The Inspector grinned. 'Right first time,' he said. 'I'm Sam Blackstone. Who are you?'

The woman returned his smile.

'Agnes McDonner,' she said. 'The family call me Miss Agnes. The servants call me the same when they're speaking to me, though God alone knows what they call me behind my back. You'll either call me Agnes or Miss McDonner.'

'And which of the two will it be?'

'I don't know yet. I'll tell you that when I've decided how well we're going to get on.'

Blackstone's grin widened. 'I await your verdict with impatience,' he said.

'That won't make it come any quicker,' Miss Agnes told him. Then the smile slowly drained away from her face. 'I hear that they've billeted you somewhere down in the darkest depths of the servants' quarters,' she continued, her voice more troubled.

'It's not so bad,' Blackstone replied. 'As a matter of fact, I quite like the smell of boiled cabbage.'

Agnes shook her head in disgust. 'Now isn't that just typical of some of the petty-mindedness that goes on around here,' she said. 'I've a suggestion. Why don't you come up to the schoolroom with me, and I'll brew you a cup of tea just like the ones your landlady makes for you back home.'

Blackstone raised an eyebrow. 'My landlady?' he said.

'Now don't you go trying to pretend to me that you're married,' Agnes said. 'I can spot a single man at fifty yards through a snow storm. Would you like that cup of tea or not?'

'It sounds delightful,' Blackstone admitted.

The tea party to which Sir Roderick had been invited was held in a conservatory which ran most of the length of the back of the chateau. Though there were tables and chairs set out at intervals under the tropical ferns and palm trees, the point of the gathering was not to sit down at all. Instead the intention was, Sir Roderick quickly perceived, to walk – to stroll up and down the conservatory, followed by a liveried servant whose sole responsibility it was to hold the guest's teacup and a plate of delicacies that he or she might care to partake of.

It was almost, the Assistant Commissioner thought, like being on the grand promenade in Nice – though without any of the inconvenience of actually being outside – and this illusion was further aided by a small brass band gathered at one end of the building, and a stall dispensing ice cream at the other.

Though he was not a man to accept guilt lightly, a certain uneasy feeling did descend on Sir Roderick. When he'd been talking to Georgie in the library, he reminded himself, he'd been quite rude about the Russians. Now, coming upon this scene as he had, he accepted that they were quite as civilized – in their own Slavic way – as any gathering of the Quality anywhere else.

'Ah, ze gentleman policeman,' said a voice just behind him.

Sir Roderick turned to find himself looking at the Duc de Saint-Cast and his companion.

'I'ave the honour to present to you Mademoiselle Durant,' the Frenchman said.

'Delighted,' Sir Roderick told the woman.

And indeed he was. Mademoiselle Durant had seemed

75

very attractive when seen from the balcony, but viewed from close range she was truly stunning. Sir Roderick tried to resist the temptation of running his gaze up and down her slim body, and failed miserably. And when he focused instead on her doe-like eyes, slim nose, and inviting mouth, he felt himself quite overcome.

'We 'ave an appointment later, do we not?' he heard the Duc say, seemingly from a great distance away.

'*Truly* delighted,' Sir Roderick told Mademoiselle Durant, aware that he was almost dribbling. 'A great privilege.'

The Duc laughed, and poked him in the ribs. 'Only a fool lusts after what 'e cannot afford,' the Frenchman said. 'Where is zis appointment of ours? In ze library?'

'What?' Sir Roderick asked, his mind still not quite back in the normal world. 'The library! Oh yes, that's where we're supposed to meet.'

'And would you like me to bring Mademoiselle Durant wiz me?'

Sir Roderick shook his head. It would be difficult enough keeping his mind on this sordid case at all, he thought, without having the distraction of this lovely creature in the room.

'Ah, *mon ami*, your mind is just like an open book to me,' the Duc said.

'Is it?'

'*Naturellement.* You are not ze first man to succumb to ze lady's charms. You would not so much like to make 'er talk as to make 'er *moan*, eh?'

'I beg your pardon?' Sir Roderick said.

'It is understandable,' the Frenchman said, with a shrug, 'but I am afraid it is not to be.'

Sir Roderick was starting to feel very hot under the collar. 'If you will excuse me,' he said.

'Of course,' the Duc agreed. 'Until later, zen.'

'Yes, until later,' Sir Roderick mumbled confusedly.

He made his way quickly to the other end of the conservatory, where the Grand Duke Ivan was standing.

'Todd, isn't it?' the Grand Duke asked.

'It is indeed, Your Highness,' Sir Roderick said. 'You were kind enough to entertain me at your palace in St Petersburg, as you no doubt remember.'

'Entertain you?' the Grand Duke repeated. 'What did I *do* to entertain you? Juggle? Ride around on a trick cycle?'

Sir Roderick looked mortified. 'I . . . I perhaps expressed myself badly,' he stuttered. 'What I meant to convey was—'

'Can't say I recall you ever being at the palace,' the Grand Duke interrupted, 'though I expect that if you say you were then you were. But we're not here to reminisce about the times when I balanced a ball on the end of my nose for your delectation. Wanted to know about the investigation into the theft of this blasted golden egg. How's it going?'

'It's . . . er . . . going very well,' Sir Roderick said.

'Excellent. So we should be able to leave soon, should we?'

'Very shortly, I hope,' Sir Roderick said optimistically. 'Did you receive my note requesting an interview, Your Highness?'

'Certainly did. Most extraordinary thing. Perhaps I was wrong to think you imagine I'm some kind of music hall entertainer. Maybe you see me more as a trained chimpanzee. Is that it? Think I swing from ropes and will do tricks in return for bananas, do you?'

Sir Roderick swallowed hard, and wished he'd never decided to accept the Count's invitation.

The school room was on the top floor of the house. There was a large wall-mounted slate board at one end of it, and Miss Agnes's desk at the other. In between were the children's desks, a nature table, and several bookcases.

'I'd entertain you in my own parlour – if I had one,' Miss Agnes said, as she made the tea at the samovar in the corner of the room. 'But since my status falls into some ill-defined space between servant and member of the family, such luxury is not to be afforded to me. Still, this is a pleasant enough room in which to sit, is it not, Sam?'

'Very pleasant,' Blackstone agreed. 'I take it that you're the children's governess.'

Miss Agnes laughed. 'You should be a detective.'

There was only one adult-sized chair in the room, and Miss Agnes insisted that Blackstone should have it, while she herself perched – rather uncomfortably – on the back of the largest of the children's chairs. The tea she had brewed had none of the delicacy or subtlety of the Russian tea which Blackstone had been drinking ever since he got off the boat. It was, instead, very hot and very strong – and the Inspector thought it was wonderful.

'So how do you come to be here?' he asked.

'I arrived in the same way that you did, I expect,' Miss Agnes replied, matter-of-factly. 'A boat from Tilbury to St Petersburg, then a train, then a bone-shaking carriage.'

Blackstone grinned again. 'Now you know that's not what I meant at all,' he said.

'I was born in India,' Miss Agnes told him. 'My father was an officer, serving in the Argyles.' A sudden look of sadness came into her dark eyes, and then was gone again. 'If he'd lived, I expect I'd have stayed in India, married one of the more ambitious younger officers in the regiment, and ended up as the Colonel's Lady,' she continued. 'But he didn't live. He caught a fever and died. After we'd buried him, my mother and I returned to Scotland. And what was I to do there – a young lady with a good background but very little formal training? Work in the dark satanic mills for twelve hours a day? That's no kind of life for any woman, and certainly not one I wanted for myself. So I used what education I had, and came to Russia to work as a governess. I've been here for twelve years now, and I've been working for this family for the last two. It's not a bad life.'

'Tell me about the family,' Blackstone said.

'I thought I just had.'

'The *Count's* family.'

'That would be a very indiscreet thing for a loyal retainer to do, don't you think?' Miss Agnes said. She paused, and smiled again. 'Be very careful of the Count. He might be a bore and a crashing snob, but that's not the same as saying that he's stupid. Not by any manner of means.'

'So what *is* he?'

'He's a courtier down to his fingertips, and – inasmuch as the Autocrat of All Russia is allowed to have one – he's a personal friend of the Tsar's.'

'What about the rest of the family?'

'The Countess is a wee bit out of her depth, to tell you the truth. Very well-meaning, in her own woolly headed way, but really not very bright. And the Count doesn't exactly go out of his way to help her with her difficulties. The marriage was a true love match, you see. He loved the size of her dowry! And now he's got his hands on it, he pretty much ignores her. The children are fine, as long as they're ruled with a firm hand – and my hand is *very* firm.'

'I'm sure it is,' Blackstone said. 'I understand you weren't here when the Prince of Wales made his visit.'

'No, I missed out on the opportunity to catch Tum-Tum's notoriously roving eye for a well-turned ankle,' Miss Agnes agreed. She raised her hand to her mouth in mock horror. 'Oh, I do hope that I haven't offended your royalist sensibilities, Inspector.'

'You need have no worries on that score,' Blackstone assured her. 'Monarchism's never been one of my vices.'

'You strike me as a man who has very few vices at all,' Miss Agnes said. 'Very much a man in control of himself.'

Was she flirting with him? Blackstone wondered.

And if she was, did he object to it?

He forced his mind back to the case, which – although she probably didn't realize it – Miss Agnes was helping him with.

'I expect the reason they sent you and the children away for the duration of the royal visit was because they didn't want them getting in the way of their guests,' he said.

Miss Agnes laughed. 'You really don't know Russians at all, do you, Sam?'

'Perhaps not. But I will if you tell me about them.'

'They dote on their children, and they dote on showing

them off to their friends. To be honest with you, I was quite surprised when the Count said that he'd arranged for us to make a visit during the house party. I'd have expected him to jump at the opportunity of presenting the children to the Prince of Wales. And they weren't too pleased about going, either, I can assure you of that. In fact, they kicked up quite a fuss. But for once the Count wasn't his usual indulgent self. They were to go, whether they liked it or not.'

'It's almost as if he knew the robbery was going to happen,' Blackstone mused. He feigned sudden concern. 'Maybe I shouldn't have said that. Perhaps you don't know—'

'That the Prince had his precious golden egg stolen from him? That there'd been a murder under this very roof – though, admittedly, since it was only a peasant who was killed, it doesn't really amount to a murder at all? Yes, I knew. In a household like this, there are very few secrets.' Miss Agnes took a sip of her tea. 'That wasn't really a slip of yours, was it?'

'What wasn't?' Blackstone asked innocently.

'Mentioning the robbery. You were testing to see how well versed I was with the affairs of the house. You were aware that the guests knew about it, and probably aware that the servants did, too. But what about the eccentric Scottish lady? you asked yourself. She's neither fish nor foul. Does she really have any idea about what's going on? Now isn't that the truth?'

'It's the truth,' Blackstone admitted.

'I'll go even further,' Agnes said. 'The reason you wanted to know was because you wished to ascertain how valuable I might be as a source.'

'Perhaps,' Blackstone agreed cautiously.

'There's no perhaps about it, Inspector Blackstone,' Miss Agnes said, matter-of-factly. 'You're doing your damndest to investigate a serious crime, but half the people involved won't speak to you, and you wouldn't understand the other half if they did. You need help, and while I would not have been your first choice in most circumstances, I'm the only choice available in this particular case. Now come on, be honest with me! Isn't that just about the long and short of it?'

Blackstone found his mind travelling back in time – retreating two years which seemed like an eternity – to a tea shop in London's Little Russia, where he'd first met his beloved Hannah. She'd spoken words similar to those Miss Agnes was speaking to him now – and look where that had led!

'It's very kind of you to offer, but I really don't want to involve any civilians in my investigation,' he said.

'Of course you don't,' Miss Agnes agreed easily. 'But, as I've already told you, you've no choice if you want to bring the investigation to a successful conclusion. And that *is* what you want, more than anything else, isn't it?'

'Yes.'

'I thought so. From the second I first saw you, I had you marked down as the kind of man who doesn't excuse failure in himself, even if there are very good reasons for that failure.'

For perhaps half a minute, Blackstone was silent. Then he said, 'Do you speak Russian?'

'Passably well,' Miss Agnes told him. 'Certainly well enough to ask the questions you'll want answering.'

Agnes could free him from the tyranny of always working through Sir Roderick, Blackstone thought. Agnes could take him to places that Sir Roderick would never think of going – like the village.

'And will you have the *time* to help me?' he asked, half-hoping that she would say no.

'I have all the time in the world,' Agnes replied. 'My job – as we've already established – is to look after the children, and since the children aren't here, I have absolutely nothing to occupy me.'

'Why *aren't* the children here?' Blackstone asked.

'Because they're still with the friends they were visiting when the robbery and murder occurred.'

'So why aren't you there, too?'

Miss Agnes frowned. 'I don't really know,' she admitted. 'Captain Dobroskok sent some soldiers to escort me back, and I thought no more about it at the time. But now I stop to consider it, it does seem a little strange, doesn't it?'

'No,' Blackstone said.

'No?' Agnes repeated quizzically.

'It doesn't seem a *little* strange,' Blackstone told her. 'It seems *very* strange indeed.'

Eleven

The Duc de Saint-Cast was smaller than Blackstone had taken him to be when watching him from the balcony, which, if anything, made his heavily waxed and elaborate moustache seem even larger than it had when viewed from above. In many ways, he could be considered almost a slightly ridiculous figure, but if he was aware of creating such an impression he gave no indication of it, and when he entered the library it was with the air of a man who owned the place.

'It's very kind of you to agree to spare us some of your time, Your Grace,' Sir Roderick said in a voice which reminded the Inspector of the trail of slime left by a snail. 'Very kind indeed.'

'Sink nossing of it,' the Duc replied. 'Eet is certainly a better use of my time zan talking to zose empty-headed people I 'ave just left.'

It was almost blasphemy – in Sir Roderick's eyes – to talk of people of quality like that, Blackstone thought. But since the Duc was undoubtedly a person of quality himself, the Assistant Commissioner did no more than blink, and then offer Saint-Cast a chair.

'I will try to make this as short as possible,' Sir Roderick began, 'but there are some questions that I feel I must—'

'No, no, no,' the Duc interrupted him, turning round to look at Blackstone. 'I am 'ere to talk to ze organ-grinder, not to ze monkey.'

'I beg your pardon!' Sir Roderick said.

'To ze professional, not to the *dilettante*,' the Duc amplified. 'If I am to be questioned, I wish to be questioned by an expert.'

Sir Roderick swallowed hard. 'I see,' he said. 'Well, if you think you'll feel more comfortable talking to Inspector Blackstone—'

'I will,' the Duc said firmly.

Sir Roderick waved his hands ineffectively in the air. 'Then, perhaps, Blackstone, you might as well . . .'

Blackstone crossed the room, walked round the table, and took up a standing position next to Sir Roderick. 'Could I ask you how you come to be in the house in the first place, sir?' he asked the Duc.

The Frenchman shrugged. 'I was invited,' he said. 'Not only zat, but ze Count insist on paying my travelling expenses.'

'And why do you think he did that?' Blackstone wondered.

'Per'aps because 'e 'oped it would give 'im the opportunity to ravage my beautiful mistress?' the Duc said. He laughed. 'No, not zat,' he continued, a little more seriously, 'because I do not sink a Russian like the Count would know 'ow to handle a woman 'oo is capable – in ze *boudoir* – of both lying on her back and moving at ze same time.'

Even without looking at him, Blackstone could sense that Sir Roderick was blushing.

'So what's the *real* reason for the Count's inviting you, sir?' he asked the Duc.

'I am 'ere, I suppose, because my very presence in ze 'ouse gives zis little party the Count is throwing a small dash of *cachet*.'

'Would you mind explaining that, sir?' Blackstone asked.

Saint-Cast looked surprised. 'What is to explain?' he

83

wondered aloud. 'My family 'as been noble since ze reign of Charles X. Ze Count's family . . .' he shrugged again, '. . . well, ze title "count" 'as only existed in Russia since ze eighteenth century. It was imported – like so many unpleasant things in Russia – from ze Germans.'

'So, on the whole, you're not very impressed by the Russian aristocracy,' Blackstone said.

'Zay are *nouveau riche*, in ze worst possible sense. Did you know zat ze Count 'as a strongroom?'

'No, I didn't,' Blackstone admitted.

'A big room wiz bars on it as thick as your arm,' the Duc said. 'And why does he 'ave it? To protect his valuables? *Non! Absolument non!*'

'Then why?'

'As soon as I arrive, 'e takes me to see it. "Your jewels will be quite safe 'ere," he says. But what he means is, "See 'ow rich I am. See what a large room I need to store all *my* jewels." He try too 'ard to impress. Zat is what new money always does.'

'And did you in fact entrust your jewels to his safe-keeping?' Blackstone asked.

The change was remarkable. The Duc's air of confidence evaporated, and he was suddenly looking rather uncomfortable. 'No, I did not entrust my jewels to 'is safe-keeping,' he admitted.

'Why not?'

'I do not travel wiz mere trinkets,' the Duc said, sounding fairly defensive now. 'The only jewel I carry wiz me is my family name.'

Which is another way of saying that you're broke, Blackstone thought. And the reason you sponge off people you claim to despise is because you have very little choice.

'Could you tell me more about the impressions you've formed of Russia?' he said aloud.

'I could talk on ze subject for hours if I chose to, but why should you wish to listen?' the Duc asked suspiciously.

'You're a man who's seen something of the world,' Blackstone said. 'A sophisticated man.'

84

'It is true,' the Duc agreed, nodding.

'Whereas I'm only a simple English policeman, completely lost anywhere outside the confines of London,' Blackstone said. 'So, as you'll appreciate, anything that I could learn would be of great value to me. And you seem just the man to teach me.'

Saint-Cast relaxed a little. 'Very well, since it amuses to me to do so, I will consent to be your *professeur* in Russian affairs,' he agreed.

'I appreciate it,' Blackstone said.

The Duc ran his finger delicately over the edges of his waxed moustache. 'Ze lesson begins,' he announced. 'Ze Russians speak passable French, but zey are barbarians at 'eart. And where zey are not barbarians, zey are simply *gauche*. You 'ave only to look at the man 'oo leads them.'

'You're talking about the Tsar?'

'We 'ad Napoleon,' the Duc said. ' 'E was an upstart, it is true, but which of us was not an upstart at some time in ze past? And what an Emperor 'e became! My one regret in life is that I was born fifty years too late to serve 'im.'

'We beat him in the end,' Sir Roderick pointed out.

Saint-Cast shot him a look of contempt. '*You* beat 'im?' he asked. '*Mais non*. It took the combined armies of ze rest of Europe to bring 'im to 'is knees.' The Duc turned his attention back to Blackstone. 'So we had Bonaparte,' he continued. 'An' what do ze Russians 'ave? Nicolas ze Second! A man 'oo might 'ave made a very good shoe salesman in a small provincial town, but 'as no business trying to run a country like Russia.'

'Look here, Your Grace, I really think you've gone a bit too far there,' said Sir Roderick, who, in spite of the Duc's impressive lineage, was no longer able to restrain himself.

The Duc gave him a glare which would have frozen glowing charcoal. 'It is a new experience for me to 'ave anybody – especially a mere *chevalier* – tell me I 'ave "gone too far",' he said.

'I'm sorry,' Sir Roderick mumbled. 'I didn't mean to—'

'Ze Tsar rules zis country as if it were a small bakery 'e

was running,' Saint-Cast told Blackstone. 'Zat is not ze act of a strong man.'

'You've met him, have you?' Blackstone asked.

The Duc smiled. 'Of course I 'ave met 'im,' he said. 'I am no snob. I will rub shoulders with even a *Russian* monarch if 'e is prepared to go out of 'is way to be amenable.'

'And the Tsar was?'

' 'E was not such a fool as to fail to recognize 'oo was being honoured by our meeting,' Saint-Cast said.

There seemed to be little point in prolonging this excursion into the Duc's megalomania, Blackstone thought. Besides, he was not sure how much longer deference and outrage would continue to battle in Sir Roderick's breast before outrage won.

'Tell me about the night of the robbery, sir,' the Inspector suggested.

'Zer is very little to tell. My mistress, she play the pianoforte, and all eyes are on 'er. Your Prince, 'e might need a winch to lower 'im over 'er, but zere is no doubt zat zat is where 'e would like to be.'

There was a spluttering sound from Sir Roderick. It might have been the onset of a coughing fit – but Blackstone did not think so.

'You went straight to bed when the party broke up?' the Inspector asked hurriedly.

'*Mais oui*,' the Duc agreed. 'My own eyes follow ze lady's curves as much as anybody else's, and I could not wait to pleasure 'er.'

'Were you sleeping in the same wing of the house as the Prince?'

A look of disappointment came to the Frenchman's eyes. 'No. Unfortunately, I arrive after most of ze others, and so I am 'oused in ze ozer wing.'

In the less *prestigious* wing, Blackstone translated – the one in which Major Carlton had been billeted.

'So you heard nothing during the night?' he asked, without much hope of a helpful answer.

The Duc smirked. 'I 'ear many groans of satisfaction,' he said, 'but of ze robbery I 'ear nussing.'

'And in the morning?'

'I 'ear all ze disturbance, but I am not an early riser, and I ignore. Besides, I 'ave other matters to consider. Ze lovely Mademoiselle Dupont, she is getting restless again.'

'Thank you for sparing us your time, Your Grace,' Sir Roderick said, standing up and bowing.

The Duc ignored him. 'We 'ave finish 'ere?' he asked Blackstone.

'I think so, sir,' the Inspector replied.

The Duc stood up. 'Zen I will return to ze charming company of ze empty-'eads,' he said.

'The man's an absolute swine!' Sir Roderick said when the Duc had left the room. 'I mean . . . er . . . his manners might be misinterpreted by those unfamiliar with the ways of the aristocracy,' he added quickly, when he remembered who it was that he was talking to.

Blackstone wouldn't have phrased it in quite that way. He saw the Duc as a man perfectly willing to exploit his social standing in front of those who really thought it mattered. And good for him!

'I couldn't comment on the Duc's manners—' he began.

'Quite right,' Sir Roderick interrupted. '*You* couldn't.'

'. . . but I did find what he had to say quite useful,' Blackstone continued.

'You did?' Sir Roderick asked, clearly amazed. 'I must admit, I fail to see how. Quite frankly, I thought that all his talk about his lady friend was a little . . . a little . . .'

'I was referring to what he said about the strongroom.'

'What *did* he say about the strongroom?'

'Well, for a start, he said that there was one. He also said that the Count invited him to deposit his valuables in it.'

Sir Roderick mopped his brow with his silk handkerchief. 'I remember now,' he admitted. 'The Duc thought the Count was merely showing off.'

'He may *well* have been merely showing off,' Blackstone

agreed. 'But wouldn't he also have shown off to the Prince of Wales?'

Sir Roderick continued with his mopping. 'Afraid I'm not following you, Blackstone,' he said.

'The strongroom has bars as thick as your arm,' Blackstone said, quoting the Duc de Saint-Cast. 'And the Prince of Wales had in his possession a precious golden egg which was a personal gift from the Tsar.'

'True.'

'So why didn't he entrust it to the Count for safe-keeping?'

'Don't know,' Sir Roderick admitted. 'Could have been all sorts of reasons for it.'

'Can you think of one?' Blackstone wondered.

'Not off-hand,' Sir Roderick confessed.

'Doesn't matter,' Blackstone said. 'We can ask the Count himself about it, the next time we interview him.'

'Ah, we could have a problem there,' Sir Roderick said.

'A problem?'

'I wasn't just wasting my time while I was taking tea, you know,' Sir Roderick said aggressively. 'I used the occasion to have a full and frank discussion with the Grand Duke Ivan. I argued very forcibly the case that he should allow himself to be questioned, but he was adamant in his refusal. And where the Grand Duke leads, the others will follow – including the Count, who feels he's said all he needs to say already.'

'So we're not to be allowed to talk to *any* of the guests,' Blackstone said grimly.

'Oh, don't look so down in the mouth,' Sir Roderick said, almost jovially. 'After all, it's not much of a loss, is it?'

'Not much of a loss?' Blackstone repeated, hardly able to believe he'd heard the words.

'Just consider for a moment what we've achieved from our interviews so far,' Sir Roderick said. 'We got damn all out of talking to young Georgie Carlton, and even less from that absolute bounder, the Duc de Saint-Cast, unless you consider his amorous exploits to be of interest, and—'

'The Duc told us about the strong—'

'. . . and we've no reason to believe we'd get any more out of the Russians if they were willing to talk, which – as I've already explained – they're *not*. The way they see it – and I'm inclined to agree with them – you'd be wasting their time. What you should really be doing is either questioning the servants or interrogating the peasants in the village.'

'I thought we'd agreed that neither the peasants nor the servants could have carried out the crime,' Blackstone said coldly.

Sir Roderick ran his handkerchief over his brow again. It was already fairly saturated with his sweat.

'You did put up quite a good argument for excluding them from the investigation,' he admitted, 'and for a while I was almost convinced. But then I got to listening to what people had to say over tea and – do you know – your argument didn't seem *quite* as strong as it had earlier.'

'And what *did* they have to say?'

For a moment, Sir Roderick looked lost for an answer. 'It's not so much what they *said* as what they *were*,' he admitted. 'They're all extremely refined people. Of course, I wouldn't expect that to mean anything to you, but it means something to me. Take my word for it, Blackstone, none of those people would be capable of committing this particular crime. And given that, I can't see what harm it would do to pursue another line of investigation. It might be taking you up a blind alley, but isn't that useful in itself?'

'How?' Blackstone asked stonily.

'Well, if you can prove the peasants in the village *didn't* do it, you'll have eliminated one possibility. And isn't the essence of good police work to eliminate possibilities?'

'The essence of good police work is to investigate the likeliest leads before the trail goes cold.'

'Why don't you take some soldiers into the village and see what you can find?' Sir Roderick asked, in a tone which was almost pleading.

Oh, I'll certainly go into the village, Blackstone thought. Now that most other lines of investigation have been cut off from me, I don't have a lot a choice. But it won't be soldiers I take with me. I'll go with someone much more likely to help me get results.

Twelve

The moon was nearly full that night. Which was just as well, Blackstone thought. Because without the moon to guide them, only blackness lay between the bright lights of the Count's elegant mansion and the dim lights in the string of shacks which passed as a village.

'The man I'm taking you to see is called Demitri Igorovitch,' Agnes said, as they walked side by side through the night. 'That's to say, he's Demitri, the son of Igor.'

'What made you pick him out as the one we should talk to?' Blackstone wondered.

'You said you wanted information, though you had no idea *what* information it was that you wanted,' Agnes replied, and he could sense that there was an amused smile playing on her lips.

'You still haven't answered my question,' he said.

'If you don't know exactly what it is you want to hear, then you need to hear a great deal. And the people likely to talk most freely – and at the greatest length – are the ones who bear a grudge against the Big House.'

'Does this Demitri have a grudge?'

'He has one the size of a bear.'

'A justifiable one?'

Agnes's clothes rustled as she shrugged. 'Perhaps. He used to work up at the Big House as one of the outside servants, you see. It wasn't a very grand job – he spent half his time up to his elbows in shit – but for someone like him it was the end of the rainbow.'

Blackstone's work habitually brought him into contact with any number of women who swore, and it neither shocked nor offended him. Which made it even more surprising that when Agnes said the word 'shit' he felt himself wince.

'I take it Demitri was dismissed,' he said.

'That's right.'

'On what grounds?'

'The Count – *being* the Count – need give no reasons for his actions if he chooses not to. But on this occasion he let it be known that he was dismissing Demitri for drunkenness.'

'And *did* he drink?'

Another shrug. 'All Russians drink,' Agnes said. 'And to excess, when they can afford it. There is a saying in Russia that you need three full days for drinking. The first is to *get* drunk, the second to *be* drunk, and the third to sober up again. You should see this village street in the days following the end of the Easter Fast. They're all out of their minds – women as well as men. It's not uncommon for one of them to die through the excess of drink during the second day, but it doesn't stop the others. They probably don't even notice he *is* dead until the third day. And that's at the *earliest.*'

They had reached the village. In most of the shacks there was only one tiny light in the window, but ahead of them they could see a hut which was brightly illuminated and had a number of crude tables outside it, around which were hunched perhaps two dozen peasants.

'The village inn,' Agnes explained. 'Not much of a place, but then in this village *nothing* is much of a place. At any rate, it's where they all go when they want a drink.'

'I thought you just said they only drank on special occasions,' Blackstone said.

Agnes laughed. 'No, I didn't. I said they only drank *vodka* on special occasions. They daren't take such a risk at harvest time, when every hour of daylight is vital, because once they've started, they know they won't be able to stop. Besides, they couldn't afford it.'

'So what are they drinking?'

'A foul brew called *kvass*. It's a kind of beer, though not beer as you'd recognize it.'

As they drew level with the inn, one of the men called across to them. Blackstone had no idea what the words meant, but he could tell from the tone that they were not meant to be complimentary.

Agnes came to a halt, and shouted something back. Most of the men sitting around the table roared with laughter, but the man who had actually spoken to her only looked angry. Satisfied she had the result she'd been seeking, Agnes started walking again.

'What was that all about?' Blackstone asked her. 'What exactly did he say to you?'

'He called me a capitalist lackey, and pus-oozing carbuncle on the backside of the working man,' Agnes said simply.

'He called you *what*?' Blackstone asked.

Agnes giggled. 'Don't sound so offended, Sam. Peter – that's his name – is a member of the Social Democratic Party, which is another way of saying that he's a revolutionary. He's always spouting slogans. I doubt if he understands half of them himself, though they undoubtedly *do* sound somewhat impressive to the other peasants.'

'Does he have a large following here in the village?' Blackstone asked.

'He has no following at all. He promises them nothing but social justice and equality – and they have no interest in that.'

'So what *are* they interested in?'

'Land! It is the only thing a peasant ever really cares about. He marries so that the village council will allot him more strips of it, he has children to increase the size of his holdings. And when his wife or children die, he mourns not for them, but because it will lose him some of his precious earth.'

'Land can't really be *all* he cares about,' Blackstone protested.

'It is,' Agnes said firmly. 'Before they were emancipated, the serfs used to freely acknowledge they were their masters' property. "Beat us, if that is your will!" they'd say. "Brand us with red-hot irons! Sleep with our daughters and our wives until you have sated yourself on them. We are yours to do as you wish with. But the land is *ours*." That's how they thought back then. And that, my dear Sam, is how they *still* think.'

His darling Hannah had been a revolutionary, Blackstone recalled. More than that. She'd been a dedicated fanatic, willing to sacrifice any number of lives – including her own – if that would advance the revolution even an inch.

'How do you feel about it?' he asked Agnes.

'How do I feel about what?'

'About freeing the peasants from their lot through revolution.'

'The peasants wouldn't know what to do with their freedom,' Agnes said, without a moment's hesitation. 'They lead pretty miserable lives now – and I pity them for that – but left to their own devices, they would destroy themselves.'

'Is that what you told Peter the Revolutionary?'

'Not exactly,' Agnes admitted.

'So what did you say to him?'

'I employed a level of debate that his friends would understand and appreciate.'

'And what do you mean by that?'

'I told him that his mother was a whore, and that even the sows in the fields wouldn't let him rut with them unless he got them drunk first,' Agnes said sweetly.

Thirteen

They reached a hut at the far side of the village which looked – if anything – even more ramshackle than the rest of the hovels.

'This is Demitri's *izba*,' Agnes announced.

'How do you know he's in?' Blackstone said.

'Why wouldn't he be?'

'Isn't it possible that he could be down at the village inn, with the rest of the men?'

Even in the pale light of the lamp in the window, he could see the almost pitying look come to Agnes's face.

'He sold his rights to share in the village's land when he got a job at the Big House,' she said. 'It was a foolish thing to do, but Russian peasants are invariably foolish. So now he has neither job *nor* land. He'll get by working for the richer peasants when they're short-handed, but *kvass* – even at village inn prices – is a luxury he can't afford.'

She walked up to the door and – with surprising firmness for a woman of her size – rapped on it with her fist.

The door swung open. The man standing there had long hair and a thick beard. His features were blunt and his eyes were cunning. Though Blackstone despised the members of the British aristocracy whom he had overheard saying that they couldn't tell one working man from another, he was ashamed to admit to himself that this peasant looked to him exactly like all those he had seen at the inn.

'*Da?*' the Russian asked suspiciously, and with not a hint of welcome in his voice.

Agnes gave no verbal answer. Instead she reached into

94

the folds of her sheepskin jacket, produced a bottle of vodka, and held it up for the man in the doorway to see.

Demitri beamed with pleasure, opened the door wider, and gestured that they should enter.

The hut was dimly lit by oil lights. At one end of the room was a crudely constructed table, with benches running around it. The woman and three children who were sitting there did not look up when they entered, or even talk about it among themselves.

At the other end of the hut was a brick stove, which would have seemed large anywhere, but in this cramped place looked enormous. It was about five feet long and four feet wide, Blackstone estimated. The top was flat, and resting on it were some shabby blankets and pillows stuffed with straw.

'The children and old people sleep on the stove,' Agnes said, reading his mind.

'And what about the rest of the family?'

'On the floor, amongst the straw.'

The only fixtures in the hut were a series of shelves holding pots and pans, and an icon in one corner, which had an oil lamp of its own.

'That's the "red" corner,' Agnes said.

'Red?' Blackstone repeated.

'Or beautiful,' Agnes said. 'The words mean the same in Russian. Have you noticed the stink in here?'

How could he not have? Blackstone wondered. He'd visited some pretty foul holes in the East End of London in his time, but the particular mixture of sweat, dirt and decay which was assailing his nostrils at that moment was truly in a class of its own.

'It's not always like this,' Agnes said. 'The whole village goes to the communal steam bath once a week. That's where they cleanse both themselves and their clothes. But at busy times of the farming year, like this is, the bathhouse remains closed.'

'Aren't we perhaps being a little discourteous to them?' Blackstone wondered.

95

'Discourteous? How? They can't understand a single word of what we're saying.'

'Maybe not,' Blackstone agreed. 'But they can't have failed to notice that we're ignoring them.'

'They're peasants,' Agnes said, her tone more matter-of-fact than contemptuous. 'They recognize us as their betters, and they expect to be kept waiting – even in their own homes – until we're ready to deal with them. Still, perhaps you're right, and we should get on with our business – before the smell completely overcomes us.'

She held up a cupped hand to Demitri, who nodded, then walked over to one of the rickety shelves and returned with three cracked and chipped glasses in his hand. He placed the glasses on the table, filled them to the top with vodka, and had downed his own before Blackstone had even had time to reach for his.

'Now we're here, where would you like us to start?' Agnes said to Blackstone.

'What was the name of the peasant who had his throat cut outside the Prince of Wales's room?'

'His name was Paul.'

'Then ask Demitri who he thinks is responsible for Paul's death.'

Agnes spoke a few words in what, Blackstone supposed, was remarkably confident Russian. Demitri thought for a moment, then replied slowly and carefully, as if he wished to use the minimum number of words to earn his vodka.

'He doesn't know,' Agnes said when he'd finished. 'But he's pretty sure it was one of the *dvorianstvo*.'

'What does that mean?'

'One of the aristocrats. But he doesn't necessarily mean someone with a title, you should understand. Anyone up the Big House who is not a servant is a *dvoriane* to him and his kind.'

'Why should he automatically assume that one of the aristocrats is the murderer?' Blackstone asked.

Agnes conveyed the question.

'He asks, "Who knows the ways of the *dvorianstvo*?

96

Besides, who else would have done it?"' Agnes said. 'All the men from the village call each other *brat* – brother – and one *brat* does not kill another, unless, of course, it is in a dispute about land. Paul – like he himself – *had* no land, so none of the villagers had any *reason* to murder him.'

This was rapidly turning into a complete waste of time, Blackstone decided. Even though Demitri had spent some time at the Big House, and seen a little of its ways, he was incapable of examining any incident – understanding any event – other than through a peasant's eyes.

'What can he tell me about the morning after Paul was killed?' the Inspector asked, without much hope of hearing anything useful.

'Those who had no stomach for the killing fled like frightened rabbits,' Demitri said through Agnes. 'First there was the big coach with the blinds pulled down, and then there was the "bird" coach with the fat man in it.'

Blackstone felt his heart begin to beat a little faster. So there *were* two coaches after all, just as Captain Dobroskok had inadvertently let slip on the journey from the railway station. Not a coach and a baggage cart, as Major Carlton had so ineptly tried to suggest, but *two* bloody coaches!

He forced himself not to display his growing excitement. Two coaches. The fat man Demitri had talked about was almost definitely the Prince of Wales, but before he went any further it would be best to make sure.

'What makes Demitri refer to the second coach he saw as the "bird" coach?' he asked.

The Russian shook his head in wonder that anyone could be so stupid as to need to ask, then sketched out his answer in the air, as he spoke.

'He calls it the "bird" coach because it had a painting of three feathers on the side of it,' Agnes said.

The Prince of Wales's feathers! His bloody crest!

And what about the first coach? Blackstone asked. Was there anything painted on the side of that?

Demitri shook his head, then shook it again, as if to contradict himself.

97

'Why does he seem so confused?' Blackstone asked.

'Because he thinks that there *had* been something painted on it – perhaps more feathers – but it had been *over*-painted entirely in black, so that only the vaguest outline could be seen,' Agnes explained.

It was still possible that the big coach – the one which came through first – had been carrying the Prince's luggage, Blackstone cautioned himself. Perhaps the Prince had borrowed it from the Count, and – since he was using it as his own – had had the Count's crest blacked out.

'Ask him if the first coach was some kind of baggage coach,' he said to Agnes.

No, it was not, Demitri replied.

How could he be so sure of that? Blackstone wondered.

He could be sure for several reasons. The first was that the coaches had been some time apart.

How long apart?

As long as it would take an old man with a sack on his back to walk to the Big House.

Roughly half an hour, Blackstone calculated.

The second reason was the big coach had at least fifty soldiers escorting it, Demitri said – and what in the world could be so valuable that it needed so many men to guard it?

'Is there a third reason?' Blackstone asked.

Yes, there was a third reason, Demitri answered. Though the blind had been down, he had clearly seen a man peeping from around the corner of it.

What kind of man? Blackstone wanted to know. Young or old? Large or small? Foreign or Russian?

He had only caught the briefest of glances of the man, Demitri said, surreptitiously filling his glass from the bottle. It was impossible to say anything about his age or his size, but if he were a gambling man, he would be willing to wager that the passenger was a Russian.

Blackstone was not convinced. Demitri would say anything to ensure that the vodka kept flowing, he thought. But he *did* believe that there had been two coaches – if only because he didn't think that the peasant was bright enough to have made that up.

Which meant that the Captain had definitely lied when he'd said that the Prince of Wales and his party had been the only ones allowed to leave the house. Someone else had fled even earlier – someone who had had his crest hastily painted out to avoid being recognized. But who could that be?

'Ask him if he knows any of the *dvorianstvo* who attended the party,' Blackstone said.

'They were very important people,' Demitri replied. 'And rich. Almost as rich as the Little Father.'

'Who's the Little Father?' Blackstone asked when Agnes had translated. 'The Count?'

Agnes laughed. 'No,' she said. 'The peasants call the Count "Father" when they're talking to him, but for them there's only one *"Little* Father".'

'And who's he?'

'The Tsar himself, of course. They've never actually seen him, you must understand – he's not one for touring the country, as Catherine the Great did – but despite that, they feel they know him as well as they know the members of their own family.'

'Because of what they've been told about him?'

'Because of what they've *made up* about him. The Tsar, according to the peasants in this village – and according to millions of other peasants in thousands of other villages – really cares about his muhziks, and it is only the landowners they actually come into contact with who make their lives a misery. They believe that he knows them all personally, and if one of them were to go to his hut – which is, of course, much, much grander than any of their huts – he would greet the visitor by name, and invite him inside for a glass of *kvass*, which, no doubt, the Empress herself would be delighted to serve to them.' She saw the expression on Blackstone's face, and said, 'You find that strange?'

'I find it incredible,' Blackstone admitted.

'But true,' Agnes said firmly. 'These are simple people,

Sam, much simpler than agricultural labourers back in England, and if you don't understand that, you will never understand *them*.'

They were getting away from the point of the questioning, Blackstone realized. 'Does Demitri know the *names* of any of the people who attended the party?' he asked.

Demitri did not, though, as if to compensate for a lack of knowledge in this particular field, he put forward the theory that some of the guests might have been even *richer* than the Little Father.

'I think you've got out of him everything that you're likely to get,' Agnes said.

'I'm sure you're right,' Blackstone agreed.

'Well, then, there's no point in staying in this stinking hovel any longer than we have to.'

Agnes turned, and said a few words to Demitri. A look of deep sorrow came over the peasant's face, and he gazed down at the vodka bottle which was standing on the table. Agnes repeated what she had just said. Demitri picked up the bottle, and clutched it tightly to his body.

For perhaps half a minute the two stood facing each other aggressively – the powerful peasant towering over the governess – then Agnes repeated herself a second time.

Slowly, as if it were costing him a great deal of both mental and physical anguish, Demitri wrenched the bottle away from his body, and handed it over to Agnes.

Once they were out on the street again, Blackstone said, 'I thought things were going to turn violent in there.'

'Did you?' Agnes asked, as if the remark were of absolutely no interest to her.

'Indeed I did,' Blackstone told her. 'I saw myself having to defend you against him, and I didn't fancy my chances of winning.'

'False modesty again,' Agnes said lightly. 'Demitri might be strong, but he's no fighter – at least, not in the way you are.'

'How are we different?'

'He is not surprised if he loses. It is just the way of things,

100

as far as he is concerned. You, on the other hand, always expect to win.'

She was a remarkable woman, Blackstone thought. Perhaps even as remarkable as his beloved Hannah.

'I still think you should have left him the bottle,' he said. 'After all, he did try to help us as much as he was able.'

'If I had left it, he would have taken that as a sign of weakness,' Agnes said. 'And the next time we wanted to bargain with him, it would have been all the more difficult.'

'You're a hard woman, Agnes,' Blackstone said, only half-joking.

'I'll tell you another old Russian saying,' the governess replied. 'It's this: "Another man's tears are only water." Can you work out for yourself what that means, Sam?'

'That you *have* to be hard, because it's a hard world we live in?' Blackstone guessed.

'Exactly,' Agnes agreed. 'And living in Russia is harder than living almost anywhere else.'

Fourteen

They walked back up the drive towards the Big House, close enough to touch each other, yet rarely doing so – and then only by accident. Ahead of them, the upper storeys of the house were ablaze with light, and from one of the salons came the sound of music and laughter.

'A party!' Agnes said. 'And tomorrow there will be another, and another the day after that. An endless string of frivolous encounters which will end only with the grave.'

Blackstone laughed, though perhaps a little uneasily. 'You sound as if you disapprove,' he said.

'I *do* disapprove,' Agnes replied. 'I'm a lowland Scot, and we lowland Scots understand that life is a serious business. You have to work at it, Sam, and there's little time left over for self-indulgence.'

'And that's your philosophy, is it?'

'Indeed it is. If you're bad at something, you must make an effort to improve. If you're good at it, you should strive to be even better. That's what I believe – and that's why I'm such a good governess.'

Blackstone was becoming uncomfortable. He was normally a serious man himself, but alone with this intriguing woman in the darkness of the Russian night, he wanted to forget that for just a short while – wanted, perhaps, to be as frivolous as the people upstairs.

'I'm sure you're a good governess – and no doubt a very frightening one!' he said, almost teasingly.

'You'd do well to believe it,' Agnes told him, still serious.

The woman was having a strange and unsettling effect on him, he thought, and wondered why that might be.

Though she was by no means ugly – or even merely plain – she certainly couldn't be described as beautiful. And though she was witty when she wanted to be, her wit was no greater than that of many other women he had known in his life. So what the hell was it about her that was making him react as he did? What was that special quality which she seemed to have?

He couldn't put his finger on it, however much he tried, but he didn't need to pin it down to know that he would feel a tiny pang of sadness when they reached the house and went their separate ways.

They arrived at the impressive main door. Blackstone wondered whether he should kiss her lightly on the cheek, or merely shake her hand and thank her for her help. But his body had already decided he should do neither, and he felt his legs move him some distance away from her.

'Where are you going?' Agnes asked.

Blackstone pointed to a spot further down the building. 'The servants' entrance,' he said.

'The servants' entrance,' Agnes repeated thoughtfully. 'Will you answer one question for me, Sam?'

'If I can,' Blackstone promised.

'You're as good as any of the people in this house, Sam. No, I'd go further than that – you're *far* better than most of them.'

Blackstone smiled. 'That's not really any kind of question at all, now is it?' he asked.

'Perhaps not, but you can certainly read a question into it, should you choose to,' Agnes countered.

'Are you asking me if I've ever thought it might be nice to go in through the front door for a change?'

'Exactly.'

'It's not important which door you walk through,' Blackstone said, growing serious, even though he didn't want to.

'Then what *is* important?'

'The only thing that really matters is *how* you walk through it – whether or not you're your own man on both sides of it.'

'It's easy to say that – words come cheap – but you'll never really *know* whether it's true or not until passing through one door is as normal to you as passing through any other,' Agnes said.

'Then I *will* never know,' he said, 'not unless the world turns itself upside down.'

'*We* could turn it upside down – at least for one night,' Agnes said, reaching for the bell-pull.

'And what would be the point in doing that?'

'What would be the point in *not* doing it?'

A liveried footman answered the door. Agnes addressed him in Russian, and he gave her a small bow, then moved to the side. Agnes stepped into the magnificent hallway as if she'd been born to it. She did not specifically ask Blackstone to follow her – but he did anyway.

They were in Agnes's bedroom. Blackstone was sitting on the only chair – were they doomed to perpetually meet in

103

rooms where there was only one chair? – and Agnes was perched on the edge of a bed which seemed so large that her body could have got quite lost in it.

The Inspector looked around the room. It was not, he assumed, as luxuriously furnished as the rooms the family used themselves, but it was still the most opulent place he'd ever been invited into as a *guest*.

As Agnes poured them two glasses of vodka from the bottle she'd wrenched away from the reluctant Demitri, Blackstone focused his attention on the impressive row of medals which hung in a large frame on the wall.

'Are those your father's medals?' he asked, as the governess handed him his glass.

'Yes, they are.'

'He must have been a very brave man,' Blackstone said.

He expected her to be pleased by the remark, but instead she seemed to be vaguely dissatisfied.

'Finish it,' she said.

'Finish what?'

'Your thought.'

'How do you know I didn't?'

'I just do.'

Blackstone swallowed slightly. 'To have earned so many medals, he must have been a very brave man, as I said before – or else he must have been a very foolhardy one.'

Agnes nodded, satisfied. 'We should always be honest with each other, you and I, Sam,' she said.

'So which kind of man was he?'

'A little of both, I suspect. Like all good soldiers are. Like I'm sure you were yourself.'

'You admired him.'

'I *worshipped* him. I wanted to be just like him when I grew up. Then, when I was around five or six years old, I started to realize that – as a girl – I never could be. And it broke my heart.'

'But you got over it.'

'Not really,' Agnes said. 'There are times when I regret not having gone to university, and times when I regret not

104

having married. But I *always* regret that I could never become a soldier.'

'You could *still* marry,' Blackstone said.

Agnes shook her head. 'I don't think so. The time for that has passed. I have other things to absorb me now.'

He wanted to tell her that she was wasted as a governess out in this Russian wasteland – that there were so many other things that she could do if she threw in the cards that life had dealt her and went off in search of an entirely new deck.

He wanted to say it – but he didn't. Because what he *didn't* want was for her to hate him – and he was afraid that if she was not brave enough to follow his advice, that was exactly what she would do.

Agnes stood up, and walked over to the window. She stood looking out into the darkness, then turned and crossed the room to the door.

It was almost as if she were *parading* herself before him, Blackstone thought, but even as the idea was passing through his mind, he was beginning to condemn it as unworthy.

Something seemed be absorbing Agnes's attention, he noted, and shifting his head slightly, he could see it was the keyhole – or rather the key protruding from the keyhole – on which her gaze was fixed.

Half a minute passed, and her gaze never faltered.

He found himself wondering what it was she saw when she looked at the key. Was it, to her, merely a piece of metal, cunningly fashioned to fit perfectly into a lock? Or had it suddenly become something more significant? Had this commonplace object taken on a new meaning for this woman who, half an hour earlier, had told him that he would never know what it felt like to walk through a new door until he had tried it for himself?

Another minute passed.

'Is anything the matter?' Blackstone heard himself ask.

A tremble ran visibly through Agnes's whole body. Then she squared her shoulders, reached forward with her right hand, and turned the key in the lock.

The click seemed as loud – and as significant – as a gunshot. Agnes stayed where she was for a moment longer, then turned around to face him.

'We both of us know why we're here in this room, don't we, Sam?' she asked.

'Do we?' Blackstone responded.

She looked deep into his eyes. 'Honesty, Sam,' she said. 'We must always be honest with each other.'

Blackstone met her gaze. 'Yes, we both know why we're here in this room,' he agreed.

Agnes nodded – and then she began to slowly unbutton her blouse.

It was the sunlight streaming in through the window that Blackstone became aware of first. It played on his eyelids with something between a sting and a tickle, as it urged him to open them and face a new day.

The sounds came next – birds chirping happily, several men's shouted exchanges somewhere below, the click-clacking of horses' iron-shod hooves on cobblestones.

The world was calling to him, but he was not ready to answer that call quite yet. He let his hand grope blindly to the part of the bed where Agnes should have been lying – and found it empty.

Had it all been nothing more than a dream, then? he wondered.

When he did finally open his eyes, would he find that he was not in Agnes's bedroom at all, but instead in the cupboard of a room that the Count deemed worthy of his status as a servant?

Perhaps it went even further back than that. Perhaps the whole Russian expedition had been a dream: the fight on the train merely the result of eating too richly immediately before going to bed; Agnes no more than a product of his own imagination – born out of his desire to fill the yawning gap in his life which Hannah had left.

Yet if any of that were so, he was prepared to swear he was *still* asleep, because the bed he was lying on was far more comfortable than any he could ever remember calling his own.

With a sigh he opened his eyes, and looked around him. Yes, he was in Agnes's room, but of Agnes herself, there was no sign at all.

His wandering eyes fell on a note, written in immaculate copper-plate script and propped up on the night-table, where he was bound to see it.

We can't all lie abed all morning, Inspector! Some of us have tasks we must be going about!

What time was it? he wondered.

He glanced out of the window at the sun which had been teasing him earlier. Eight o'clock, or a little after, he decided.

No doubt Agnes could find plenty to occupy her in the schoolroom, whether her charges were there or not. But he had no worries that Sir Roderick would be waiting for his arrival with a growing impatience. No, it was far more likely that the Assistant Commissioner – after the previous evening's excesses of drugs or alcohol – was still trying to muster the strength to face the day.

He looked at the note again. Agnes had signed it, and then, as an afterthought – perhaps because she was worried he would take her humour as criticism – she had added as a postscript.

I hope that this investigation takes you a long time, Sam. I hope you never have to go away.

He felt a smile creep across his face, and tried not to let it turn into a complacent smirk.

It had certainly been a night to remember, he told himself, as he swung his legs out of the bed and reached for his clothes, which were lying in a hastily discarded heap on the floor.

Agnes was not the most skilful lover he had ever taken

to his bed – far from it – but never had he known a woman to throw herself into her love-making with such fervour and intensity.

There was a bowl of water on the washstand. The water was cold to the touch. No doubt Agnes had already used it herself, before setting off for the schoolroom. But after all they'd shared the night before, it did not bother him that the water now touching his skin had previously caressed hers.

His toilet complete, he dressed with the speed and efficiency of the man of action that life had so often compelled him to be. Yet once he was dressed, he was in no hurry to leave the room. Rather, he lingered by the door, committing all the details to memory, as if he hoped that he would return to it – but had a secret, hidden, fear that he might not.

His gaze fell idly on the bed. The sheets and blankets were in great disarray, as though a desperate struggle had taken place beneath them. And in a way, he supposed, it had.

He was reluctant to obliterate the evidence of the night of passion he had spent with Agnes, but – whilst he was proud of it and grateful for it – it might not be a sight that the governess wished the servants to see.

He crossed the room, stripped back the bedding – and froze in something like horror.

Midway down the mattress – where Agnes had been lying during the first of their couplings – there was a thin red stain.

The detective in him wanted to get closer to it – to examine the stain in all its forensic detail. But the *man* in him had no need to do any such thing.

The *man* in him already knew that the stain was blood – and what the source of that blood was.

He felt suddenly very giddy, and clutched frantically on to the bedhead for support.

He had not known.

He had never even so much as guessed.

And Agnes had certainly never told him.

Yet there was all the proof he needed that the woman he had taken into his arms the night before had been a virgin.

Fifteen

The 'Quality' were probably still at their leisurely break-fast – and a gargantuan meal it would be, if Blackstone knew anything about the upper classes – but the dozens of servants who were employed to answer their every whim had already been at work for hours.

A team of gardeners was busily engaged in rebuilding the floral calendar with dozens of new plants, straight from the hothouses. Another team had begun the never-ending task of polishing the scores of windows until they gleamed in the sunlight. There were servants with brushes and servants with hoes; servants scrubbing the paving stones and servants buffing up the brass fitments on the impressive main door. A veritable army was at work. And that, Blackstone reminded himself, was only the servants carrying out their tasks *outside* the house. God alone knew how many more of them were involved indoors!

He ambled over to the stables, and watched the grooms and blacksmiths at work. Money had never meant much to him. Though his police salary would have seemed pitiful to any of those people sitting at the breakfast table, he still gave at least half of it to the orphanage in which he had been brought up. Yet looking at these fine horses – so noble and so spirited – he found himself wishing that he had suffi-cient funds to own one.

'You've got the bearing of a military man about you,' said a voice behind him. 'Seen service, have you?'

Blackstone turned around, and saw that the man who'd addressed him was George Carlton. Even at that early hour of the morning – early, at least, for the Quality – the Major already glowed with a health and vigour which his drug-soaked godfather, Sir Roderick Todd, would have envied.

'Sorry if I derailed your train of thought by speaking out,' Carlton said apologetically. 'It was just, seeing you standing there like that, I thought you might have been a soldier at one time.'

'I was,' Blackstone said.

'I'm very rarely wrong on such matters,' Carlton said, obviously pleased with himself. 'What the Army stamps on a man very rarely wears off, even with time. Might I enquire where it was you served?'

'India. And Afghanistan.'

'My father was in Afghanistan,' Carlton said. He put his hand to his mouth, as if he had been struck by a sudden revelation. 'Hold on there, a minute! Your first name wouldn't happen to be *Sam*, would it?'

'That's right, it would.'

'And when you were serving in Afghanistan, were you a sergeant, by any chance?'

'I was.'

'Sergeant Sam Blackstone,' Carlton said wonderingly. 'My father's often spoken about you. You saved his life, didn't you!'

Blackstone shrugged. 'He would have done the same for me, if I'd been in his position.'

And it was no lie, Blackstone thought – no attempt on his part to flatter a member of the officer class.

Mad Horatio Carlton hadn't been like many officers, who saw the men who served under them as mere cannon fodder. True, he wouldn't tolerate insolence, and would have any man who showed a sign of it flogged to within an inch of his life. But out there on the battlefield, all those fighting with him – whatever their rank – were his comrades.

'I say, it's a tremendous honour to meet you,' George Carlton said enthusiastically.

'As I told you, I only did for him what your father would have done for me if our positions had been reversed,' Blackstone said, as he felt his skin start to itch and realized that this was one of the rare occasions in his life when he was actually embarrassed.

'You do ride, I assume,' Carlton said, his boyish enthusiasm still very much in evidence.

'Yes, I ride a little,' Blackstone replied cautiously.

Carlton roared with laughter. 'Listen to the man,' he said, as if addressing an invisible audience. ' "A little", he says. I'm sure you're just as splendid in the saddle as you seem to be in most of the things you do. What say we take a couple of horses and go out for a gallop on the steppe?'

Ah, to be young, Blackstone thought – and then it suddenly occurred to him that despite his boyishness, George Carlton was not that much younger than he was himself.

Ah, to be privileged, he corrected himself. To assume that something could happen just because you wanted it to.

'What's the matter, Old Man?' George Carlton asked. 'Don't tell you're afraid you won't be able to keep up with my pace, because I shall simply refuse to believe that.'

'I'm not sure the Count would take kindly to someone like me borrowing one of his horses,' the Inspector said.

'But you won't be, don't you see?' Carlton countered. 'It's simply that I'll be borrowing *two* of them, and since the Count's my cousin, he can't really object to that, can he?'

'Possibly not,' Blackstone agreed, 'but I'm not sure Sir Roderick would like the idea much, either.'

'In case you need reminding, Sir Rodder's my *godfather*!' Carlton said. 'Always indulged me tremendously when I was a sprog, and I don't see any reason why he shouldn't continue to do it now I've grown to man's estate. So if he gives you any grief on the matter, just refer him to me.'

Blackstone looked beyond the house to the everlasting steppe. 'It's tempting,' he admitted.

It was more than tempting, he told himself. It was a golden opportunity to get close to one of the house guests

– to question him without Sir Roderick Todd constantly interfering.

The peasants were already labouring in the fields – and probably had been ever since first light – although 'fields' was probably the wrong term to apply to what they cultivated, since each man was toiling over only a small strip of land.

'Got rid of this kind of agriculture in our own country nearly two hundred years ago,' George Carlton commented. 'Good thing too, in my opinion. Look how much land is being used simply to divide one strip from another. Grow twice as much if they amalgamated their plots.'

But they wouldn't, Blackstone thought, remembering what Agnes had told him the night before.

To a peasant, his land – *his* land – was the reason for his existence, the very essence of his being. He wouldn't share it with others, even if, in the process, he were to become better off.

They were not more than a hundred yards beyond the village when they spied the military cordon which Captain Dobroskok had thrown around the area. It had seemed impressive enough from the coach, but observed from horseback it was truly awesome. The last time he had seen it, Blackstone had compared it to a band of iron around the village. Now it seemed more like a ring of fire – ready to burn anyone who dared to draw close to it.

'Quite a sight, isn't it?' Major Carlton asked.

It *was* quite a sight, Blackstone agreed silently. And all for the sake of a little golden egg.

The mounted soldiers had seen them approaching. The ones closest to the point that the new arrivals were obviously heading for had already reached down and unsheathed their rifles.

'I rather think we'd better turn round,' Blackstone said.

'Whatever for?' Carlton asked.

'Picket lines make me nervous,' Blackstone explained. 'They've strict orders not to let anyone through. If they think we're trying to break out, they might start shooting. And while I'm not afraid of death, I don't want to hasten it through a stupid misunderstanding.'

Carlton reached into his uniform jacket, and produced an impressive-looking piece of paper.

'Safe conduct or – as the French call it – *droit de passé*,' he said, with all the enthusiasm of a public schoolboy eager to show off the parcel of goodies he has received from home.

'Safe conduct!' Blackstone repeated thoughtfully. 'And is it bullet-proof, sir?'

Carlton laughed, as if he really thought his riding companion had been making a joke.

'You're worrying unnecessarily,' he said airily. 'These chaps aren't going to shoot us. That would be more than *their* lives are worth.'

It was the true officer mentality, Blackstone told himself.

They all believed – from the most elevated general, right down to the greenest lieutenant – that an enlisted man would never dare to shoot an officer. Which was why it always came as such a shock to them to learn that a hot lead cylinder is no respecter of rank.

'I think it still might be wisest for us to head back to the stables, sir,' Blackstone said.

'Nonsense!' Carlton replied. 'Can't give these horses a proper run within the military cordon. Need miles of open country for that.'

As they got closer – as it was possible to distinguish their faces – the soldiers sheathed their rifles.

'See what I mean?' the Major asked complacently.

The mounted soldiers at the point closest to where they would pass through the cordon came to attention – bodies and faces rigid, eyes fixed firmly on the horizon. They did not even blink when Carlton saluted them.

'Now how was that managed?' Blackstone asked, when he and the Major were clear of the line

'How was *what* managed?' Carlton asked innocently.

'Why did they let us through?'

'You saw my safe conduct, didn't you?'

113

'Yes, I did,' Blackstone agreed. 'But *they* didn't!'

'Of course they did. Had it in my hand all the time. They'd have to have been blind to miss it.'

'They *saw* it, but they didn't *examine* it. It could have been your laundry list, for all they knew. Besides, how do you come to have a safe conduct at all, when Captain Dobroskok assured me that no one – not even a Grand Duke, a member of the Russian *royal family* – is allowed to leave the area?'

Carlton grinned sheepishly. 'My father told me that you were a smart fellow. I should have listened to him. You've really caught me out, haven't you?'

'Undoubtedly,' Blackstone agreed. 'But what exactly is it that I've caught you out *in*?'

'Not sure I should tell you,' Carlton admitted. 'And if I *do* tell you, I'm not sure *how much* of it I should tell you about. Matter of fact, stuck out in the middle of nowhere as we are, I'm not even certain how much you're *entitled* to know. Not making much sense, am I?'

'Not a great deal,' Blackstone agreed.

'Tell you what, then,' Carlton said. 'Let's go for a ride, as we originally intended. In my experience, a good gallop does wonders for clearing the brain. I'll probably know exactly what to do when I've given my steed her head for a while. So what do you say? Shall we try a little hell-for-leather?'

Blackstone nodded.

There didn't seem to a lot else he *could* do.

Sixteen

Major George Carlton was an even finer horseman than his father, Sir Horatio, had been, and the steppe was the perfect terrain for him to display his ability to get the best out of a horse. Blackstone found it impossible to keep up, and for half an hour could do no more than follow in Carlton's wake, as he galloped past villages, circled small forests, jumped brooks and forded streams.

Finally, Carlton decided that he'd had enough and brought his horse to a halt.

'She's got a big heart, and she's earned a rest,' he said, patting the beast affectionately as Blackstone drew level with him. 'It's a pity you can't always rely on people as much as you can rely on horses.'

Blackstone felt he could use a rest himself – it was a long time since he'd ridden so hard – but the questions which had been intriguing him since they left the soldiers behind them were now demanding an answer.

'I'd like to know why it was so easy for us to get through the cordon, sir,' he said bluntly.

'We'll come on to that presently,' the Major promised him. 'But first, if you don't mind, I'd like to talk more generally. You *don't* mind, do you, Sergeant Blackstone?'

'That's *Inspector,* not *Sergeant,* if *you* don't mind, sir,' said Blackstone, who'd worked hard to get where he was.

'Ah, but that's just the point, don't you see!' George Carlton explained. '*Inspector* Blackstone is a London policeman, and I don't know much about the police or how they work. But *Sergeant* Blackstone is a soldier, like me. A soldier, furthermore, who saved my father's life. And if I'm going to confide in anybody – if I'm to say more than I probably should – I'd like it to be to *Sergeant* Blackstone. D'you understand what I'm saying?'

There was something about Carlton's boyish earnestness which made Blackstone grin, despite himself.

'That distinction's all well and good, sir,' he said, growing more serious again. 'But I can offer no guarantee that *Sergeant* Blackstone won't tell *Inspector* Blackstone what he knows.'

'Of course you can't,' Carlton said solemnly. 'I'd *expect* Sergeant Blackstone to tell Inspector Blackstone. It's his

115

duty. Still, if you've no objection, I'd be happier calling you "Sergeant".'

'I've no objection,' Blackstone told him.

For perhaps a couple of minutes, Major Carlton gazed intently at the horizon, then he turned to his companion and said, 'You know, Sergeant Blackstone, I really *do* worry about the future.'

'Your own future? Or the future of your family?'

Carlton laughed nervously. 'Nothing so trivial as that, I'm afraid. What's got me worried is the future of my own country – and the future of Europe in general.'

'That's a lot for any man to have on his plate,' Blackstone said, not quite sure where Carlton was going with all this, but certain he was going *somewhere*.

Carlton frowned. 'The problem is, you see, that we soldiers have got so good at killing.'

'We've *always* been good at killing. It's what we've been doing since time immemorial.'

'Perhaps so. But we've not always had the means to do it so *effectively*. The outcome of battles – of whole wars, come to that – used to turn on the deaths of a few thousand – or even a few *hundred* – soldiers. After all, there are only so many men you *can* kill when all you're armed with is a sword or a spear. But it isn't like that anymore.'

'Isn't it?' Blackstone asked, although he could now see the lines on which the Major's thoughts were running.

'No, it isn't. You remember me saying I was in the Sudan with General Kitchener?'

'Yes.'

'Well, it changed my view about a lot of things, but especially about warfare.' A shudder ran right through Carlton's frame. 'I don't think I'll ever be able to forget what I saw there.'

'Are you talking about the campaign in general, or the Battle of Omdurman in particular?'

'Omdurman. The Dervishes who attacked us were armed with spears, and bows and arrows. Some of them had no more than copies of the Koran in their hands. On our side, we had machine guns and repeater rifles. The poor devils never got closer to our lines than three hundred yards away. Killing them was easy. It was like scything down wheat. And when it was all over, and we had time to assess the damage, we calculated they'd lost eleven thousand men, with another sixteen thousand wounded. And what do you think the losses were on our side?'

'Very low, I should imagine.'

'We had forty-eight casualties in total.'

Blackstone nodded, but said nothing.

'It was a terrible sight to behold,' Carlton continued, 'but it would have been even worse if the Dervishes had been as well-armed as we were, because then there would have been huge losses on *both* sides.'

'What's the point you're making?' Blackstone wondered.

'The European powers – especially France and Germany – *are* as well-armed as we are, and if we have to fight them, it will be a real bloodbath which will make Omdurman seem like no more than a skirmish.'

'What do you think the chances are that we *will* have to fight them?' Blackstone asked.

'Very high! Far *too* high! I know you could say it's forty years since we fought the Russians in the Crimea. But forty years isn't *that* long in the larger scheme of things.'

'True,' Blackstone agreed.

'And think of the wars which *might have been*! Which almost *were*!' Carlton continued. 'It's just *two* years since we nearly went to war with the Germans because of their support for the Boers in southern Africa. And it's less than *one* year since there was talk of us declaring war on France because it wanted to annex part of the Sudan. So who'll be the next enemy? Russia again? Or will we revive our quarrel with the French or the Germans? Nobody knows! The way I see it, everything's so delicately balanced between the Great Powers that it'll only take the slightest shift, one way or the other, to upset the whole blasted apple cart.'

'Then everybody had better learn to tread very carefully, hadn't they?' Blackstone said.

117

'But that's just the point, you see. They're not treading carefully at all! There are any number of high-ranking officers in all the countries I've mentioned who see themselves as the next Napoleon and are just itching for a fight. And their rulers are sometimes no better. Her Majesty the Queen, thank the Lord, is willing to be guided by her government, but the German Kaiser's always looking for trouble, and as for the Tsar of Russia – he's well-meaning enough, but he's a very weak man, and the last chap you want in charge of a loaded gun is one who'll fire it through pure bloody loss of nerve.'

'You talk as if you know the Kaiser and the Tsar personally,' Blackstone said.

Carlton laughed nervously. 'Is . . . er . . . that the impression I gave you?' he asked. 'I never meant to. But I do know their *sort*, if you understand what I'm saying. I've served with all kinds of men in the Army, and there's plenty of indecisive ones like Nicholas of Russia, and plenty of mad buggers like William of Germany.'

They'd been dancing around the main point long enough, Blackstone decided. 'Tell me about the second coach that left the Big House on the morning of the robbery,' he said.

'The second coach?'

'The one that had its crest masked over with black paint.'

'How did you . . . how did you know about that?' Carlton gasped.

'It doesn't matter *how* I know,' Blackstone told him. 'The point is, I don't know *enough* to conduct my investigation properly. And unless you choose to enlighten me, I'll probably never find this infernal golden egg.'

Carlton looked more shocked now than he had when Blackstone had mentioned the blacked-out coach.

'The golden egg!' he echoed, as if his brain were incapable of any other response. He made a determined effort to pull himself together. 'Is that what you think this whole affair is all about?'

'Isn't it?'

'I knew you were being kept in the dark about some

118

things. You have to be when you're dealing with matters of national security. But it never even occurred to me that they'd keep you *so* much in the dark. Damn it, it's not fair! It's not fair at all! It's like sending a man into enemy territory wearing a blindfold.'

'You have the power to remove that blindfold if you choose to,' Blackstone pointed out.

'And I will!' Carlton said firmly. 'I'll do it whatever it costs me personally. They can court-martial me, if they like. I don't care. It's unforgivable to treat a front-line soldier like you as if he were . . .'

'As if he were what?' Blackstone asked.

But Carlton was no longer looking at him. Instead, the Major's eyes were scanning the middle distance.

'I don't like that,' he said worriedly.

'What are you talking about?'

Carlton pointed his finger in the direction of his gaze. 'I'm talking about them!'

A group of riders was approaching, Blackstone saw. There were six of them, and they were moving at a gallop.

Carlton drew his sword. 'What, in God's name, was I thinking of, to let us get cornered like this?' he said angrily. 'How could I ever have been so completely stupid?'

'Put your sword away,' Blackstone advised. 'You don't know yet that you're even going to need it.'

'Don't I just? Haven't you seen the bloody fur hats that they're wearing, man!'

'Yes, but—'

'That means they're Cossacks, you idiot. They're the nearest thing that Russia's got to the Mongol Horde.'

'Are they out to rob us?'

'Of course they're not. They're out to bloody kill us! And it's all my fault. I set it up for them.' Carlton slashed his sword through the air. 'Listen, Blackstone, I'll hold them off while you make a run for it.'

'I'm not running,' Blackstone said firmly.

'But you're not even armed.'

'Then give me your pistol, and I will be.'

'I'm *ordering* you to go!' Carlton screamed.

'I'm not in the Army any more, so your order's not worth a tuppenny damn,' Blackstone told him.

The Cossacks were drawing ever closer, and Blackstone had seen enough men riding into battle in his time to be sure that Carlton had been right in his assessment of their intention.

'Look here, Sergeant, you really have to go while you still can,' Carlton said desperately.

'No!'

'But don't you see, it doesn't really matter if I'm killed, whereas it will be an absolute disaster if they lay their hands on you.'

'Why?' Blackstone demanded. 'What's so special about me?'

'We've no time to talk about that now. Just get the hell out of here.'

'The pistol, Major!' Blackstone said. 'Give me the bloody pistol, for God's sake!'

Carlton unbuckled his holster with his free hand, took out the gun and passed it to Blackstone. 'If my father had ordered you to leave, you'd have gone without question,' he said miserably.

At the rate the Cossacks were moving, they were not more than a half a minute away. They had still not drawn their swords nor unsheathed their rifles, but that meant nothing. Because what they did have in their hands were their short whips, and a Cossack's whip was a lethal weapon.

Blackstone sighted the pistol, and loosed off a round. It went over the riders' heads, as he'd intended it to. A warning shot. He knew, even as he fired it, that it was probably a waste of a bullet, but at least he'd given the Cossacks a *chance* to back away.

The riders kept on coming. Suddenly – without any warning at all – Carlton spurred his horse forward, then wheeled it around sideways. He was deliberately presenting a barrier that the Cossacks would have to deal with before

120

they could get at Blackstone, but he was also effectively blocking the Inspector's line of fire.

'Get out the way, you bloody idiot!' Blackstone shouted.

'And miss all the fun?' Carlton yelled back. 'There's only six of them, Sergeant. I don't need any help from you, so I'd really appreciate it if you'd get the hell out of here.'

It was British-officer-class bravado at its most extreme, and neither the man who spoke the words nor the one who heard them spoken believed them for a moment. Like his father before him, Major Carlton was putting his own life at risk in an attempt to save a man he considered to be serving under him.

The Cossacks had been riding in a tight formation, but now they parted, so that two were approaching Carlton from his left flank and two from his right. The remaining pair separated – again one to the left and one to the right – and cut an even wider swathe, avoiding the confrontation completely. Their job, it seemed obvious, was to deal with Blackstone.

The Major slashed out at the leading Cossack coming at him from the right, but the man had been ready for such a move, and veered his horse to the side. Carlton swung around to deal with the first of his attackers from the left – but too late. The handle of the Cossack's whip caught him in the throat. He tried to scream, but couldn't. He tried both to hold on to his sword and to avoid falling backwards in his saddle, but his body betrayed him in both respects. The sword fell to the ground, and the Major lurched towards the hindquarters of his mount.

He might have been able to stage some kind of recovery, given time, but the Cossacks were intent on seeing that did not happen, and only moments after being struck by the whip, he was being dragged off his mount.

The two remaining Cossacks were clear of the melee, and coming at Blackstone. The Inspector took careful aim and shot at the one approaching from the left. He was aiming for the chest, but his target was moving deliberately erratically, and he only succeeded in hitting him in the shoulder.

121

There was no time to loose off a second shot. Even as his brain was noting the success of the first, he felt a huge weight crash into him, and then was flying towards the ground with the second Cossack's powerful hands already locked tightly around his throat.

The two men hit the earth with considerable force, though since Blackstone was on the bottom, it was his body which absorbed most of the impact.

The air knocked out of him – and feeling as if every bone in his body had been broken – Blackstone fought back, thrusting his outstretched fingers at his opponent's eyes. But his aim was off and he only succeeding in jabbing the Cossack in the forehead.

The Cossack shifted position, so that now he was straddling his opponent. He had released his grip on Blackstone's throat, but only so he could reach for the knife he carried in his belt. Blackstone clawed up and grabbed at the descending knife-arm. Yet even as he did so, he knew it was a wasted effort, because the Cossack had both position and leverage on his side.

As Blackstone gasped and struggled, the knife, aimed at his chest, drew closer and closer.

Experience of other knife wounds, received in the past, told him that he would probably feel no more than a gentle prick at first. Then the knife would dig deeper, slicing its way through his flesh. And if it did not encounter resistance from a rib in its journey, it would go on until it reached his heart.

For less than a single beat of that heart, his body would scream at him that this should not be happening – that it *could* not be happening. Then it would be forced to accept that it *had* happened, and give up the ghost. The heart would stop beating – and he would be dead.

A terrible cacophony of noise filled what Blackstone took to be the last few moments of his life. There was his own laboured breathing – as loud, to his ears, as a cannon's blast. There was the grunting of the man on top of him, as he strained to bring the conflict to its final, bloody conclusion.

The horses' hooves pounded on the ground, the men riding them shouted loudly, as men always will in battle. And when yet another sound was added to the fearful din going on around him – this time a single loud crack – Blackstone could not be entirely sure what it was. But he thought it might have been a shot.

The Cossack who was straddling him suddenly went rigid, and then – almost immediately – limp. His burning eyes glazed over. His heavy breathing was transformed into a desperate gurgle, and then stopped completely. The knife fell from his hand.

With some considerable effort, Blackstone pushed the dead Cossack clear of him, and then tried to struggle to his feet. But it was no more than a pointless exercise. The fall from the horse, the pressure that had been exerted on his windpipe, the tremendous fight he had put into trying to keep the knife away from his heart, now finally proved too much for him. As he pressed down on the ground with his hands, hoping it would give him the necessary leverage, his brain informed him that it had had enough – and shut down.

Seventeen

It was the sun which had gently awakened him when he had been lying in Sweet Agnes's bed only a few hours earlier, and it was the same sun – though far hotter and more unforgiving now – that he was aware of as he regained consciousness on the hard, but springy, ground of the Russian steppe.

Blackstone's first thought was to wonder why he was still alive. His second was to ask himself whether it was intended that he should continue in that state, or if he was merely experiencing a temporary reprieve.

Where were his enemies?

Were they watching him, even at that moment?

If they were, then they probably thought he was still unconscious, and hence no threat. It was not much of an advantage he had over them, but it was the only one he'd got – and he was damned if he was going to squander it by moving before he was completely ready.

He cautiously opened one eye, and saw the pistol Major Carlton had given him, lying on the ground a few yards away.

Good, he told himself. He at least had a weapon with which he could kill one or two of the Cossacks before the rest inevitably cut him down.

He listened for the telltale sounds which would reveal the enemy's position to him. But there was only the noise of the wind, whistling through the grass. He waited, expecting to hear one of the Cossacks break the silence, but none did.

Had they gone? That didn't make any sense. The Cossacks were not the kind of men to confuse unconsciousness with death. And even if they had, they would surely not have left Major Carlton's pistol behind them.

He listened again. A horse snorted, and pawed its hoof on the ground, but still no one spoke.

Perhaps the Cossacks were waiting for him to make the first move. Perhaps they had been wagering about how long it would take him – or whether he would have the courage to move at all.

He tensed himself for action, then rolled over several times and grabbed the pistol. Once he had it firmly in his hand, he forced himself up into a crouching position. His chest hurt like the devil. So did his arms, his legs and his head. But he already had the gun cocked, and he was more than ready to take the Cossack bastards on.

There were no Cossacks *to* take on! Save for the two horses – his own and the Major's – which were quietly munching at the grass, the vast plain seemed to be totally empty.

Why were the horses still there? Left to their own devices, they should have wandered off, because with horses – as with men – the grass was always greener in some other place.

'There's no time for this idle speculation,' he told himself with all the anger his weary frame could muster. 'No time at all! You've got to get back to the redoubt. Your men will be waiting for you there.'

His mind was wandering, he realized, and wondered if he had a fever. Fever or not, he had to get back – and to the Big House where the robbery had taken place, *not* to the military redoubt back in India.

He could understand now why the horses had stayed where they had. There'd been no choice in the matter. A peg of some kind had been hammered into the ground, and the beasts had been tethered to it.

But where was Major Carlton? What the devil had happened to Major Carlton?

He shifted his gaze a little to the left and got his answer. Carlton was lying on the ground a dozen yards from the tethered horse.

'Are you all right, Major?' Blackstone shouted in a cracked voice. 'Do you think you can stand up?'

The Major made no reply.

Blackstone slowly straightened up. Rising to his feet brought on temporary giddiness. Walking towards the Major made him acutely aware of aches and pains he'd only suspected while he'd been lying on the ground. But it was the unanswered questions which were troubling him the most.

What was it that Major Carlton had been about to tell him when the Cossacks appeared from out of nowhere?

Why had the Cossacks appeared *at all*?

Had it been their intention to kill anyone at all they came across, or were they on a definite mission?

And if they had been on a definite mission, why had they

failed to accomplish it, when there seemed to be absolutely nothing standing in their way?

Even before he bent down to touch Carlton, he knew that the other man was dead, but he went through the motions of searching for signs of life anyway.

The slash of the whip across his throat had probably been what killed him, Blackstone decided. It would have crushed his windpipe, and from then on it was only a matter of time before he choked to death. But his attackers had made doubly sure that their assault had accomplished its aim – the deep red stain around his heart was proof of that.

So why not me? Blackstone asked himself again.

Why was *I* spared?

For all his boyish good looks, the Major had possessed a manly figure, and – deadweight – it would have been a hard enough task for a Blackstone feeling on the top of his form to hoist the corpse over the saddle. Blackstone as he was now, found it almost impossible. Each attempt to heft Carlton up brought on new bouts of agony, and the horse – as if through pure malevolence – kept shifting its position every time the operation looked like being successful.

In the end, however, Blackstone did achieve his objective, and once he had Carlton hanging over both flanks of the horse, he tied the dead man's wrists to his ankles, in order to ensure that he did not slip off again.

The ride to the point at which they had encountered the Cossacks had been fast and furious. Covering the same ground in reverse was a much slower process. Blackstone – partly as a result of his own injuries, partly in deference to the dead major – never let the two horses go beyond a gentle trot.

And all the time he was making his way back to the military cordon, he kept expecting the Cossacks to reappear – to correct the mistake they made earlier and finish him off.

But no Cossacks *did* appear, and at just after two o'clock – as nearly as he could tell by looking at the sun – he caught sight of the cordon, outlined against the horizon.

Did they know there was a renegade band of Cossacks on the loose, he wondered hazily.

And if they knew, did it concern them?

Probably not. The military mind is an inflexible mind at best. The soldiers had been ordered to seal off the area around the village and the house, and that was what they had done superbly. Why, then, should they care if bloody murder had been committed beyond their range of operations?

But *Blackstone* cared.

He did not know what secrets Major Carlton had been keeping close to his bosom, nor what role the Major had been meant to play in this whole affair of the golden egg. But he *did* know that when danger had appeared on the horizon, Carlton had told him to run. And that when he refused to flee, the Major had done all that he could to protect him.

Major George Carlton had died a soldier's death. An honourable death, of which his father could have been justly proud. But it was also a death which had to be avenged – and Blackstone was determined he would be the instrument of that vengeance, for who else was there?

The soldiers on the cordon line had spotted him, and two of them detached themselves and began to ride towards him. They seemed to Blackstone to be taking an inordinate amount of time, but that was probably because – as far as he could tell – they were not letting their horses' hooves touch the ground, but instead, and in a most unmilitary manner, were making them tread air.

He watched their slow progress with a growing impatience. Why couldn't they get there quicker, so he could tell them what he was going to do to the men who killed Carlton?

They were still some distance away. In fact, they seemed to be moving backwards. Very well then, if he couldn't tell them all about it, he would just have to settle for telling God.

He looked up at the sky and shook his fist. 'I'll get the bastards!' he bellowed.

127

Then he swayed and, for the second time that day, fell off his horse.

Eighteen

It was when the man had reached a point roughly half-way between the village and the Big House that he began to think about operational matters in general and his own mission in particular.

An operation should resemble a smooth piece of machinery, he told himself. From its very inception, infinite care should be taken in constructing it. Then, before it was ever activated, each part should be thoroughly tested to make sure it would properly fulfil its function. That having been done, the operator should be able to just sit back and let it run its course.

But it never *was* like that – at least for him. Because however meticulous the preparations – however thorough the checking – factors over which he had no control were constantly jamming up the works.

And then what happened?

Then he was forced to improvise, just as he was being forced to improvise now.

If only those for whom he was working would listen, he thought. If only they would leave matters to the experts. But they were convinced they knew best – convinced that their own involvement was all the lubrication the machine needed. And when the cogs finally refused to mesh, these same people turned to him, and told him to fix it – as if it were the easiest thing in the world!

At least the moon was shrouded in cloud for the moment, he noted. At least the weather seemed to be co-operating, even if the human side of the operation was not.

There were no soldiers standing on guard in front of the Big House, and whilst he was grateful for that omission, he could not but feel contempt for those who had thought security was unnecessary.

He had a plan of the house clearly mapped out inside his head, so at least there would be no problem finding his way around. Yet there were plenty of other difficulties which *might* arise.

Say, for example, he encountered one of the guests during the second phase of the operation. What would he do then? Well, he supposed, if it were an *unimportant* guest, he would simply kill the unfortunate man or woman. But if the guest in question *were* important, it would present him with a real dilemma, because even *he* could not assassinate a grand duke or grand duchess with impunity.

Fortunately, there would be no such problem during the first – more difficult – phase of the operation, because that would take place on the ground floor, where there were only the kitchens, workshops and servants' dormitories.

He had heard that in England, where the policeman came from, the servants slept at the top of the house, while the aristocracy occupied the lower floors. But then the English did not have the violent flash floods which were so common during the Russian spring thaw, else they would no doubt have decided – as the Russians had done – that it was better to have servants drowned in their sleep than risk damage to valuable carpets and furnishings.

The impressive main door to the house might have severely tested his lock-picking skills, but the door to the laundry room presented no difficulties at all. Once inside he made his way quietly down the corridor until he reached one of the sets of steep, narrow stairs which connected the servants' world with that of their privileged masters.

He had not been told who was sleeping in which room – his informant had thought that collecting such information would be bound to point the finger of suspicion in the morning – but that did not really matter. Since the object of the exercise was to spread alarm through the *whole* of

129

the West Wing, any starting point would be as good as any other.

He had reached the first-floor corridor, which was so much wider and grander than the one which ran directly below it. As luck would have it, the moon chose, just at that point, to emerge from behind the clouds, and the floor was suddenly bathed in a pale yellow light.

Good, he would not have to use the lantern that he'd brought with him after all.

He took his time inspecting the corridor, before selecting a window half-way down it as the spot at which to begin his work. He examined the thick crimson curtains – heavy with elaborate embroidery – which hung from the ceiling to the floor. Excellent!

This one set of curtains alone, he thought, would have cost more than a peasant in the village could earn in a lifetime. But he felt no sympathy for the peasants in question. If they acted like sheep, they deserved to be treated like sheep. If they did not fight back when they had the chance, they had no cause for complaint when they saw the butcher's knife hovering over them.

He unstrapped the pack he had been carrying on his back, and spread out the contents on the floor. Powder, liquid, wadding and a timing device – all he needed for his night's work.

He set about his task. It took him less than three minutes. There were others who could have completed the job even quicker, he realized – but they had not been available, and he had.

The work completed to his satisfaction, he quickly made his way to the servants' stairs. As he passed along the lower corridor, he heard one of the male servants groan in his sleep, and chuckled softly at the thought that the man would soon be wide awake and driven by panic.

There was no real need to re-lock the door by which he had entered the house, but he knew that he had time – and that it would add to the confusion later – so he did it anyway.

The moon had retreated behind the clouds again, so maybe God – if such a being existed – was working with him to help him confound his enemies.

He did not run as he covered the ground between the house and the main gate, but neither did he dawdle, and it was only when he reached the gate itself that he permitted himself to stop and look around.

The house was now completely in darkness, except for a faint – but spreading – glow by the upper window in the West Wing.

Excellent, he thought – and had to resist the temptation to start whistling.

Nineteen

At one point in the course of his delirium, Blackstone recalled seeing Sir Roderick Todd standing over him, purple with rage and screaming that he would break him for what he had allowed to happen. At another, he was conscious of Agnes mopping his brow with a damp cloth – and sobbing softly to herself. Mostly, however, he was unconcerned with anything that belonged to the real world. Instead, he lived within his own mind – in a swirling, multi-coloured, many-shaped fantasy which answered every single question he had ever asked, and yet at the same time told him absolutely nothing at all.

On the morning of what he was later told was the third day of his confinement, he awoke to find that his brain had finally returned to something like its normal functioning.

He was almost sure that he could now distinguish between what had been real and what had not. He knew, for example, that both Sir Roderick and Agnes had been to see him, but he doubted very much that a huge eagle with golden teeth had flown around the room, advising him to forget all about its egg and worry about the nest instead.

Yet there was one incident over which his uncertainty still persisted. At some time during the previous night, he was *almost* convinced, he had heard a loud bell ringing incessantly in the distance. Other sounds had followed – horses' hooves and men screaming at the tops of their voices. And though he was quite prepared to be told that it had all been part of a grand delusion, he still could not shake off the belief that he had definitely smelled acrid smoke.

He was still lying there, deliberating over the problem, when the door swung open and Agnes walked in.

'Do you like the room?' she asked, wafting cheeriness about her much as an orthodox priest wafts incense. 'It's a pleasant change, isn't it?'

He had not even noticed the room, but now he saw that it was neither the cupboard in which he had spent his first night in the Big House, nor Agnes's bedroom, in which he had spent the second.

'They wanted to put you in some dismal little room off the servants' quarters, but I was having none of that,' Agnes continued. 'I said that you'd been injured in the line of duty and that you were entitled to the very best the house could offer. Well, of course, they'd never have given you anything that grand – not even if you'd almost laid down your life for the Count himself – but what they *have* given you isn't bad at all, now is it?'

Blackstone looked around. No, it *wasn't* bad at all.

'Where exactly am I?' he asked.

'East Wing. The floor they keep for minor guests. Still, even being a *minor* guest is something of a promotion for you.'

She was being just a little *too* chirpy, he thought.

And why was that?

Because she'd been worried about him, and this was just a way of expressing her relief?

Or, and this seemed more likely to him, was it that she

was embarrassed? Embarrassed – and perhaps even ashamed – about what they had done together in her room. So embarrassed, in fact, that she was using her cheeriness as a cloak, to disguise just how uncomfortable she felt.

'And it's certainly just as well they didn't put you in the *West* Wing, isn't it?' Agnes continued.

'Why?'

'Because if they'd forgotten about you – and they may well have done in all the confusion – you might possibly have burned to death.'

'What are you talking about?' he asked.

She looked at him strangely. 'The fire!'

'What fire?'

'The one in the West Wing. Didn't you know? Hasn't anybody told you about it?'

'You're the first person who's been to see me seen since I came round,' Blackstone admitted.

'The servants were supposed to check on you every half hour!' Agnes said, outraged. 'I'll give them hell when I catch them.' Then she softened a little. 'I suppose I can't blame them completely,' she continued. 'Everything has been at sixes and sevens since they put the fire out.'

'Was it a big fire?'

'Big enough. Several of the rooms have been badly damaged, though the structure as a whole doesn't seem to have suffered too much.'

'What caused it?'

'Nobody knows. Or, at least, nobody's told me.'

It might have some connection with the robbery, Blackstone thought, with a sudden quickening interest. Then again, he cautioned himself, it might not. At any rate, there were other matters of more concern to him at that moment.

'What about Major Carlton?' he said – hoping to hear Agnes reply that the Major's death had been no more than a part of his delirium, yet knowing deep inside him that it had been all too horribly true.

'The poor man,' Agnes said. 'They packed him in ice almost as soon as you'd brought him back, and then the

133

soldiers took him to the railway station. They put him on the first train that came through, and he should be nearly in St Petersburg by now.'

There was no time to mourn for Carlton, however much he wanted to, Blackstone told himself.

Not now. Not yet.

'What do people here think happened to us out on the steppe, Agnes?' he asked.

The question seemed to surprise the governess. 'They *know* what happened,' she said. 'You ran into some brigands. They robbed you, and killed Major Carlton. That *is* what happened, isn't it?'

No, Blackstone thought. It most definitely isn't.

Brigands would have taken the horses, not tethered them so they'd be waiting for him when he eventually came round.

Brigands would never have murdered one of their own to prevent him from killing the man he'd attacked. And that, Blackstone was starting to realize, was what they *must* have done! There was no other way to explain what had happened to the Cossack with the knife – no other reason why he wouldn't have pressed on and driven the knife through the English policeman's heart.

'We need to have a serious talk,' he said.

'What about?'

'I have to know what's been going on in the house while I've been fighting off the fever.'

'I've told you all I've heard about the fire.'

'Not *just* the fire. *Everything* that's been going on. Who's been acting strangely . . .'

'These people are Russians. They always act strangely.'

'. . . any unusual occurrences, any variation from the usual routine of the house . . .'

Agnes held up her hand to silence him, and tut-tutted disapprovingly.

'I'm sure it all seems very important to you at the moment, Sam,' she said, 'but you're simply not strong enough to deal with anything of that sort yet. What you need is a good long rest. There'll be plenty of time to get back to your investigation later.'

The detective in him knew that was not true – had learned from experience that the colder a trail gets, the harder it is to follow.

'What are you doing now?' Agnes asked sternly.

'I'm getting out of bed,' Blackstone told her, swinging his legs awkwardly on to the floor.

'You'll do no such thing,' Agnes told him.

But he already had, and when he took a few tentative steps towards her, he was pleasantly surprised to find that he did not fall over.

'Where are my clothes?' he asked.

'The state they were in, where do you *think* they are?' Agnes replied, her hands now bunched into angry fists and resting firmly on her hips. 'I had them burned.'

'You had them *burned*!'

He could only imagine the expression on his own face from Agnes's reaction to it. At first she tried to maintain her stern countenance, but then she gave up and burst into laughter.

'Don't worry, I'm not expecting you to walk around in your underclothes for the rest of the time you're here,' she said.

'But I only have two suits to my name, and the other one's back in London,' he protested.

'That's probably why I couldn't find it, then,' Agnes said, still chuckling to herself. 'But you've no need to fret. I've begged one of the Count's old suits off him. It should fit you well enough, and it's probably better quality than you've ever felt on your back before. So if you insist on getting up, when any man with an ounce of sense would keep to his bed . . .'

'I do.'

'. . . if you *absolutely, positively,* insist, you'll find the Count's old suit in the wardrobe over in the corner.'

'I meant it when I said we needed to have a serious talk,' Blackstone told the governess. 'And it has to be soon, because, what with the fever, I've wasted far too much time already.'

Agnes nodded. 'All right,' she agreed reluctantly. 'If you're recovered enough to dress yourself, and can find your way up to the schoolroom, we'll talk. Be there in ten minutes. I'll have the samovar on the boil, so there should be a nice hot cup of tea waiting for you.'

'You couldn't lay your hands on some whisky as well, could you?' Blackstone asked hopefully.

Agnes gave him a reproachful look, then softened again and said, 'I'll see what I can do.'

Twenty

Getting dressed was not as easy as Blackstone had anticipated. The trousers he was attempting to climb into were being most uncooperative – or so it seemed to him. And when he tried to cover his aching torso with the jacket, the arm-holes deliberately shifted around so he could not find them. The socks alone were willing to be compliant, but pulling them on caused his body to scream out that such stretching and tugging was both cruel and unnecessary. These were all signs that he should have stayed in bed after all, he told himself – but then he'd never been much of a one for paying attention to signs.

When he finally reached the schoolroom, he found Agnes gazing at a map of Europe on the wall.

'Swotting up for the first lesson you'll give when the children get back?' he asked, using jocularity as a cover for the fact that his difficulties in dressing had caused him to arrive ten minutes later than he'd promised he would.

Agnes jumped, as if he'd startled her.

'What?' she said.

'I was asking you if you were swotting up for some future lesson.'

'No, I wasn't,' Agnes said seriously.

'Then what *were* you doing?'

'I was thinking.'

'About something important?'

'Perhaps.' Agnes stepped clear of the map, so that Blackstone could have a better view of it. 'One of the exercises I give the children is to take a map of Europe, cut out all the countries with scissors, mix them all up, and put them back together again as if they were a jigsaw,' she continued.

'It sounds like fun.'

'It's *educational*,' Agnes said, with just a hint of school ma'am creeping into her voice. 'Yet sometimes I can't help wondering whether I'm giving them the wrong idea.'

'What do you mean by that?'

'I worry that I might be helping to create the impression in their minds that Europe is somehow fixed and unchangeable. But it isn't, is it?'

'History would suggest not,' Blackstone said.

'Exactly!' Agnes agreed. Still standing to the side of the map, she began tracing out shapes on it with her index finger. 'This bit of Russia – Vistula Province – was part of an independent Poland until not so long ago.' The finger moved on. 'All these states were free, too, until they became part of the German Empire, less than thirty years ago. And *this* part of Germany,' she indicated Alsace–Lorraine, 'belonged to France until the War of 1870. So will I still be teaching from this same map in twenty years time? Or will war and conquest have changed the whole picture again by then?'

'You mean, will something have happened to upset the balance of power in Europe?' Blackstone asked, thinking of Major George Carlton's words, just before the poor man died.

'Precisely! Alliances seem to change almost from day to

137

day. The countries we counted as our friends last year are now virtually our enemies, though by next year they may well have become our closest allies again.' Agnes sighed. 'But you didn't come up here to discuss *real politik*, did you?'

'No, I didn't.'

'Then take a seat, and I'll bring you your tea.'

'And the whisky?' Blackstone asked hopefully.

'We'll see about that after we've talked for a while,' Agnes said sternly. 'If I think you're up to it, you shall have a small glass. And if I don't . . .'

'Then I can whistle for it?'

'Exactly.'

Blackstone smiled. 'I'll be up to it,' he promised.

And he hoped that he was right.

Agnes gave him the tea, then perched on the edge of the table. 'What do you want to know?' she asked.

'Let's begin with the fire,' Blackstone suggested. 'When and where did it start?'

'I don't know *where* it started, but it was about three o'clock when the church bell in the village woke me up, so I suppose that it must have been some time before that?'

'Why did they ring the church bell?' Blackstone wondered.

'To rouse the peasants.'

'I can't imagine they particularly *wanted* to be roused, not after a day's back-breaking work in the fields.'

'I'm sure they did not. But they have the same duty to protect the Count's property as they had when they were his serfs.'

'And what if they refuse?'

'They'd never refuse.'

'Because they'd be afraid of the consequences?'

Agnes shook her head wonderingly. 'You really *don't* know Russia, do you, Sam?' she said. 'Consequences have nothing to do with the way they act. They wouldn't refuse to help the Count, because it would never occur to them that they could. They fast throughout Lent – no meat, no

138

milk, no eggs – even though they have only the vaguest idea of what religion is all about. They get drunk after Easter, because that's what people do. And they come to the Count's assistance whenever they're called to do so. "Why" simply doesn't enter into it. That's the way it is, the way it always has been, and the way it always will be. They can't even imagine any other life.'

'So they came and helped to put out the fire,' Blackstone said. 'What happened next?'

'The peasants went back to the village – no doubt cursing the Count under their breath when they were close to the house, and being much louder about him once they were clear of it. Then all the servants set about moving the belongings of the guests who were staying in the West Wing into rooms in the East Wing. I don't know what happened after that, because I went back to my lonely bed.' Agnes paused again. 'I'm getting rather bored with the fire,' she said. 'Let's talk about something else, shall we?'

'Like what?'

'I've been doing some thinking about the golden egg, and also about the mysterious carriage which left the house at roughly the same time as the Prince's carriage did.'

'Oh, yes?'

'We know the Prince didn't steal the egg. What would be the point in his taking something that was already his?'

'Agreed.'

'But what about the occupant of the other carriage?'

'You think *he* might have taken it?' Blackstone asked. 'In other words, you think the egg is no longer here?'

'That *is* what I thought might be the case at first,' Agnes admitted. 'But it just wouldn't make sense if it were.'

'Explain yourself,' Blackstone suggested.

'Everybody knew the egg had been stolen by then, yet the other carriage was still allowed to leave. Why was that?'

'You tell me.'

'Because the person in the carriage – whoever he was – was as much above suspicion as the Prince himself!'

'And who might that person be?'

Agnes frowned. 'That's a very taxing question. Under normal circumstances, I'd say it had to be someone who was so important that no one dared question him – even if they did suspect he was involved in the robbery. That's certainly what I thought at first.'

'And why don't you think it anymore?'

'Because Grand Duke Ivan's important – he's a member of the Russian Royal Family – and he hasn't been allowed to leave. So the only way I can see the soldiers ever agreeing to let anyone else go is if the Prince of Wales was prepared to vouch for him personally.'

'So you think this man was a friend of the Prince's?'

Agnes shook her head, not so much in denial but as if she were impatient with the slowness of his mind.

'It doesn't really matter *who* he was,' she said.

'Doesn't it?'

'No! What's important is that the Prince must have been convinced that he didn't have the egg. So, in all probability, he didn't. Which means that the egg is still here!'

'You're a governess, not a policeman. Why are you showing so much interest in this matter?' Blackstone wondered.

Agnes smiled, almost enigmatically. 'There are several reasons,' she said. 'The first is that I like you, Sam, and want to see you succeed. The second is that this whole affair is damaging the Count's reputation. And while I may not like him very much myself, I am a member of his household, and feel a certain responsibility to help him in any way I can.'

'Anything else?'

Agnes's smile broadened. 'But the third reason – and possibly the most important of all – is that I was born with an incredibly curious nature, and love solving puzzles.'

Blackstone felt a slight pang of disappointment, the cause of which he couldn't quite pin down.

'Now I've offended you,' Agnes said mischievously. 'You'd have liked me to say that my first reason was the most important one – that what I wanted more than anything

140

else in the world was to see you gain another feather in your cap.'

Yes, that was it, Blackstone thought with self-disgust. That was *exactly* what it was.

He had seduced this woman – this virgin – but in the process he had somehow managed to allow himself to be seduced as well. Now, instead of using her purely as a sounding board – which had been his original plan – he was taking everything she said in personal terms.

And that had never happened to him before!

Even with Hannah – his beloved, worldly-wise Hannah, who'd had so much more control over him than this until-recently virginal woman could ever hope to exert – he had managed to maintain some distance. Even with Hannah, he had learned to be a lover when they were in bed together, but a policeman during the time they were out of it.

'I was just teasing you a little,' Agnes said contritely. 'I never wanted to upset you.'

'You didn't upset me,' he told her.

But what he really meant was: I'll do my level best to see it never happens again.

There was a roaring below – a great bellow of excitement and anticipation. It was the sort of noise only normally heard at an important football match – or at a public execution.

Agnes went over to the window and looked down. 'I can see what's got them so worked up,' she said. 'Some soldiers have just arrived, and they've brought a prisoner with them.'

'A prisoner!'

'Yes. The poor blighter's got one end of a rope tied around his wrists, and the other end's tied round one of the soldier's saddle horns. They must have brought him from the village. How he must have suffered! I know soldiers, and they won't have ridden any slower than they would normally just because they were bringing a prisoner in. And running behind them, he'll have known that if he lost his footing, they'd simply have dragged him the rest of the way.'

141

'What makes you think they've brought him from the village,' Blackstone said pensively. 'Is he one of the peasants?'

'Of course he's one of the peasants! You don't think they'd treat anyone else in that way, do you?'

'I suppose not.'

Agnes must have realized, from his muted response, how her words might sound to him, because she turned around and said, 'Sam?'

'Yes?'

'I'm sorry, Sam. I truly am. I didn't mean to sound abrupt. It's just that I've lived here for so long that I take many things for granted, and I'm amazed when I discover that I have to explain them to you.'

'It's understandable,' Blackstone said, more because it bothered him to see her look distressed than because he *did* understand.

Agnes turned round and looked down again. 'The Count's there. Well, he would be, wouldn't he? He relishes this kind of situation. It's the perfect opportunity to show everyone just how powerful he is.' She held her hand over her eyes, to shield them from the sun. 'The soldiers have dismounted now, and they're frog-marching the poor bloody peasant towards the Count. They're turning him, so that the Count can get a proper look at him, and . . . . Oh, my God!'

'What's the matter?'

'It's . . . it's Peter.'

'Your friend the Social Revolutionary?'

He had not meant the remark to antagonize her in any way, but it very clearly had, and when she swung round to face him again, her hands were set almost like claws.

'He's *not* my friend,' she hissed.

'It's just a manner of speaking,' Blackstone protested. 'I never meant to suggest that—'

'How *could* he be my friend? I'm a Scottish governess and he's a Russian peasant. We have absolutely nothing in common. Besides, he's only been in the village a few days.'

'Has he, now?' Blackstone asked, as he felt the detective in him take control again. 'Only a few days, you say?'

142

Agnes caught the change in his tone, and it seemed, in some peculiar way, to calm her down.

'Well, yes, he's only been here for a few days,' she said lamely.

'So he wasn't born in the village?'

'No.'

'And he's never lived here?'

'No. For God's sake, Sam, he's a *political agitator*. Don't you know what that means?'

'I'm not sure that I do.'

'It means that he constantly travels from village to village, partly so that he can speak to as many of the peasants as possible, and partly to avoid being caught up with by the police.'

'You never mentioned this before,' Blackstone said accusingly.

'But I *did*. I distinctly remember telling you he was a revolutionary. We were outside the inn at the time.'

'You might have told me that,' Blackstone conceded, 'but you certainly didn't tell me that he'd only recently arrived in the village.'

'Didn't I?'

'No, you didn't.'

'Then perhaps . . . perhaps I just didn't think to. Perhaps it didn't seem particularly important.'

'A suspicious character arrives in the village just before the theft of the golden egg, and you don't think it's important enough to mention?' Blackstone asked sceptically.

'If someone had tried to assassinate the Count, I might have thought Peter was involved in it,' Agnes argued. 'But it honestly never occurred to me that he might have anything to do with the robbery. And why should it? Whatever else he is, he's no thief!'

'He might be willing to do all kinds of things to finance his revolution,' Blackstone said. 'That the ends justify the means is pretty much the revolutionary's motto.'

'He's *not* a thief,' Agnes said firmly.

'How can you be so sure of that? You've only known the man for a few days.'

'I have a gift for understanding people the moment I see them,' Agnes said passionately, as if pleading with him to believe her. 'And I'm always right. Look how I spotted you.'

But what did you see in *me*? Blackstone wondered. I thought I knew, but now I'm not so sure.

Tears had appeared in Agnes's eyes and began to roll slowly down her cheeks. Blackstone wanted to comfort her – to ask what he could do to ease her pain – but when he spoke it was the voice of the policeman which was in control.

'Why should it distress you so much that this man, who is almost a stranger to you, has been arrested?' he demanded.

Agnes's head jerked back as if he'd slapped her.

'I'm not crying for Peter,' she said.

'Then who are you crying for?'

'I'm crying for myself!'

'Why?'

'Because I thought I'd found someone who would understand me. Someone I could put my trust in, and who would trust me in return. But I was so wrong, wasn't I? You don't understand me at all! And you'd rather trust the Police Handbook than believe what I have to say!'

'I didn't mean . . . I was only trying to . . .' Blackstone began.

But it was too late for any more words. Lowering her head so she didn't even have to look at him, Agnes ran through the door and rushed down the passage.

Twenty-One

Blackstone walked over to the schoolroom window, and looked down on the drama being played out below. It was just as Agnes had described it before she'd fled the room in tears. Everyone connected with the Big House – from the indoor and outdoor servants to the Grand Duke Ivan himself – had congregated in the courtyard to observe the exchange between the master of that house and the peasant whom the soldiers had dragged from the village.

The Count was sitting astride his horse, the prisoner standing perhaps a dozen feet from him.

Had the Count already been mounted and out riding when Peter was being brought in? Blackstone wondered.

No, probably not. At that time of day he was much more likely to have still been working his way through his gigantic breakfast when he'd received news of the arrest.

So why was he mounted now?

Because when members of the aristocracy appeared before the lower orders, they were, by their very nature – and by the nature of the system that they embodied – *theatrical*. And what could be *more* theatrical than to gaze down on the miscreant from the back of a mighty steed?

The Count was speaking – or perhaps, from his stance and gestures, it would have been more accurate to say that he was *speechifying*. Blackstone was too far away to hear any of the actual words – and wouldn't have understood them however close he'd been – but he'd witnessed enough examples of oratorical over-indulgence in his time to have a fairly good idea of what the Count was saying.

'I look after my muhziks,' the Count was probably telling the peasant revolutionary. 'They call me "father", and that is exactly what I am to them. They are my children, and they love and respect me for it.'

And he possibly at least *half* believed it, Blackstone thought, because even the hardest heart needs to employ a little self-deception in order to justify its owner's excesses.

The Count was addressing the rest of his audience now. 'Isn't that true?' he seemed to be saying. 'Don't I treat all of them – ungrateful wretches though they are – better than their real fathers would ever treat them?'

The Quality assembled there nodded their heads gravely.

145

The servants nodded too, but, aware that their masters' eyes were on them, they did it with considerably more vigour.

The Count turned his attention to Peter again. 'And this is how I am repaid?' he appeared to be asking. 'Is this the thanks that I get for all my kindness and my bounty?'

He didn't know he wasn't addressing one of the peasants from his own village, Blackstone thought. They had no individual identity to him, and he was simply assuming that Peter had lived in the shadow of the Big House all his life.

But Peter hadn't!

According to Agnes, Peter travelled around the country and had only been in the village for a few days.

But if the Count had unwittingly cast himself in the wrong role as betrayed father, there was also something not quite right in the way Peter was playing his part in the drama. Standing there, with his head bowed, shoulders slightly hunched, and eyes pointed firmly at the ground, he was, as Blackstone well understood, merely *acting* the part of Count's peasant in order to hide his real identity as a revolutionary. Yet even taking that into account, this performance was flawed. He wasn't even playing the part of a revolutionary playing the part of a peasant with any real conviction, the Inspector decided.

Here was a man who'd been dragged behind a horse, all the way from the village. Here was a man who'd been arrested for starting the fire – for what else was likely to have brought about his arrest? – and could look forward to a savage punishment once the Count had finally finished his harangue. Yet he simply did not look anything like concerned enough about the fate which was almost certainly awaiting him.

Blackstone descended the stairs to the courtyard with as much speed as his aching body would allow him. By the time he reached the door the Count had apparently finally tired of hearing his own voice, and was barking an order to the soldiers standing on each side of the peasant revolutionary.

The soldiers immediately began to half-drag, half-carry Peter towards the house. But they were dragging him because they *wanted* to drag him – because that was the way this particular scene had been mapped out – Blackstone thought. The truth was that no such force was necessary – that Peter seemed more than willing to go wherever it was they wanted to take him.

From his new vantage point, Blackstone was afforded a better view of Peter than he'd had from the schoolroom window. He could see now that while the revolutionary had the long hair and thick, matted beard of a typical peasant, he did not exactly have the build. He was taller and less square than most of the men from the village, and even as the soldiers pulled and tugged at him, there seemed a certain elegance in the way he moved. But it was the face that struck Blackstone the most, because though he could not say where he had seen it before – or even been sure he had ever seen it *at all* – it looked oddly familiar.

The Count spurred his horse, and trotted off in the direction of the stables. Prisoner and escort disappeared into the house. Now that the show was over, the servants scurried back to their work, and the guests ambled gently towards yet another morning of relaxation and self-indulgence.

Soon the only two people left standing in the courtyard were Blackstone himself and Sir Roderick Todd.

Todd, noticing him for the first time, strode angrily over to where the Inspector was standing.

'You got my godson killed, you reckless bastard!' the Assistant Commissioner said angrily.

'He was the one who invited *me* to go out riding on the steppe,' Blackstone pointed out.

'So you're blaming him, are you, you coward? You're blaming a man who can no longer answer for himself?'

'No,' Blackstone said. 'I'm blaming the Cossacks – and whoever set them on to us. Why do *you* think the Major was murdered?'

'I have no idea,' Sir Roderick replied. 'But if one of you

147

had to be killed, why did it have to be him – a young man with so much promise?'

Several responses came unbidden to Blackstone's mind – none of which he could deliver to a superior officer.

'Why was that peasant arrested?' he asked. 'Did it have anything to do with the fire?'

'But of course it had something to do with the fire, you idiot! What else could it possibly have had to do with?'

'How did the soldiers know that he was to blame?'

'Not all peasants are as completely ungrateful as *he* seems to be,' Sir Roderick said, inadvertently revealing his own ignorance of Peter's origins. 'There are some who know where their loyalty lies, and who wish to see justice done.'

In other words, Blackstone translated, the Count has paid informers in the village.

'And what will happen to the man now?' he asked.

'If there's any justice, he'll be hanged for attempting to destroy this beautiful house,' Sir Roderick said fiercely. 'And even if he isn't hanged, he'll get twenty-five years hard labour in Siberia – which, don't you worry, is as good as a death sentence in itself.'

'I wasn't worried,' Blackstone replied mildly. 'Do you think there's any chance that the fire had something to do with the robbery, sir?'

'Anything's possible with these people,' Sir Roderick said, contemptuously. 'They don't think like we do. But I can't honestly see *how* the two things are connected. The robbery was committed for personal gain. The fire was an act of pure, malicious envy by an animal who couldn't bear the thought that other people live surrounded by beauty.'

'So why did he start the fire on the first floor of the West Wing?' Blackstone wondered.

'I'm not following you,' Sir Roderick said.

Well, that certainly made a change, Blackstone thought.

'I assume the bedrooms in the West Wing are pleasant enough – though I haven't had the privilege of seeing one of them myself,' he said, 'but if the man was merely envious – as you seem to think he was – then why didn't he start the fire in one of the reception rooms? Surely they're the most self-indulgent rooms in the whole house.'

'Self-indulgent?' Sir Roderick repeated, as if he had no idea of what Blackstone was talking about.

'Ornate, then,' Blackstone substituted. 'Elaborate. Spectacular. Call them what you will.'

'What you're trying to say is that if he was out to destroy beauty, he would have attacked the most beautiful example of it.'

Blackstone sighed. 'Yes, that's what I was trying to say.'

'I'm sure that coming from a stinking hovel, as he undoubtedly does, the whole building seemed dazzling beautiful to him.'

'And there's another point to consider,' Blackstone said. 'Most arsonists choose one of two possible spots to start their fire. The first is an area where there's a great deal of flammable material. From that point of view, I would have thought the best place would have been somewhere on the ground floor – either the laundry or boiler room.'

'Yes, yes,' Sir Roderick said impatiently.

'Or they choose some central spot inside the structure, from which the fire can spread out and engulf the whole building. This arsonist didn't do either of those things.'

'The man's a peasant, not a professional fire-raiser, like the kind you're used to dealing with!' Sir Roderick said exasperatedly. 'He'd probably have no idea where the best place to start a fire was.'

'In which case, you'd have thought he'd have chosen to do what was easiest,' Blackstone pointed out. 'You'd think he'd start the fire close to where he broke into the house, and then get out as quickly as he could. But he didn't do that, did he? Instead, he took the risk of going up to the first floor. Why? What could he possibly hope to gain from that?'

'Back in London, they told me you were clever,' Sir Roderick said, almost wearily. 'And they were right. You're far *too* clever for your own good, Blackstone. You take a simple incident, and you worry it to death. Who knows why the bloody peasant went up to the first floor? He probably doesn't even know himself. And if you could step back for a moment, and take a wider view of things, you'd see that it doesn't really matter one way or the other.'

But it *did*, Blackstone thought. There was only one way to explain the fire – and that was to see it as having been started with no other purpose than to *throw light* on the robbery.

'Do you think you could persuade the Count to give me permission to speak to the arsonist, sir?' he asked.

Sir Roderick looked at him as if he suspected he'd lost his mind. '*Speak* to the arsonist?'

'That's right.'

'Good God, man, he's nothing but an ignorant peasant. What do you think he'll be able to tell you that can be of any possible use?'

'I won't know until I've spoken to him.'

'And who do you expect will translate for you? The Count himself, I suppose! Or do you think that the Countess would rather relish the thought of being confined in a room with a stinking peasant, while she does your donkey-work for you?'

'I wouldn't wish to put either the Count or the Countess to any inconvenience,' Blackstone said. 'In fact, I'd much prefer to speak to the prisoner alone.'

Sir Roderick shook his head. 'You really have lost your mind,' he told the Inspector. 'You speak no Russian, do you?'

'No.'

'And the prisoner – a stinking, ignorant peasant – will certainly speak no English. How do you expect to communicate with him? Through gestures? Through grunts?'

'As long as he is convinced that we have absolute privacy for our discussion, I'm sure that communication between us will present no problem at all,' Blackstone said.

'If I do convey your ludicrous request to the Count, he'll think you're a fool,' Sir Roderick pointed out.

'He *already* thinks I'm a fool. How could a man wearing one of his cast-off suits be anything else?'

'That's certainly true enough. But more to the point, he'll probably think *I'm* a fool.'

And he wouldn't be far off the mark in that particular assessment, Blackstone reflected.

'I think I've found a solution to your dilemma,' he said.

'You have? And what is it?'

'You could tell the Count that you need an opportunity to allow me to make an idiot of myself.'

'And why would I want that?'

'So you'll have an excuse to send me back to London.'

The idea, now it was clearly spelled out, appealed to Sir Roderick, just as Blackstone had known it would. Because while there were times when the Assistant Commissioner was aware of how much he needed his Inspector, there were others – many more of them – when the arrogant bastard was just *looking* for an excuse to send his subordinate packing.

'Very well, I'll talk to the Count,' Sir Roderick said, his tone making it clear that, in giving Blackstone enough rope to hang himself, he was, in fact, doing the other man a huge favour.

'That's very good of you, sir,' Blackstone said, doing his best impersonation of a humble, grateful subordinate.

'But if it turns out to be a mistake,' Sir Roderick continued, 'then I shall expect you to take the full consequences of your impetuous action. Is that clearly understood?'

'It's understood, sir,' Blackstone replied.

'In that case, I will speak to the Count immediately.'

'Thank you, sir.'

'Don't thank me,' Sir Roderick said witheringly. 'All I'm doing, Blackstone, is to make quite sure that when you get back to London you have no possible grounds for saying that I, at least, didn't play my part.'

He turned, and strode towards the stables. When speaking of the Tsar, the late Major Carlton had said it was a frightening thing to put power in the hands of a weak man. And watching Todd's progress, Blackstone knew exactly what he had meant.

The Inspector lit a cigarette. The case was still far from solved, he thought, but at least it was becoming a little clearer. And it would become clearer yet when he talked to the arsonist. Because despite what Agnes thought, the man was far from being a revolutionary. Nor – whatever else it might be – was Peter his real name. And though Blackstone had no idea of what his true name actually was, he did at least now know where they had met before.

Twenty-Two

The arsonist had been incarcerated in one of the rooms on the ground floor of the wing in which he had set his fire. There were two soldiers on guard outside the door. They were standing back-to-back, so that one was looking up the narrow corridor and the other was looking down it. Blackstone approached them with caution, his outstretched arm holding the piece of paper which the Count himself had signed, and which Sir Roderick had assured him would gain him access to the cell.

The Inspector came to a halt a few feet from the closest soldier, who, he now saw, had a corporal's stripes stitched to the arm of his jacket.

'Please read this,' he said.

Though he did not understand the words, Blackstone's intention was obvious enough, and the soldier craned his head slightly forward. He did not find it an easy process to read what the Count had written, and while his eyes travelled slowly across the page – and his lips moved as he spelled out the words – Blackstone took the opportunity to examine the holding cell.

The door was made of steel, he noted, and was probably

at least two inches thick. Perhaps it had been used as a cell before, or perhaps only as a secure storeroom, but whatever the case, there was no way that the man inside would ever be able to escape through it.

The corporal had finished reading the note, and said a few words to the man behind him. The second soldier took a couple of steps back, raised his rifle, and aimed it squarely at the centre of the door. Not until the manoeuvre had been completed did the corporal unhook the key from his belt and insert it in the keyhole.

The corporal turned the key twice, then twisted the handle. He pushed the door open and took two quick steps back, so that the only person standing in the open doorway was Blackstone himself.

The Inspector peered into the cell. There was no lamp in the room, and no window, either. A little light did find its way in from the corridor, but not even enough to allow Blackstone to see the far wall. It was, he thought, like gazing into a deep dark cave.

He turned to face the corporal. 'I can't see anything at all in there,' he complained.

The corporal looked at him blankly.

'I need some kind of light!' Blackstone told him, then mimed striking a match and lighting a lantern.

The corporal first checked that his comrade still had his rifle trained on the door, then he took a cautious step forward, pushed the door closed, and immediately locked it again.

'I still want to see the man inside, but I'm going to need more light,' Blackstone explained.

The corporal nodded, to show that he had understood. With one hand he gestured that Blackstone should stay where he was; with the other he indicated that he would go in search of what the Inspector needed.

Blackstone thought about the prisoner on the other side of the thick steel door.

Most men, having been left alone in total darkness, would not have been able to resist calling out something when the door was opened. They might have pleaded for mercy. They

153

might have demanded to know what was going to happen to them. They might have spoken for no other reason than to elicit some response from their guards – a few words which would prove to them that they still existed. But not this man. This man had said nothing.

What self-control the arsonist had! What iron self-discipline!

Yet it was no more than Blackstone would have expected of him.

The soldier returned with a lantern. He handed it to Blackstone, then removed the key from his belt and unlocked the door a second time. Once the Inspector had stepped over the threshold, the soldier shut the door again with a loud clang.

Blackstone held the lantern up high and shone it around the room. There was no furniture at all – nothing to break up the monotony of the four bare walls and the rough stone floor. No ventilation, either, so the air was both hot and sticky, and had already begun to smell of sweat and other – even more unpleasant – bodily functions.

He could not find the prisoner at first, and for a moment speculated that – against all odds – he had somehow managed to escape. Then he saw the man, sitting on the floor with his back against the wall. It was scarcely a dignified position to be discovered in, but given that the prisoner's hands were tied behind his back – and his ankles bound together in front of him – it was perhaps the best option available to him.

'Hold the light closer to yourself so that I can see your face,' the prisoner said, and when Blackstone had done so he chuckled and continued, 'Have you only just worked out who I am, Inspector?'

'The long hair and beard had me fooled for a while,' Blackstone admitted. 'Are they real?'

'They are real in the sense that, until a few days ago, they were a fixture of the head of a real peasant,' the prisoner said.

'And what happened to him?'

'He was not harmed. At least, not permanently. But there

154

was not time for me to grow a disguise, so the peasant in question had to sacrifice – albeit reluctantly – his precious growth, and I had to glue it on. And now, I must tell you, that glue is itching abominably.'

'You've endured much worse in your time,' Blackstone said unsympathetically.

'Yes, I have,' the prisoner agreed. He chuckled again. 'You know, Inspector Blackstone, you disappoint me. I had expected that long before now you would have realized that the reason – the only possible reason – for you to be in Russia was that I wished it.'

He's right, Blackstone thought. That *is* the only possible reason, and I *should* have been able to work it out.

He remembered the last time they had met. It was at the end of a case which had almost cost both his own life and the life of a person far more important – by any standards – than he could ever hope to be.

He had been walking along the Thames Embankment, mourning the loss of the only woman he'd ever loved. He'd stopped walking and looked down at the river.

He'd heard the gentle swish of the tidal waters. He'd seen the lights of ships anchored midway between the two shores. And he'd been tempted to walk down the nearest set of steps, and keep on walking.

Until he was drowned.

Until he had made himself at one with the heart of the city which had been his home for most of his life.

And then he had realized that he was not alone.

'Do not turn around, Inspector Blackstone,' a voice from not far behind him had said.

'Vladimir?' Blackstone had asked. 'Is that you? Have you recovered from falling off the roof?'

'The common people below cushioned my fall. That is, after all, what the common people are for – to cushion the fall of those who matter. But why do you call me Vladimir? Do you mean Vladimir Bubnov? How could I possibly be him, since he does not exist?'

155

'But you still don't want me to look at you?'

'I have already exposed myself to you far too much for my liking.'

'So now you're going to kill me,' Blackstone had said, not entirely certain whether he cared one way or the other.

'No, I am not here to kill you.'

'But you've got your pistol pointing at me right now, haven't you?'

The Russian had not denied it. Instead, he'd said, 'My Tsar and my country owe you a debt. Since you have undoubtedly saved us from a ruinous war, I have been authorized to offer you a reward of five thousand pounds, provided, of course, that you agree to sign an undertaking to never again mention the name of Count Turgenev.'

'He offered me ten thousand pounds to let him go ahead with his plan,' Blackstone had countered.

'Perhaps we could match that.'

'And if I asked for fifteen?'

'That might be considered a little greedy.'

Blackstone had laughed. 'You're already sighting your pistol at me, aren't you? There's no need for it. I promise not to tell anyone about Turgenev – but I don't want your money.'

'I did not take you for a fool.'

'I've been a fool all my life. But even a fool can learn his lesson, given time. I'm sick of the games you people play. Sick of being a pawn in them – and of the people around me being pawns. I'm tired of the whole pack of you.'

'Isn't there a saying in English that you must either run with the fox or the hounds?' Vladimir had asked.

'Yes, there is.'

'The wise man will always choose the hounds.'

'The truly wise man will stay at home and tend his vegetables.'

'I am not sure my superiors will accept that,' Vladimir had said. 'They would be much happier if they knew you were on our side. And the best way to prove that you are is to take the money.'

156

*'I'm going to walk away,' Blackstone had told him.
'There's no one around, so if you're going to kill me, now's
the time to do it.'*

He had walked away – and there had been no shot.

'The moment this matter blew up in my face, I began
plotting the ways I might get you to Russia,' Vladimir said.

'Why?'

'Because you had all the qualities which I needed for this
particular operation.'

'And what qualities are they?'

'Your lack of avarice was certainly one which ranked
highly. A man who seeks power or wealth would have been
no good to me, you must understand, since I would inevitably
have been putting him in a position which he could have
used to advance his own ambitions. But you, my dear
Inspector Blackstone, do not care for such things.'

'Don't I?'

'Most certainly you do not, or you would have taken the
money when I offered it to you on the Thames Embankment.
Nor do you fear death – though you will avoid it if you
possibly can. And that must be an advantage when you are
involved in an operation during the course of which several
people have already died – and more may yet. So you see,
my dear Blackstone, you are – all-in-all – the ideal candi-
date for the task I have in mind.'

Yet no task had yet been mentioned, nor any operation
outlined. Vladimir was toying with him, Blackstone decided.
Like the expert hunter he was, he was not chasing his prey,
but encouraging his prey to come to him.

Well, sod that for a game of soldiers! the Inspector told
himself. If the Russian wasn't going to say what it was he
wanted, then he was buggered if he was going to ask.

'Are your bonds hurting you?' he said, changing the
subject.

'Somewhat,' Vladimir conceded. 'The Count instructed
his soldiers to tie me up tightly, and they have followed his
orders to the letter.'

'Then why don't you ask me to loosen them for you? That's what most men in your position would have done.'

'True, that is certainly what most men *would* have done.'

'But not you.'

Vladimir nodded. 'But not me,' he agreed.

'Because you feel it might put you in my debt?'

'Because it would be a waste of both your time and mine. The moment you had left me, the guards would come into the cell and re-tie my bonds even tighter than they were before. Besides, we both know very well that I am *not* like most men. I can brush pain, and other such inconveniences, aside. I am single-minded. And so are you.'

'Am I?'

'Of course you are. For the moment, your pride is putting a brake on your single-mindedness, but it will not be able to hold it for ever. Why not admit it, Inspector – you are almost bursting to know what task it is that has made me go to all the trouble of bringing you here.'

'But I already know why I'm here,' Blackstone said, not quite ready to concede that all Vladimir had said was true. 'A golden egg has been stolen, and I am here to recover it.'

Vladimir laughed. 'I would be truly disappointed if I thought you believed that,' he said. 'But you don't, do you? The convenient fiction, which was designed to fool duller minds than yours, will not have held you in its sway for more than a short time.'

'So I know this isn't about the golden egg,' Blackstone admitted. 'Then what *is* it about?'

'It is about the goose which laid it,' Vladimir told him.

Twenty-Three

'The Prince of Wales had in his possession a certain document,' Vladimir said. 'A wiser man than he – his father, Prince Albert, comes immediately to mind – would no doubt have taken better care of it. Perhaps Albert would have entrusted it to the Count for safe-keeping in the strong-room. Failing that, he would at least have seen to it that a number of guards were posted, rather than putting his security in the hands of one peasant. But the son is not like the father. He prides himself, foolishly, on his own manliness. Besides, after so many years of being kept out of the process of government by his mother, he is desperate for anything that will make him feel important. And what could make him feel *more* important than having sole charge of a precious document?'

'Does the Count know what was really stolen?' Blackstone asked.

'Yes, he does.'

'Then he can't actually believe it was taken by one of the peasants from the village.'

'A man would have to be very foolish indeed to believe that an illiterate muzhik would place any value on a piece of paper.'

'So why is he always ranting on about riding into the village and whipping the peasants?'

'Because that is how people would expect him to behave if a golden egg *had* been stolen. By his histrionics, he is merely maintaining the fiction.'

'What does this document contain?' Blackstone asked.

Vladimir gave as much a shrug as his bonds would allow

159

him. 'If you are attempting to recover stolen silver bullion, you do not ask where it was mined,' he said. 'Why then, should you worry about the words on this piece of paper I am asking you to retrieve?'

'Is it some kind of land title deed?' Blackstone persisted. 'Is it a bank transfer?'

Vladimir laughed. 'If you were an archer, I would have to tell you that you are facing in completely the opposite direction to the target you are supposed to be aiming at,' he said.

'What's in the document?' Blackstone demanded angrily.

'Why should that be any concern of yours?'

'Because it's important enough to have inspired two attempts on my life, you bastard!'

'I think that is something of an exaggeration,' Vladimir said. 'It is certainly true that someone tried to kill you on the train from St Petersburg, but my men prevented that quite easily.'

'Quite easily!' Blackstone repeated. 'If they'd have arrived ten seconds later, I'd have been bloody well dead!'

'Ten seconds was an ample margin for men like you and I, who take pleasure in cutting things fine,' Vladimir said blandly.

'Who was it that attacked me?'

'Would you like me to give you *the names* of the men who attempted to garrotte you?' Vladimir asked.

'Stop playing games!' Blackstone said impatiently. 'I want to know who sent them.'

'I imagine they were sent by whoever stole the document. Like me, he appears to have great confidence in your ability to recover it.'

'And what about the attack on the steppe?

'*What* about it? You are surely not trying to tell me that was also an assassination attempt, are you?'

'Why wouldn't I?'

'Because if that had been the intention of your attackers, you would already be dead.'

He'd forgotten how intelligent Vladimir was, Blackstone

160

thought – had forgotten that, in so many ways, the Russian's mind worked in much the same way as his did.

'It wasn't your men who saved me?' he said.

'No, regrettably not. I am ashamed to admit that, on that particular occasion, they let us *both* down rather badly. But rest assured, they will not go unpunished for their error.'

'So if they didn't step in and save me, why did I survive?'

'That, I must admit, I am at a loss to explain,' Vladimir said.

'And that doesn't bother you?'

'There are so many little mysteries in life which are never explained. All a simple man like myself can do is to deal with those for which an explanation is possible.'

'Why are you pretending to be a peasant?' Blackstone demanded.

'I would have thought that was obvious. I do not wish anyone here at the chateau to know that I am member of the *Okhrana*.'

'But *why* don't you want them to know? If you revealed who you really are, you would have all the authority you needed to conduct this investigation in a proper manner.'

'Next question,' Vladimir said, in a tone which made it quite plain that he was not prepared to discuss that particular matter any further.

'What's your connection to Miss Agnes?' Blackstone asked.

'Who?'

'The governess.'

'Oh her! There is no connection at all.'

'You must think I'm a complete fool!' Blackstone said angrily. 'She *spoke* to you when we were in the village together. When she saw you'd been arrested, she was in *tears*! So don't pretend you don't know her.'

'Ah, I see what you mean,' the Russian conceded. 'When I told you that I had no connection with her, I was speaking as Vladimir, the secret policeman. Peter the revolutionary is an entirely different matter. Though they have only exchanged a few words at most, she is enthralled by him.'

161

'And why should that be?'

'I think she has developed a romantic view of the peasants, and sees Peter as one of the instruments for freeing them.'

Agnes hadn't seemed at all a romantic in Demitri's *izba*, Blackstone thought, remembering the way she had spoken about the peasants back then. But perhaps that had been no more than an act – perhaps the hard shell had only been a protective cover for the virgin–idealist.

'You are always taken in by pretty women, my dear Blackstone,' Vladimir said, his amusement evident in his voice. 'Remember how easily Hannah managed to run rings around you?'

In Blackstone's mind's eye, he was suddenly transported back to a photographer's shop in a run-down area of London. He could see himself standing at one end of the room, and Hannah at the other. And though the Russian was not yet visible, he was aware that Vladimir was lurking somewhere near the doorway. He knew what would happen next – knew because it had already been enacted a thousand times in his head – and as he once again relived those painful moments which followed, he felt a sudden surge of rage course through his body.

In two furious strides, he had crossed the room and was towering directly over the helpless Vladimir.

'If you ever mention Hannah's name in my presence again, I'll kill you!' he promised.

'I'm sorry. That was a mistake on my part,' Vladimir admitted. He sounded contrite – and perhaps a little afraid. 'But we are professionals, you and I,' he continued. 'We must not let what has happened in the past deflect us from our present purpose.' He paused, as if wondering whether, after he had made such a huge blunder, he dare say more. 'Why don't you ask me why I set fire to the West Wing of this house?' he said tentatively.

He was right when he said it was a mistake to dwell on what had happened in the past, Blackstone thought – because such memories were the first step on the road to madness.

162

'Why did you set fire to the West Wing of this house?' he asked, in a dull flat voice.

'When they brought you in off the steppe, you were in a very poor condition,' Vladimir said, his confidence starting to return. 'I had every expectation that you would recover, but I had no idea how long that recovery would take. And I was not at all sure that I could afford to wait – because the longer I *did* wait, the longer the thief would have to find a way to break through Captain Dobroskok's military cordon. So I set the fire as a way of possibly bringing a speedy end to the case.'

'You thought that whoever had stolen the document would have hidden it somewhere, and that the moment he knew there was a fire, he would rush to retrieve it,' Blackstone said.

'I knew I would not need to spell it out for you,' Vladimir said delightedly. 'I'm now more certain than ever that my confidence in you was justified. Yes, that is exactly what happened. I set the fire in the hope that it would panic the thief.'

'But it didn't work.'

'Indeed it did not. Our man – whoever he is – has more nerve than I ever gave him credit for. I expected him to run straight to the hiding place. Instead, he feigned the same panic as the other guests were displaying – acted as if his own life was the only thing that was important to him. And as a result, I am no closer to finding him now than I was before I embarked on what turned out to be a very rash course of action.'

There was something in Vladimir's story that did not quite add up, but for the moment Blackstone couldn't quite put his finger on it.

'Tell me why the document is so important,' he said.

'Regrettably, I cannot.'

'Why?'

'Because if you knew that, you would also come to see the wider picture, and then, I'm afraid, I would have to kill you.'

'Look at yourself,' Blackstone said contemptuously. 'You're in no position to threaten to kill anyone.'

Vladimir laughed. 'You surely don't imagine that this state of affairs will be allowed to continue, do you?'

'Won't it?'

'Of course not. In a day or two – three days at the most – this whole incident will be over. More than that – it will never have happened. Everyone involved will have forgotten that there was ever a revolutionary called Peter who tried to burn down the chateau. They will have forgotten because that is what they will have been ordered to do.'

'If you still have sufficient power to get yourself out of this mess, why do you need me at all?' Blackstone wondered.

'For the same reason that I always needed you, my dear Inspector. Because it is of vital importance that this case be solved, but I cannot be seen to be the one who solves it.'

'And I'm supposed to do the dirty work.'

'Exactly.'

'Why should I?'

'Because it is dirty work which *needs* to be done. And because there will be disastrous consequences – *for both our countries* – if it is *not* done.'

'Why should I believe you?' Blackstone asked.

'Because you know that I do not lie.'

'You've been lying to me since I walked into this room,' Blackstone said. 'I don't know which specific lies you've told me, but I'm willing to bet there were at least two or three of them.'

'At least that number,' Vladimir agreed. 'Let me put it another way, then. I may lie to you over operational matters, but when it comes to the big things – such as the security of our two countries – I have always told you the truth. You believe that, don't you?'

I shouldn't, Blackstone told himself. I don't *want* to. But – damn and blast it – I do!

'Assuming I do agree to do your dirty work for you . . .' he said.

'Yes?'

'How would you suggest I go about it?'

'You are the true policeman – the detector of crime,' Vladimir said. 'It is not for me, someone who you think of as a mere political thug – and perhaps you are right to do so – to tell you how to go about your business. But I do perhaps have one suggestion.'

'And what might that be?'

'You will need help to conduct your investigation. I suggest you continue to use this Miss Agatha.'

'Miss Agnes,' Blackstone corrected him.

'Just so,' Vladimir agreed. 'Use her. Just as I get you to do my dirty work for me, so you can get her to do your dirty work for you.'

'And how might I go about that?' Blackstone wondered.

'Use your imagination – and her romantic gullibility. Tell her that you are working for me, and that we are both working for the good of the peasants. She will believe you, because she *wants* to believe you.'

'I'll probably be putting her in danger,' Blackstone said.

'Naturally.'

'But that doesn't matter to you, does it? Because as far as you're concerned, she's expendable.'

'We are all expendable, my dear Blackstone,' Vladimir said. 'Surely you should have learned that by now.'

Twenty-Four

As Blackstone stepped out into the corridor, the corporal slammed the heavy steel door behind him and turned the key in the lock.

The Inspector wondered how the clang of metal would

sound from inside the cell – what feelings it would evoke, whether it might bring just a moment of self-doubt to the man he had left there. Probably not, he decided. Even if he were staring certain and inevitable death in the face – even at the point where all others would long ago have given up hope – Vladimir would still be working feverishly on a plan to extricate himself from the situation.

Blackstone stepped out into the courtyard. He was not surprised to find that his head was spinning, and his brain ached. After fifteen minutes with the Russian, that was only to be expected.

What he needed, he told himself, was a quiet room in which to mull over their conversation – somewhere he could be alone, as he attempted to unravel the complex web of deals and double-dealing which passed as Vladimir's thought processes. But where should he choose?

His mind ran through the possibilities, and settled on the schoolroom, since the children were away, and Agnes – who had so recently left it in considerable distress – would be unlikely to return for quite some time.

Agnes, looking pale and drawn – but also determined – was sitting at her desk. She raised her head when Blackstone entered the room and – with just the tiniest of quakes in her voice – said, 'You look surprised to find me here.'

'I am,' Blackstone admitted.

'You wouldn't be, if you knew me better. My father once said that we should always return to our old battlegrounds, especially the ones on which we were soundly beaten. He said we should do it in order to face our mistakes squarely on – and perhaps learn from them. That's what I'm doing here now – facing my mistakes.'

'Agnes . . .' Blackstone began.

She held a hand up to silence him. 'I made a fool of myself right here in this very room, didn't I?' she asked. 'And even worse, I showed myself up to be the coward I truly am.'

'I don't understand.'

166

Agnes put her hands to her forehead. 'How could you, when I've lied to you so much?' she asked anguishedly. 'I said that we should always be honest with each other, and then immediately began to pretend to you that I was something I was not.'

'I'm still lost,' Blackstone confessed.

'I pretended to be indifferent to the plight of the peasants in the village, but it isn't true at all. It breaks my heart to see the way they're forced to live – in such filth, in such poverty – and I'd do anything I possibly could to improve their condition.' She paused, and looked down at her desk. 'Or, at least, that's what I used to tell myself,' she continued, almost in a mumble.

'What's changed your mind?'

'Peter's arrest. When I saw him being dragged before the Count, down in the courtyard, the first thing I should have felt was pity for a poor man who's dedicated his life to helping the muhziks. But it wasn't pity I felt.'

'No?'

'No! It was fear! Fear for *myself*. I was terrified that the Count would find out I'd been talking to Peter, and that I'd be dismissed from my post. Isn't that terrible? My fate would be mild in comparison to what awaited Peter, yet it was still myself I thought about. What kind of person am I?'

'I think you're a person who judges herself too harshly,' Blackstone said, and even as he spoke the words he was wondering: Am I saying that because I wish to comfort her – or because I need to pull her out of this state before I can even begin to *use* her?

'Poor Peter,' Agnes said.

'You needn't worry about him,' Blackstone assured her.

'You have no idea what the Count's like, Sam. You don't know the kinds of things he does to those weaker than himself – the kinds of things I've actually *seen* him do.'

'Peter has friends.'

'Friends! How do you know? You've never met him – and you couldn't understand him if you did.'

'Do you trust me?'

'Of course I trust you, Sam. I'd trust you with my life.'

And that's just what you may be doing, Blackstone thought.

But aloud, all he said was, 'Then trust me on this. Peter will be fine, and no one will ever know you had any connection with him.'

'But if they torture him . . .'

'They won't.'

Agnes smiled. 'Do you know what you are?' she asked.

'What am I?'

'You're one of those people who promises that everything will be all right – and somehow usually manages to keep his word.' Agnes squared her shoulders and raised her head. 'Well, now that's out of the way. I'm not worried about Peter, because you've told me I shouldn't be. So let's return to your problems, shall we. How on earth are we going to find this missing golden egg?'

He had reached a crossroads, Blackstone accepted. Either he trusted Agnes completely or he didn't trust her at all. Either he told her the truth now, or he would never be able to tell her.

'We're not looking for a golden egg,' he said. 'It wasn't stolen, because it never actually existed.'

'Was *anything* stolen?'

'Yes.'

'What was it?'

'A document.'

'A piece of paper!' Agnes asked incredulously. 'All this fuss is over a piece of paper?'

'It's a very important piece of paper.'

'What makes it so important?'

'I don't know.'

'So how can you be so sure it *is* important? How can you even know it's gone missing at all?'

'I trust the man who told me about it.'

Agnes looked at him sceptically. 'And who was that man? Was it Sir Roderick?'

'No, not him.'

168

'Then who?'

It would be a mistake to tell her about Vladimir, he thought. More than a mistake – if she knew the man's real identity, it might be putting her life more in danger than it already was.

'The Count has confided in me,' he said.

But he was thinking that not only was that a lie for a moment, but that there was not even the remotest possibility that circumstances could ever change to eventually make it something closer to the truth.

It had *never* been considered necessary to tell him what was missing, because he'd never been expected to recover it. *His* job had been to find the thief, and then hand him over to the Count – who no doubt had a hundred unpleasant ways of making the man reveal his hiding place.

And what if the Count *did* find out that he knew it was actually a document which had been stolen? The fable of the golden egg had been created because even knowledge of the document's existence was a top-secret matter. So would the Count ever allow him to go back to England, with that knowledge in his head?

Of course not! He would have to be killed. And so would Agnes!

'You mustn't tell the Count you know that I know about the document,' he said urgently.

'Very well,' Agnes agreed.

She was so trusting! So very, very trusting! It almost broke his heart.

Agnes had begun to slowly pace the room. 'This is a big estate,' she said thoughtfully. 'A *huge* estate. Looking for a piece of paper here would be like looking for a needle in a haystack.'

'I know,' Blackstone agreed.

By lighting the fire, Vladimir had contrived to make the thief lead him to the document, instead of searching for the document himself. It had been a good idea, but it hadn't worked, because the thief's nerve had held. Yet that nerve must have become a *little* frayed in the process, and if it

169

were possible to put the same kind of pressure on the man again . . .

'If only we had a golden egg,' he said wistfully.

'You want a Fabergé golden egg?' Agnes asked, incredulously.

'Not a *Fabergé* egg, just an egg I could pass off as one.'

'I think I could get my hands on something that might serve,' Agnes said.

'You could?' Blackstone asked excitedly.

'Yes. But what would be the point? I thought you said there was no such thing as the golden egg.'

'There isn't,' Blackstone agreed. 'But as long as most of the people in this house *think* there is, there might as well be.'

Twenty-Five

The workshops, which were located on the ground floor of the house, came as a revelation to Blackstone. He had already known they were there, of course, but it was seeing the extent of them which took his breath away. They ran under the entire East Wing and seemed to employ nearly a score of craftsmen. There were carpenters and French polishers, iron-smiths and painters, all bent over their workbenches, completely engrossed in their tasks.

Agnes laughed at his obvious perplexity. 'This isn't London, you know, Sam,' she said. 'Look at where we are. It's not a question of deciding whether it's to Harrods or Fortnum and Mason's that we'll take a short carriage ride. The nearest equivalent we have to those stores is in St Petersburg, and even then it's not *that* equivalent.'

'Even so . . .' Blackstone began.

'Besides, this is the way the Russian aristocracy have always done things. And there is a certain cachet, don't you think, in having things made for you, rather than buying them off even the most *expensive* shelves?'

'I suppose so,' Blackstone agreed.

They had passed through the main workshops, and reached a small one at the end. Through the open door Blackstone could see a tiny, shrivelled man, sitting precariously on a high stool and examining something through a huge magnifying glass.

'His name's Yuri,' Agnes said softly. 'No one knows exactly how old he really is, but the general feeling is that he must be at least ninety.'

'Ninety!' Blackstone echoed.

'In his time, he was the best jewel-maker in Russia. The only reason he is here now is because he was born in these parts, and this is where he has decided he wants to die.'

'He may once have been a great jeweller, but the older we get, the more our skills slip away from us,' Blackstone said sceptically. 'Are you sure he's still up to the job?'

'When the Countess needs her most precious jewels repairing, she doesn't send them away to Fabergé, as she so easily could. Instead, she has them brought down to Yuri,' Agnes said. 'Does that answer your question?'

'Yes,' Blackstone admitted. 'I think it does.'

Agnes tapped lightly on the door, then stepped inside. When the old man turned round to face her, Agnes lightly rubbed the top of his bald head with her hand, then planted a kiss on his forehead.

'Everyone else treats him with such solemn respect,' she said to Blackstone. 'I think he rather likes it that I don't.'

'Tell him what we want,' Blackstone instructed her.

Agnes spoke for three or four minutes, and the old jewel-maker listened to her in complete silence. It was only when she was finished that he spoke a few words in reply.

'He wants to know how good it has to be,' Agnes said.

'As good as he can make it,' Blackstone said.

Agnes snorted. 'He is a master craftsman. If he makes

the best egg he could, it will be absolutely *perfect*. If he makes the best egg he could, it would fool even the experts at Fabergé itself.'

'Well, then . . .?'

'But it would also take him months to complete the work. Perhaps even years.'

'What can he do in a couple of days?' Blackstone asked.

A twinkle came into the old man's watery eyes as he answered the question, and Agnes laughed out loud.

'What did he say?' Blackstone wanted to know.

'He said that in two days he could produce an egg which would fool *you* completely . . .

'That's all I want.'

'. . . but would not convince a man with any discrimination or taste even for a split second.' Agnes paused. 'He likes you, you know. That's why he's being so rude to you.'

'Ask him if he could produce an egg in two days which would fool a man of discrimination and taste from a distance,' he said.

Yes, the old man agreed, he could do that.

Another long exchange followed in Russian.

'He wants to know whether or not you will be providing the gold,' Agnes translated.

'And what did you say?'

'I asked him if he really thought that a man who is wearing one of the Count's cast-off suits would have access to so much gold. He agreed that it was unlikely, so now he wants to know where the gold is coming from.'

'Couldn't he use a cheaper metal?'

'He's a true artist. To ask him to work with a cheaper metal would be an insult. Besides, even if I could persuade him, it wouldn't do any good. The people upstairs wouldn't be fooled by an egg made of an inferior metal for a moment – not even if they were looking at it from the other end of a very long ballroom.'

'Then we can't do it,' Blackstone said gloomily.

'Of course we can.'

'But where will we get the gold from?'

'From Yuri. A jeweller of his skill cannot work with gold for fifty years without some of it sticking to his hands. He'll be perfectly willing to supply his own gold, as long as he's certain of getting it back.'

'Did he say that?'

'Naturally not. What he *did* say was that it will be completely impossible for him to lay his hands on so much gold. But he didn't mean it. It's just part of the negotiation.'

Agnes returned to her conversation with the old man. Blackstone, though he did not understand a single of word of Russian, could still tell that the balance of it was swinging back and forth. Twice Agnes stroked the old man's head, and once she gently twisted his ear. On three separate occasions she looked as if she were about to walk away, but Yuri did not seem as if he were seriously concerned she would carry out the threat.

Finally, the old man lifted his hands up and cupped them on his scrawny chest. Agnes shook her head firmly. A pleading note came into Yuri's cracked voice. Agnes shook her head again. A third appeal from him brought the same reaction from Agnes, but after she had finished shaking her head, she spoke to Yuri in a very soft – almost seductive – voice. The moment the words had sunk in, the old man nodded happily.

'We can go,' Agnes said to Blackstone.

'You've struck a deal?'

'We've struck a deal. It will be ready in two days – or possibly earlier now he has the incentive to work hard.'

They left the workshop, and stepped out into the bright autumn sunshine of the courtyard.

'How much money did he want?' Blackstone asked.

Agnes laughed. 'Money!' she repeated. 'What good is money to an old man like him? He hasn't left the Big House for the last ten years, and there's nothing to buy here.'

'So what did you offer him?'

'Not as much as he wanted.'

'Not as much of *what* as he wanted?'

'A gentleman would never think of forcing me to answer that question,' Agnes said.

She was trying to sound prim and proper, but was so obviously amused by the whole situation that she was finding it impossible.

'A gentleman would never do most of the things I do,' Blackstone said, catching her amusement, though he was still unsure what there was to be amused about. 'Tell me.'

'Very well,' Agnes said. 'He wanted to play with my bosoms for an hour. I told him the excitement would very probably kill him, so he said he would settle for half an hour. When I turned him down again, he said that five minutes would probably be enough. I said that even five minutes would be too much of a strain, but if he worked hard – and I was pleased with the work he'd done – then I might think about *showing* him my bosoms.'

'And will you?' Blackstone asked, not sure whether he was still as amused as she was, or simply scandalized.

'Will I what?' Agnes asked innocently.

'Will you show him your bosoms?'

'As I told Yuri himself, I'll certainly think about it,' Agnes said mischievously.

Twenty-Six

They made love twice before they went to sleep in each other's arms, once more in the middle of the night, and a fourth time while the early morning sun was streaming in through the bedroom window. For Blackstone it was like a reawakening. When he had lost Hannah, he had lost a part of himself, too, and only now, with Agnes, did he begin to hope that he would find it again.

174

They had breakfast in the school room – where Agnes had made him that first cup of truly English tea, where he had questioned her about her relationship with Peter, and from which she had fled in tears. All that seemed so distant now. He felt as if he had known Agnes for ever – as if she had always been a part of his life.

The knock on the schoolroom door reminded Blackstone that there was another world outside. The message the liveried servant had come to deliver only confirmed it.

'Leon says that your boss is having his breakfast on the East Wing terrace, and that he wants to see you immediately,' Agnes told him, when she'd spoken to the servant. 'Do you think it could be something important?'

Blackstone nodded grimly. 'Yes, I do.'

'You've gone so pale,' Agnes said, worriedly. 'What is it you think he might say to you?'

'I think he might be about to give me my marching orders,' Blackstone replied.

There were two ways he could handle this next meeting, Blackstone told himself, as he left the schoolroom and made his way towards the West Wing terrace.

The first way was to lie – to tell Sir Roderick that he had been quite right all along, that the arsonist was no more than an ignorant peasant who hadn't spoken a word of English, and the whole thing had been a waste of time. And how would the Assistant Commissioner react to that? Probably by invoking the threat he'd made when he'd agreed to set up the meeting. Probably by ordering Blackstone to return to England immediately.

The second way – and Blackstone shuddered even at the thought of it – was to tell his superior the truth. To explain that Vladimir was a member of the *Okhrana*, that there had never been a golden egg, but there *was* a document. And he would have to go even further than that – he would have to lay out before Sir Roderick his plan to make a fool of the Count.

So he was not so much trapped between the devil and

175

the deep blue sea as trapped between the self-righteous anger and the total panic of the bloody fool he found himself working for.

He had still not made up his mind which of the two lines to take when he opened the French doors and stepped out on to the terrace where Sir Roderick was taking his breakfast.

Even from a distance, the Assistant Commissioner looked distracted by the letter spread out on the table in front of him, and he positively jumped when Blackstone coughed discreetly to announce his arrival.

'Ah, Inspector Blackstone,' Sir Roderick said. 'What can I do for you?'

'*You* sent for *me*, sir.'

'I suppose I did,' Sir Roderick admitted, vaguely. 'You know, Blackstone, this has been a very rum business right from the start. I've never really understood why they insisted on sending you here with me when there were half a dozen inspectors with considerably more *finesse* who I could have called on.' He paused for a moment. 'No offence intended.'

'No offence taken, sir,' Blackstone said, remembering the old Indian saying that an elephant does not take offence at the farting of an ant.

'I mean to say, there are officers at the Yard who could just about pass themselves off as gentlemen if the situation called for it,' Sir Roderick continued. 'But – and let's be honest about this – you're certainly not one of them.'

'True.'

'The Count doesn't like you at all. Captain Dobroskok can't stand the sight of you. And most of the guests in the house seem to think you're some kind of manservant.'

'Point taken, sir,' Blackstone said, a little impatiently – for even the elephant can begin to take umbrage if the ant farts often enough.

'So I would have thought that if anyone could be spared from this investigation, it would have been you,' Sir Roderick continued.

'That would certainly make sense, sir,' Blackstone

176

agreed, drawing just a little hope from his boss's obvious confusion.

'And yet a galloper's just arrived with this dispatch from the Foreign Office,' Sir Roderick said. 'It seems that they want me to go back to St Petersburg for what they call "further briefings", but at the same time they're most insistent that you stay here. I can't understand it.'

'It's got me mystified, too,' the Inspector said.

'You know, Blackstone, I get the distinct impression that something's going on here that we know nothing about. This golden egg business, for example. I'm starting to suspect that that's not the real issue at all. Do you have any thoughts on the matter?'

'I'm just a simple copper, sir,' Blackstone said, starting to enjoy himself now. 'I've been told to look for the golden egg, and that's what I'm doing.'

'That's just my point!' Sir Roderick explained. 'You've no subtlety, have you? Not your fault, of course – one shouldn't expect anything else, given your background . . .'

'It's very kind of you to make allowances, sir.'

'. . . but you're completely out of your depth here. Which makes it all the more strange that I'm to go and you're to stay.'

'Very strange,' Blackstone agreed.

Or at least it *might* have seemed strange to him, had he not been able to sense the invisible hand of Vladimir lurking somewhere behind the scenes and carefully pulling all the strings.

Now he had received his instructions from London, Sir Roderick was quick to act, and the carriage which was to convey him to the railway station was ready within the hour. Blackstone, feeling it was his duty to see him off – if only to make sure the bloody fool was actually going – was in attendance.

As they both stood in the courtyard, another coach pulled up. This one had none of the refinement of the carriage which would be conveying Sir Roderick. It was a stubby vehicle, painted entirely in black, and with bars at the window. The two men who descended from it were also in black, and had an air of menace about them that was detectable even from a distance.

'That's the *Okhrana*, come to pick up your arsonist friend,' Sir Roderick said.

The two secret police officers strode towards the house like men who knew exactly where they were going and had no fear of anyone ever daring to impede their progress.

'You know, Blackstone, I have to rather admire the way the Russkies conduct their business,' the Assistant Commissioner continued. 'We have to go through all the rigmarole of asking for warrants and attending magistrates' courts, but that kind of thing doesn't get in their way at all. If they know a chap's a thoroughly bad lot, they deal with him immediately. We could learn a lot from their methods, don't you think?'

'Undoubtedly, sir.'

'By the way, I never asked you how your so-called interview with the arsonist went. Didn't turn out to speak English after all, did he?'

'No, sir.'

'Never thought he would. Knew it was a waste of time right from the start. I had intended, once you'd seen how mistaken you were, to haul you over the coals for it, but I don't suppose there's much point now.'

The secret policemen re-emerged from the house with Vladimir between them. The prisoner wore manacles on his wrists and ankles, and each of the escorts had a firm grip on one of his arms.

'Nothing namby-pamby about the way they treat their prisoners here,' Sir Roderick said approvingly.

The policemen opened the carriage door and thrust Vladimir roughly into it. He didn't struggle. Why should he, Blackstone asked himself, when there was probably a bottle of excellent vodka and a plate of the finest caviar waiting for him inside the coach?

'Well, I suppose I'd better be going,' Sir Roderick said,

climbing into his own coach. 'You won't get anywhere with this investigation, you know. Even if there is a solution, it'd take a better man than you to find it.'

'You're probably right,' Blackstone agreed.

'So, bearing that in mind, the wisest thing you can probably do is try to avoid making a nuisance of yourself,' Sir Roderick advised. 'It won't do you any good to keep offending people in the way you have been – especially since I won't be here to protect you.'

'I'll bear that in mind, sir,' Blackstone promised.

'Well, goodbye, Blackstone,' Sir Roderick said. 'The next time we see each other, you'll probably be a uniformed constable back on the beat – unless, of course, they've kicked you off the Force completely.'

'I suspect you're right, sir.'

The two carriages pulled away at the same time. Sir Roderick and Vladimir would probably also be on the same train back to St Petersburg, Blackstone thought, but, if anything, the 'prisoner' would probably travel in considerably more luxury than the English policeman.

The next two days were very strange ones for Blackstone.

It felt to him almost as if he'd been placed in a bubble. His physical movements were restricted by the presence of the military cordon, his mental ones by the lack of the egg on which Yuri was still working. There was nothing to do but to float around and enjoy himself in the company of Agnes.

It should have been one of the happiest periods in his life – and in many ways it was. He and Agnes went riding together, though not beyond the bounds of the cordon. They picnicked beside a small brook which ran through the extensive grounds. They walked, and talked about the life of an India they had both known so long, long ago.

Yet all the time there was a nagging voice in the back of Blackstone's head which reminded him that this could not go on for ever. That the bubble, by its very nature, was eventually bound to burst. And when it did burst, this almost

179

make-believe world he was living in would be gone – when it burst, he would be forced to face the harsh realities which, just for the moment, he could put to one side.

At around lunchtime on the third day, almost exactly forty-eight hours after Sir Roderick's departure, Yuri produced the egg.

It was a marvellous piece of work, and even though he knew the truth, Blackstone still found it hard to believe it was a fake.

Looking at it, nestling in the palm of his hand, Blackstone felt a wave of deep sadness wash through him. The bubble had been pricked, and he felt the pin sink deep into his very soul.

Twenty-Seven

The whole house party – surrounded by the usual gaggle of servants – was seated around a long table on the South Lawn, with the Count at one end and the white-whiskered figure of the Grand Duke Ivan at the other. The Count looked as if he were trying desperately to animate the conversation, but most of the Russians wore on their faces the bored expressions of people who would much have preferred to be elsewhere. Only the Duc de Saint-Cast – who was shamelessly flirting with one of the Russian ladies despite the glares he was getting from Mademoiselle Durant – really seemed to be enjoying himself.

Positioning was everything, Blackstone told himself as he walked across the lawn. He needed to be close enough so he did not appear to be hiding anything, and yet far enough away to be able to do just that.

He came to a halt ten feet from the table, about an equal

distance from the Count and the Grand Duke. The Count ignored him, and the other guests didn't even seem to be aware that he was there.

'It's lucky that you all stayed longer than you had originally planned to, because the hunting in the next few days should be exceptional,' the Count was enthusing.

'Not much point in hunting when we can't go beyond the military lines,' said one of the Russians. 'Anyway, I've had enough of that kind of sport for one year. Rather be back in Petersburg, where it's a bit livelier.'

'Excuse me, Your Excellency,' Blackstone said.

The Count gave Blackstone a look which was clearly a command for him to go away, then turned his attention back to his guest.

'Had enough of hunting, Nicholas?' he said, with patently false jocularity. 'I shouldn't have thought a sportsman like you could ever have had too much of hunting.'

'Your Excellency,' Blackstone said.

'How dare you disturb us!' the Count demanded, rising from his seat in what could only be described as a threatening manner. 'Your superior would have been accepted here, but then he is a gentleman. Your presence, on the other hand, most certainly is *not* welcome.'

I'll be even less welcome when you hear what I've got to say, Blackstone thought.

'I apologize for intruding, and certainly would not have done so under most circumstances,' he said with mock-humility, 'but I thought you'd like to know as soon as possible that I've found it.'

'Found what?'

'The golden egg.'

The Count looked thunderstruck. 'But . . . but that's simply impossible!' he gasped.

'I can assure you, it isn't,' Blackstone replied. 'It was hidden under the hay in one of the stables.'

A new, wary look appeared in the Count's eyes. 'Is this some kind of joke, my man?' he demanded. 'Because if that's what it is, I promise you you'll pay dearly for it.'

181

'I wouldn't go threatening me, if I were you, sir,' Blackstone advised. 'I'm a British subject – and a serving police officer, which makes me a crown servant. I don't think my government would take it kindly if you had me whipped as if I were one of your peasants.'

'Such . . . such insolence is intolerable!' the Count said, now so red in the face that he looked to be on the point of exploding.

'If he says he has the egg, why doesn't he show it to us?' Grand Duke Ivan asked.

'Because he *can't*!' the Count said furiously, as Blackstone reached into his pocket. 'Because there isn't—'

And then he saw what the English policeman had pulled out of his pocket and was holding out in his hand.

'I've got to admit, that looks rather like a Fabergé egg to me,' the Grand Duke said.

'Let me see the egg!' the Count ordered Blackstone. 'Bring it over to me at once!'

But Blackstone had already slipped it back into his pocket.

'Didn't you hear what I said, you oaf?' the Count shrieked. 'I want to examine the egg.'

'I'm afraid I can't let you do that, sir,' Blackstone said, with what could have passed for genuine regret in his voice.

'You can't *what*?'

'This egg, as I'm sure you're aware, sir, is the property of His Royal Highness, the Prince of Wales. I was ordered to retrieve it, and now that it is in my custody I would be in dereliction of my duty if I gave it – even for a while – to anyone else.'

'The man has a point, you know,' the Grand Duke said. 'I certainly wouldn't want any of my servants handing over my property, just because some titled country gentleman told him to.' He turned towards Blackstone. 'Tell me, my good fellow, who stole the egg?'

'I have not been able to establish that, sir,' Blackstone said, in his best witness-box manner. 'Indeed, it was not within my remit to do so.'

'Is that so?' the Grand Duke asked.

'It is, sir. I was instructed only to *re*cover the egg. Nothing was said about *un*covering the guilty party. But if His Excellency the Count wishes me to pursue my investigations further, I'm sure my masters in London would have no objection to my doing so.'

'Get out of my sight!' the Count said in a strangled voice.

'Does that mean you don't wish me to proceed any further with my investigations, sir?' Blackstone asked innocently.

'Yes, damn it, that's exactly what it means!'

'In that case, I will leave your estate as soon as is practicable, sir,' Blackstone said. 'I apologize again for disturbing your lunch.'

Then, having given a small bow which was *almost* gentlemanly, he turned, and walked back to the house.

'Well, I'm glad that's settled,' the Grand Duke commented when Blackstone had gone. He turned to one of the servants who was hovering nearby. 'What time is it, my good fellow?'

The servant consulted his watch. 'It's a quarter past one, Your Royal Highness.'

'Then if I can whip some sort of life into my people, we should just about catch the evening train,' the Grand Duke said.

'You're surely not thinking of leaving, Your Royal Highness?' the Count asked, in a panic.

'Certainly am. Would have left two days ago, if it hadn't been for this blasted business of the egg,' the Grand Duke told him. 'Not saying you haven't put on a reasonable show for us, Count Rachinsky – or at least as reasonable a show as was possible within your limited means – but even the most lavish hospitality tends to pall after a while.'

'But you *can't* leave!'

The Grand Duke arched his right eyebrow. 'Why can't I? We were asked to remain here until the egg was recovered—'

'Yes, but—'

'. . . and, as inconvenient as that was for me, I was prepared to be gracious. But now the egg *has* been found, and I can see no reason for staying any longer.'

183

'But the egg *hasn't* been found!' the Count protested.

'What are you talking about? Of course it's been found. Saw it myself in that detective chap's hand.'

'That was a forgery. It simply has to be.'

'Does it? How would you know? Got ambitions to be a craftsman, have you? Been studying jewellery-making in your spare time?'

'No, but—'

'Anyway, it looked genuine enough to me.'

A look of loathing came into the Count's eyes, but since such looks are not to be directed at a grand duke, it was quickly gone again.

'Please stay a little longer,' he pleaded. 'Just until I can get fresh instructions from St Petersburg.'

'Don't see why you need fresh instructions. The egg's been found, and we can all go home.'

'I'm not sure the soldiers will allow you through the cordon without fresh orders,' the Count said desperately.

'Oh, you're not, aren't you?' the Grand Duke asked, his voice now very much reflecting his growing irritation. 'Well, let me make the position clear to you, Count. I'm not some jumped-up little aristocrat whose family has only held its title for the last hundred years or so. I'm a Romanoff. The Tsar is my nephew, and I am the Colonel-in-Chief of three crack regiments. Can you really see the soldiers attempting to stop me when I want to leave?'

'I . . . well . . . no,' the Count said.

'I . . . well . . .no,' the Grand Duke mimicked. 'I give you notice, Count, that I intend to leave your estate as soon as possible. And I imagine that most of my fellow guests will feel the same way.'

And all around the table, heads nodded in agreement.

Twenty-Eight

The Count stood on the balcony of his study, watching the procession of coaches which was being assembled below.

If only there had not been a grand duke present at the gathering, he might have been able to bully the other guests into staying, he told himself.

But there *had* been a grand duke present, and the Tsar's displeasure at an attempt to forcibly constrain his Uncle Ivan might have been even greater than the displeasure he would undoubtedly express when he learned that the guests had been allowed to leave.

It was all that bastard Blackstone's fault, the Count thought. He had no idea how the bloody Englishman had managed to pull off his trick, but there was no doubt that it *was* a trick – because Fabergé golden eggs could not simply be conjured out of thin air.

He now wished he had been pleasanter to the man. If only he'd been a *little* politer – if only he'd assigned the English policeman a *slightly* better room – then it was possible that, instead of blindsiding him, Blackstone might actually have chosen to confide in him.

Yet how could he have been expected to know that he should have treated Blackstone better? The man did not dress like a gentleman, nor did he speak like one. Surely anyone of breeding would have made the same mistake with the Inspector as he had made himself.

The Count heard a discreet cough behind him, and turned to find the Duc de Saint-Cast standing there.

'Yes?' he said irritably.

'I just come to tell you zat I sink the way your so-called guests 'ave thrown your wonderful 'ospitality in your face 'as been little short of a disgrace,' the Duc said.

'What are you talking about?' the Count demanded.

'I tried to persuade zem to stay, but zey simply would not 'ear of it,' the Duc continued. 'I am so ashamed for zem, zat I ask myself what I can do to compensate ze Count for such ill-breeding.'

'Did you, indeed?'

'And almost immediately, ze perfect answer comes to me. Ze others may leave if zey wish, but I will stay 'ere to keep you company. We will 'ave a much jollier time wizout zem.'

All the anger and frustration which had been building up inside the Count was suddenly – and fiercely – focused on the figure of the Duc de Saint-Cast. Here, the Count told himself, was a man whom he could hit out at with very little concern for the consequences.

'You are nothing but a blood-sucking leech,' he said with relish.

'I beg your pardon?'

'Look at you! You come to my house and you drink my wine and eat my food as if it were your own.'

'You invite me, *mon ami*,' the Duc reminded him.

'And you are not just a leech, but a lecher to boot,' the Count said. 'There is no point in attempting to deny it. I have seen, with my own eyes, the way you behave towards the ladies. Good Lord, man, I've seen the way you've behaved towards my own wife.'

The Duc shrugged. 'I was only being polite,' he explained. 'In truth, I would never dream of taking your wife to my bed.'

'So now you're saying she's not *good enough* for you, are you?' the Count asked, giving his pent-up fury full rein. 'You're saying you'd bed all the other women you've flirted with, but not the lady of the house.'

'You misunderstand me,' the Duc protested.

'I want you out of my house now!' the Count said. 'I

don't even want you to wait until *my* servants have packed *your* bags for you. Leave immediately, and I'll see to it that all your pathetic belongings are forwarded on to you.'

'You are only speaking in zis way because you are distraught, *mon vieux*,' the Duc said.

He attempted to put his hand on the Count's shoulder, but the other man brushed it angrily away.

'You will need some support in your time of trouble,' the Duc continued. 'Permit me at least to stay with you until zat English detective, 'oo annoys you so much, 'as finally gone.'

'Have you no pride at all?' the Count asked incredulously. 'Is there no level of self-degradation that you will not stoop to, as long as it provides you with free board and lodgings?'

'I excuse you for your rudeness, because I understand zat you are—' the Duc began.

'Get out!' the Count screamed. 'Get out before I call my servants in and tell them to give you a damn good thrashing.'

The Duc squared his shoulders. 'Even a tolerant man such as myself 'as 'is limits, and you have exceeded zem,' he said, with some dignity. 'I will leave within ze hour. And ze next time we encounter each other, *Monsieur le Conte*, I 'ope you will have ze grace not to acknowledge me – because I will certainly not acknowledge you.'

'Acknowledge you! I'll burn in hell before I'll ever speak to you again,' the Count said.

'Good. Zen we are agreed,' the Duc replied.

He would have liked to approach the potentially dangerous situation with more caution, but that was an option no longer open to him, the Duc de Saint-Cast thought as he entered the East Wing.

It had been a mistake to suggest to the Count that he should stay, and an even bigger one to keep insisting long after it was plain that the fool would never give way. And the result of making that mistake was that it would be no time at all before it was widely known in the house that he

187

was *persona non grata*. Worse, it might even become common knowledge the Count had threatened to have him whipped, and then even the lowest of the indoor servants would not think twice before demanding to know what he was still doing in a house where he was no longer welcome.

Thus, the unseemly haste.

Thus, the almost reckless way he headed for the smaller of the house's two libraries.

By the time he passed through the library door, the Duc had all but persuaded himself that his argument with the Count had been no mistake at all, but was, in fact, a master-stroke on his part.

For if the Count sees me as no more than vermin, he told himself, then so will everyone else on his estate.

And you do not question vermin. Nor do you search vermin. When you see a rat, your dearest wish is that it will leave your vicinity as soon as possible. It never even occurs to you that instead of the plague, the rat in question may be carrying with him something that will keep him in luxury for the rest of his life.

He glanced around the library.

When people heard the word 'document', they pictured huge elaborate scrolls, he thought.

But a document did not have to be like that at all. It could just be – as this one was – a few sheets of paper. For it was not how a document looked which mattered, but what it said. And whose signature was affixed to the bottom of it!

He marvelled at his own cunning in choosing this as a hiding place. Who would think of looking for a few sheets of paper in a library which already contained so many? Even if they did look, it could be days before they found what they wanted – and if they were just a little careless, they might not even find it at all!

How tragi-comical it would be if he had forgotten where he'd hidden the precious document which would finally give him everything he'd ever yearned for in life. But, of

188

course, he hadn't forgotten. It was stamped on his brain. Stamped on his heart!

He stood on tip-toe, grasped the heavy, leather-bound volume, and took it carefully down from the shelf.

The searcher might even have the book in his hand and still not find what he was looking for, he told himself.

He reached delicately down into the space between the spine of the book and its leather covering. For one terrible moment he thought that he might be too late – that, for all his self-congratulation, Blackstone might have been there before him. Then he felt the tips of his fingers brush against the edge of the paper.

He extracted it carefully – oh, so carefully. He was tempted to read it – to take in, once again, those beautiful words which would make him rich. But such temptation was to be avoided, and he slipped the document carefully into the inside pocket of his jacket.

'I didn't know for certain that you were the thief,' said a voice behind him. 'Except for your unusual willingness to assist me in the investigation of the crime, I had no real reason to suspect you more than any of the others. But if I'd been a betting man, you're the one I would have put my money on.'

Twenty-Nine

The Duc de Saint-Cast slowly turned around to face the tall man in the borrowed suit who was standing in the doorway and pointing a pistol at him.

'What is your problem, my good man?' the Duc asked. 'Does a gentleman not 'ave ze right to retrieve 'is own private correspondence before 'e leaves zis 'ouse?'

'It's certainly private correspondence,' Blackstone agreed, 'but it's not *your* private correspondence.'

'I am surprised zat your government would trust such a low-level official as yourself – a man 'oo has scarcely risen beyond the rank of servant – with knowledge of the document,' the Count said sneeringly.

'It didn't,' Blackstone replied. 'But I have friends in the Russian secret police.'

'I also,' the Duc said.

'I know you do. Two of them tried to kill me on the journey down from St Petersburg. Do you know about *that*?'

'How could I, when I 'ave been isolated in zis Russian *gîte* ever since ze robbery?' the Frenchman asked logically.

'But you would have approved their action if you *had* known about it, wouldn't you?'

'Since you must already know zat I arranged for ze throat of ze peasant guarding the Prince of Wales's door to be slit, it would be pointless for me to try and pretend I would 'ave shed any tears if my associates in St Petersburg 'ad dealt with you in a similar manner,' the Duc said. He paused for a moment. 'May I ask you a question, purely for my own satisfaction?'

'Why not?'

'How could you have been so sure zat, of ze thousands of places I could 'ave chosen to hide ze document on zis estate, I would select ze library?'

'I *wasn't* sure. Though, now I come to think about it, it was the logical choice – and you French have always prided yourself on your logic, haven't you? But I *was* fairly certain that wherever you'd stashed it, it would probably be somewhere in the East Wing.'

'Indeed?'

'Indeed. The reason the fire was started was to panic you into retrieving the document. But you didn't panic, did you? There was no need to, because the fire was in the *West* Wing, and unless it got totally out of hand and spread through the rest of the house, the document was perfectly safe.'

'So ze only reason zat you are 'ere now is because *I* am 'ere?'

'That's right. All the other guests seemed to have nothing else on their minds but making their arrangements to leave. But you appeared to have some other objective. All I had to do was follow you.'

The Duc sighed. 'Alas, where ze fire failed, the "discover" of ze golden egg 'as succeeded. I should 'ave been careful. I should 'ave watched my back. But I 'ave always been cursed with an impetuous nature.'

'You're taking all this very calmly,' Blackstone said.

'Why should I not take it calmly? You know as well as I do 'ow valuable zis document is, do you not?'

'Yes,' Blackstone lied.

'Zen you must also know zat zere is more zan enough money to be made from it to keep us all 'appy. Zat being the case, I suggest zat you name your price, Inspector. But please, try not to be *too* greedy.'

'Reach into your pocket, take out the document slowly, and place it on the table,' Blackstone said.

'What! You want it *all* for yourself? My friend, you truly do surprise me. I am an avaricious man myself, but zat is a level of greed to which even I would not aspire.'

'I'm going to return it to its owner,' Blackstone said.

'And 'oo might that be?' the Frenchman countered. 'Ze Prince of Wales? Or ze *Tsar*?'

The Tsar? Blackstone repeated silently. What the bloody hell does the Tsar have to do with it?

And then he remembered the coach with the blacked-out crest which had fled early on the morning after the robbery.

The Duc de Saint-Cast laughed. 'For all your protestations to the contrary, you really do *not* know what ze document contains, do you, Inspector?' he asked. 'And zat, in turn, means zat you cannot even begin to gauge just how truly rich it could make you.'

'Put the document on the table,' Blackstone said firmly.

Something had been nagging away at the back of his

191

mind ever since the Duc had first spoken, and now –
suddenly – he knew what it was.

The Duc hadn't said that *he'd* slit the throat of the peasant
who'd been guarding the Prince of Wales's room. No, his
actual words were that he'd *arranged for* it to be slit.

And that could only mean one thing.

The Duc wasn't in this alone.

The bastard had back-up!

Even as the idea set alarm bells ringing in his head,
Blackstone heard two distinct sounds behind him – one the
swish of some heavy material, the other the lightest of foot-
falls.

He swung round to face the new – and totally unexpected
– threat. If he'd made his move a second earlier, the knife
would probably have missed him completely. If he'd left it
a second later, the blade would have been plunged deep
into his back. As it was, the weapon did no more than slice
across the surface of his upper arm.

The shock came first, but the pain followed hard on its
heels. As a thousand tiny burning needles seemed to embed
themselves in his arm, Blackstone felt his fingers open and
his pistol slip away.

Fight back! his instincts commanded. Fight back while
you still have the chance!

The knife had embedded itself in the door frame, and its
wielder was attempting to pull it free. Despite his pain,
Blackstone forced his mind to assess his opponent.

His attacker was wearing a long dress and a wig which
had come askew, and was now covering one eye. But this
was no woman he was fighting. It was a slight – but strong
and determined – man.

Mademoiselle Durant – now revealed to be *Monsieur*
Durant – succeeded in pulling the knife free and lifted
back his arm to take another swing at Blackstone. But he
was not dressed for hand-to-hand fighting. His whalebone
corset – and the padding inside it – slowed him down just
enough for Blackstone to take a counter-action of his own.

The Inspector brought his uninjured arm up, and, with

the heel of his hand, struck Durant – hard – across the throat. The Frenchman started to crumple immediately.

Blackstone did not wait to see him fall – he had been in enough fights in his time to know that with a crushed windpipe Durant was finished, and there were other dangers still to deal with.

The Duc de Saint-Cast was coming across the room at him, armed with a knife of his own.

'You 'ave killed him!' the Duc screamed. 'You 'ave killed my love – *mon petit ami!*'

The pistol was on the floor, but it was covered by the body of the dying Durant, and would take too long to retrieve.

Blackstone looked around him for some other weapon he might use, but there was nothing!

Burning with rage, the Duc lunged forward. Blackstone reached out, and grabbed the wrist of the hand holding the knife.

Mistake! he told himself, as fresh waves of agonizing pain coursed through his body.

Big mistake!

He should have thought before he acted. If he had, he would never have used his injured arm to block the Duc's attack. But it was too late to change tactics now, because the good hand was needed to grasp the Duc's free hand, which was on course to gouge out his eyes.

For a moment then two men stood locked together, then they swayed and tumbled to the floor. They rolled three, or perhaps four, times – Blackstone could not be sure – before they smashed against one of the library tables.

They were both winded from the experience, but the Duc had no throbbing wound to contend with, and so it was he who recovered first. He pulled himself free from his opponent and – now on his knees – raised the knife in preparation for striking the lethal blow.

Looking helplessly up at him, Blackstone could see that whilst there was undoubtedly madness in the Duc's eyes, it was not the kind of raging madness which causes a man to make a mistake. No, it was rather a cold, determined

193

madness – a madness which would drive him on until he succeeded in his aim.

Then, suddenly, the Duc's eyes were no longer mad – because they were no longer there. The top of his head exploded, covering Blackstone with blood, brains and splinters of bone.

The Inspector dragged himself clear of the carnage, and saw Agnes standing in the doorway. She must have pulled his pistol from under Durant, he thought hazily – pulled it out, taken aim, and fired.

Agnes looked down at the gun in her hand as if she were almost surprised to find it there.

'My father taught me how to shoot mad dogs in India,' she said calmly. 'I never thought I'd have to do the same in Russia.'

Thirty

Blackstone was sitting on the teacher's chair in the schoolroom. Agnes had bandaged his wound, and though it still throbbed, the pain was becoming easier to bear. His head was starting to clear, too. And he would need a clear head, because though he had dealt with one enemy, there was another he still had to face.

The Count was, if anything, even more ruthless than the Duc de Saint-Cast, he thought.

The Duc had only tried to kill him when it was plain he couldn't be bribed. The Count, on the other hand, had a vested interest in seeing him dead, however much he was willing to co-operate. So if he was ever to leave the chateau alive, he would have to *bargain* for his life – and bargain for *Agnes's* life, too!

The door of the schoolroom burst open, and the Count stormed in.

'I have been out riding, to calm myself down a little after my guests have treated me so shabbily,' he roared. 'And when I return, what do I find? That my home has been turned into a slaughterhouse!'

It was mostly play-acting, Blackstone thought. The Count was not so much burning with *rage* as with *anticipation*. He wanted what Blackstone had taken from the dead Duc as much as he had ever wanted anything in his life.

The Russian's next words confirmed it. 'You have the document, do you not?' he asked.

'Yes, I do.'

'Then give it to me immediately!'

Blackstone shook his head as much as his aching body would allow. 'I'm afraid that I can't do that, sir,' he said.

The Count laughed heartily, as if he really did find the situation genuinely amusing.

'You are in no position to refuse it to me,' he said. 'You are in no position to refuse me *anything*. Don't you understand that I have only to click my fingers in order to have half a dozen men come into the room and take the document off you by force? And let me assure you, they will not be gentle. Why should they be gentle – with a proven criminal?'

'A proven criminal?' Blackstone repeated. 'Me?'

'Of course, you! What else would you call the man who has just murdered two of my guests?'

'I can't see why their deaths should bother you particularly,' Blackstone said, praying that he sounded as much at ease as he was intending to. 'One of the men – Durant – was here under false pretences. And as for the other – Saint-Cast – you'd ordered him to leave anyway, though perhaps not quite in the manner he did. Besides, I was only defending myself. They did both try to kill *me*, you know.'

'The document,' the Count said, holding out his hand impatiently. 'Give me the document!'

'Ah, I see. You want to return it to the Tsar,' Blackstone

said. 'You feel that in some way that will mitigate the disgrace that's befallen you for allowing it to be stolen from under your roof.'

'I am not prepared to discuss such matters with the likes of you,' the Count said haughtily.

'As soon as I'd handed it over to you, I'd be a dead man,' Blackstone pointed out.

'Why should I want to kill you?' the Count asked, as if Blackstone's words really had puzzled him.

'Why?' Blackstone repeated. 'Which reason would you like me to give you? The one you'll *tell* yourself is the truth – or the one which actually *is*?'

'This is nonsense!' the Count said.

'No, it isn't,' Blackstone contradicted him. 'You'll *tell* yourself that the reason you had to kill me was to keep the document's very existence a secret. But your real motive will be that, with me out of the way, you'll be able to claim all the credit for its recovery yourself. But before you do anything you might regret, let me ask you one question. Given all you'd done to keep it quiet, how do you think *I* knew what to look for?'

'Sir Roderick must have told you,' the Count said, off-handedly.

Blackstone laughed as heartily as the Count had earlier, though he had to force himself.

'Sir Roderick?' he said. 'Do you really think my government would have trusted that idiot with such valuable information?'

'It must have done.'

'You've had plenty of chances to speak to – and observe – Sir Roderick. Can you honestly say that you think he knew what we were searching for?'

'No,' the Count admitted. 'He would have had to be the finest actor in the world to play the fool so convincingly.' He frowned. 'But if your government wouldn't tell him, it certainly wouldn't have told you.'

'Exactly,' Blackstone agreed. 'So what's the only other place I could have got the information from?'

'The *Okhrana*?'

'Do *they* know about all this?' Blackstone asked, feigning surprise. 'I must say, you amaze me. I would have thought that if the *Okhrana* had had anything to do with it, I'd have been bumping into them all over the place.'

'You're right,' the Count admitted. 'The government was involved in what went on here, as was the military, but the *Okhrana* have not been made privy to any of it.'

'So if I didn't learn about it from my government or the *Okhrana*, then who *did* I learn it from?' Blackstone asked.

'The Tsar's court!' the Count said, astounded. 'You're claiming that you have a protector somewhere in the Tsar's court.'

'It certainly looks that way, doesn't it?'

'You're bluffing,' the Count said contemptuously.

'And are you prepared to *call* that bluff?' Blackstone wondered. 'Are you prepared to kill me now and worry about the consequences later?'

'Don't threaten me!' the Count warned him.

'I'm not,' Blackstone replied. 'In fact, I'm willing to offer you a deal from which you'll gain a great deal more than you ever would from killing me. Would you like to hear it?'

'Go on,' the Count said suspiciously.

'If you *do* kill me, there'll always be the suspicion in many people's minds that it was the dead policeman, rather than the live count, who actually recovered the document. If you let me live, I'll take the document to London and hand it over to my government – which was what the Tsar always wanted to happen. And in my report I'll say that you were the one who *actually* recovered it, and I was no more than your messenger boy. And who's going to doubt the word of the only other man who *could* claim the credit?'

'How do I know I can trust you?'

'Why shouldn't you trust me? I'm a simple policeman, who just wants to be left alone to do his job. I don't lust after power and influence, because I've seen what it does to other people.'

'What other people?'

'People like you! You have a beautiful house, a wife, children, and all the money you could ever want. You should be deliriously happy. But you're not. And why? Because it's eating you up inside that the Tsar is displeased with you. That he might not show you his usual favour – or listen to your advice – ever again. I don't want to be weighed down by those kinds of chains.'

'You insult me!' the Count said.

'I didn't mean to,' Blackstone told him. 'I thought that I was just being a realist.'

The Count paced back and fro across the floor for well over a minute before he came to a halt again.

'I have your word that you'll do what you said?' he asked.

'You have my word,' Blackstone promised.

'What will happen to Agnes? Will she be going back to England with you?'

'Yes, that's what she wants to do.'

'And she will keep quiet about this?'

'What is there for her to keep quiet about? I told her that what the Duc was trying to steal was the title deed to some land you own in France and, being a mere woman, she believed me.'

The Count nodded. 'Yes, women will believe most things that men tell them,' he said. 'Well, now that the last matter has been resolved, there is no more to be said. I will make the arrangements for your departure imme-diately. A detachment of soldiers will first escort you to the railway station, and then accompany you to St Petersburg.'

'I'd appreciate the escort to the station, but I won't need any protection once I'm on the train.'

'How can you be so sure of that?'

Blackstone tapped his nose knowingly with his index finger. 'Friends in court, remember,' he said, playing the lie for all it was worth.

The Count nodded, then walked over to the door. 'I trust you are not expecting me to shake your hand,' he said.

'No, I'm not,' Blackstone agreed. 'To tell you the truth, I don't think either of us would enjoy the experience very much.'

Besides, he added mentally, if you shook my hand you'd see just how much it was trembling.

Thirty-One

Agnes was luxuriating in one of the railway carriage armchairs and drinking the sweet Russian tea that the waiter had just brought her. Blackstone sat looking out of the carriage window, taking in the view of the vast, unrelenting Russian steppe as if he suspected that he would never see it again – and wanted to commit it to memory.

'This is wonderful,' Agnes said. 'I've never travelled in anything like this much comfort before.'

'Haven't you?' Blackstone asked, still half-absorbed by the scenery. 'You surprise me.'

Agnes laughed. 'I *surprise* you? What could ever have given you the impression that I'm used to being pampered?'

'I thought perhaps, that when you travelled with the Count, you did so by private coach.'

'We travelled in a private *compartment*,' Agnes said. 'That's not the same thing by a long chalk. This carriage is so opulent that it could almost belong to the Tsar himself.'

'I think it *does* belong to him,' Blackstone said. 'Or at least, to someone very close to him.'

'A Grand Duke?'

'No.'

'A courtier, then?'

'No, not a courtier, either. Courtiers only flatter him, and tell him how God has placed him on the throne of Russia.

The people I'm talking about are the ones who *keep* him on the throne.'

Agnes frowned. 'You seem rather strange tonight, Sam – rather distant,' she said. 'Is something wrong?'

Nearly *everything* was wrong, Blackstone thought.

But all he said was, 'Don't concern yourself. I'm just thinking.'

'What about?'

'About many things.'

The train groaned and wheezed its way into one of the rundown stations which appeared at the side of the track every thirty miles or so. There were no soldiers in evidence, but the fact that there were no passengers waiting on the platform, either, made it clear that the army was somewhere close at hand.

The only person who did seem to be awaiting the arrival of the train was a well-built, though thoroughly nondescript man who was wearing a suit which just fell short of being described as shabby. Blackstone was not surprised to see him. In fact, he'd been expecting him ever since the journey began.

The private carriage came to a halt just in front of the waiting man.

It was not by chance it had stopped there, Blackstone thought. Nothing that happens to this man *ever* happens by chance.

The man hesitated for a second, as if considering other options, then opened the door and stepped inside.

'This carriage is not available to ordinary members of the travelling public,' Agnes said severely.

Blackstone laughed, though there was not much humour in it.

'How easy it is to get used to the idea of being grand,' he said. 'But you've made a mistake, Agnes. This gentleman here isn't an ordinary *anything*.'

'He isn't?'

'Of course not. Don't you recognize your old friend from the village, Peter the Revolutionary?'

Agnes's mouth fell open. 'But he can't be Peter,' she sputtered. 'Peter's a peasant, and this man is a . . . is a . . .'

'A minor provincial official of some kind?' Vladimir supplied. 'A petty bureaucrat, so over-impressed with his own importance that he has the temerity to attempt to ride in a grand coach like this one?'

'Well, yes,' Agnes agreed uncertainly.

'I'm flattered that you're so taken in by my disguise,' Vladimir told her, 'but let me assure you that what you see before you is no more the real me than was the me you saw in my peasant costume.'

'I . . . I don't understand,' Agnes said.

'You're not meant to,' Blackstone said. 'Our friend here takes a kind of malicious pleasure from confounding other people. It could almost be called his hobby.'

'But what's he doing on this train?'

'I think he wants to talk to me. And I rather imagine he would like to keep the conversation private. So if you'd be so kind as to withdraw to the sleeping compartment . . .'

'You want me to leave you alone with him?'

'If you wouldn't mind.'

'And what if I *do* mind?'

'I'm afraid I'd still have to insist.'

Agnes stood up, and smoothed down her dress with her hand. 'I'll go, but I shall expect an explanation after he's left,' she said huffily.

'And you'll get one,' Blackstone promised her.

Vladimir followed Agnes's progress to the sleeping compartment with an appreciative eye, but it was not until she had closed the door behind her that he finally sat down opposite Blackstone.

'A spirited woman indeed!' he said. 'Are you taking her back to England with you?'

'That seems to be the general assumption,' Blackstone replied, noncommittally.

Vladimir nodded. 'It is probably for the best. There's no future for her as part of the Count's establishment. With the recovery of the document, his star hangs high in the sky once more. But soon, the people who matter will start to reflect that he should not have allowed it to be lost in the first place. And then that same star will be become a *shooting* star, and rapidly plummet to earth.'

'Why are you here?' Blackstone asked.

Vladimir produced a cigar from his waistcoat pocket, and took his time in lighting it.

'I am here because I always felt I owed you an explanation for what has gone on, and now I am finally in a position to give you one.'

'You are here to learn how much I know for a fact, and how much I have been able to conjecture,' Blackstone corrected him. 'Once you have that information, you will assess what I am likely to do with what I know. If you reach an unfavourable conclusion, then Agnes may well still be on the train when it reaches St Petersburg, but I most certainly will not.'

Vladimir blew a smoke ring into the air. 'What you say is quite true, of course,' he agreed. 'Shall we make a start?'

'Why not?'

'I suppose the first thing I should ask you is whether or not you read the document after you had recovered it.'

'Would you believe me if I said I hadn't?'

'Knowing you as I do, I do not think so.'

'Then there's no point in my lying, is there?'

Vladimir blew another smoke ring, a larger one this time, and paused to admire the effect. 'What did the document say?' he asked casually, when the smoke ring had dissipated itself.

'It's a secret treaty of mutual defence between Russia and Great Britain,' Blackstone said. 'The Tsar has already signed it. He did so, I assume, in the Count's house.'

'Indeed.'

'But no one was supposed to know that. The official explanation of his visit was to be that he'd made it on a whim – that he had heard his uncle, the Prince of Wales, was staying there, and simply decided to spend some time with him.'

'Just so.'

'That would explain why there were so many soldiers already in the area at the time of the robbery.'

'The Tsar is so deeply loved by *all* his people that he never travels anywhere without a huge number of body-guards,' Vladimir said laconically.

'But once the robbery had occurred, it became necessary to do two things. The first was to get the Tsar away as quickly as possible. The second was to deny he had ever even been a guest of the Count. He left in such a hurry that the black paint which had been used to mask the imperial eagle crest on his carriage door hadn't even had time to dry.'

'Exactly.'

'What I don't understand is why the meeting had to take place at all,' Blackstone said. 'Couldn't the treaty have been signed more safely – and more secretly – in some anony-mous government building?'

'Yes, that is how it should have been done,' Vladimir admitted. 'The two foreign ministers – mine and yours – would have found some other pretext for a meeting, and the deal would have been done without the world being any the wiser. Simple! But that scenario does not take into account the actions and desires of our glorious leader, His Imperial Majesty, Nicholas II.'

'I think I need a little more of an explanation,' Blackstone said.

'And I will be pleased to provide it. Our tsar is like a little boy who has been given a great many toys to play with – toys which are far too difficult for him to under-stand. But when older, wiser heads try to explain them to him, he becomes angry and frustrated. And there is nothing the older, wiser heads can do about it, because – when all is said and done – they are *his* toys.'

'He wants to be a statesman,' Blackstone said.

'He believes that he already *is* one,' Vladimir replied. 'He *likes* most of his ministers, but he does not *trust* them. On the other hand, while he is not particularly fond of his uncle, the Prince of Wales, he *does* trust him. So when it comes to signing a treaty, he wants to do it himself, and he wants his uncle to receive it and take it back to England, where, he fondly imagines, that same uncle will hand it directly to the Queen.'

'And would he have done?'

'Of course not. Your queen is no tsar. It would have been handed over to your prime minister. And then the Queen would have been told about the treaty itself, but not about the circumstances under which it was signed.'

'Why did the Prince of Wales agree to go along with it?'

Vladimir smiled. 'Who knows the way the minds of great ones work?' he asked.

'You do,' Blackstone said. 'Or at least, you like to *think* that you do.'

'You are quite right, as always,' Vladimir agreed. 'Your royal family does not have as large a part to play in government as ours has, but it does have *some* part. Yet the Prince of Wales has been kept out of government all his adult life. Unlike his father, he is not allowed to see important cabinet papers. Now why do you think that is?'

'Because the government does not trust him?'

'Wrong! Your government is well aware that when the frail old lady who sits on your throne finally dies, it will be the Prince of Wales who takes her place. Your government is eager to start working with him – to start *training* him – as soon as possible. They have wanted to do so for many years, but the old woman will not allow it.'

'So he jumped at the chance to do something significant at last?'

'He most certainly did.'

'If the meeting was so important, why was the Duc de Saint-Cast permitted to be at the house when it was being held?'

Vladimir looked suddenly sheepish. 'That was my decision,' he admitted, 'though, of course, since I was not even supposed to know that the meeting was taking place, you will find no written evidence to tie me in with it.'

'Of course not,' Blackstone agreed. 'But you still haven't told me why you arranged for him to be there.'

'The best way to keep a secret is to display it openly, as if no secret exists,' Vladimir said. 'I was afraid that the French government would find out about the meeting, and draw the correct conclusions. But say I had already placed a Frenchman in the house – a notorious *roué* interested in no more than his own pleasure. If the French government chose to question him – as it undoubtedly would – he could report that the Tsar had arrived at the Count's house on a whim, and that there was nothing suspicious about it. He would report, in other words, not what had *happened*, but only what he had *seen*.'

'You underestimated him.'

'That is exactly what I did,' Vladimir agreed. 'The Duc somehow learned the true purpose of the Tsar's visit, and immediately saw a way to use it to his advantage. Or perhaps it was not his idea at all. Perhaps it was his lover, Henri Durant, who came up with the plan. He is, after all, the one with the criminal record.'

'What *sort* of criminal record?' Blackstone asked.

'He was a thief before he found his way to the Duc's bed – a thief with a genius for picking locks.'

Which explained how the pair managed to get into the Prince's bedroom, Blackstone thought.

'How long have you known about Durant?' he asked.

'Not long at all,' Vladimir admitted. 'I had a background investigation carried out on all the Count's guests, but the Duc has been very discreet about his little peccadilloes, and by the time I discovered that Mademoiselle Durant was, in fact, Monsieur Durant, you had already both *unmasked* him and *dispatched* him.'

'What would the Duc have done with the document?'

'I am not sure he had even made up his mind about that. But he had several tempting options open to him. He might, for example, have sold it to the French government.'

'And what would the French have done with it?'

'They would either have used it as a tool to put pressure

on us or as an inducement to Germany to draw it into an alliance with them against the wicked Russians and British. He might have sold it to the Germans, who would have used it for much the same purpose. Or perhaps he would have kept it, and used the threat of its disclosure to blackmail my government or yours. When you have a golden egg in your hands, there are so many uses you can put it to.'

'Even though you hadn't uncovered Durant's secret, did you still know for certain that it was the Duc who had stolen the document?' Blackstone asked.

'No. If I had have done, I would have seen to it that you were pointed in his direction from the very beginning. But the truth was, the theft could just have easily been carried out by any of the decadent Russian aristocracy who were in the house at the time of the robbery.' Vladimir smiled. 'You can't imagine how much I was itching to conduct the investigation myself.'

'But you couldn't, could you?'

'No, I couldn't. I spy on my own Tsar. I do not want to, but I cannot trust him to do the right thing. And if he does do something *wrong*, it must be corrected as soon as possible. So, both for his sake and for the sake of my country, I need to be aware of what he is doing. This, of course, can sometimes create a problem. I knew exactly what had happened at the house, but I was not supposed to know about the house *at all*. Thus, as so often happens, I was forced to work behind the scenes, prodding my chosen instrument in the direction I wished him to go. And in this case, my chosen instrument was you. You should be flattered.'

'You know I'm not,' Blackstone said.

Vladimir nodded. 'I suppose I do. What was it you once said to me? "A man does not have to run with the fox *or* the hounds. He always has the choice to stay at home and tend his vegetable garden." Isn't that it, more or less?'

'Something like that,' Blackstone agreed.

'Unfortunately, my friend, in order to protect that garden,

206

it is sometimes necessary to run with both the fox *and* the hounds.'

The train began to slow down again.

'Is this where you get off?' Blackstone asked. 'Or where we *both* get off?'

Vladimir stood up. 'I will be the only one,' he said. 'I am satisfied that you have not changed since we last met in London, which means, of course, that I do not have to rob you of your life. I hope you will believe me when I say that gives me a certain amount of pleasure.'

'I believe you,' Blackstone said.

The train juddered to a halt. Blackstone looked out of the window. There was no station or any other building in sight, but there was a coach, escorted by a group of soldiers.

'If I had my choice, I would gladly travel with you all the way to St Petersburg, but there is another piece of business I must conduct in this area,' Vladimir said regretfully.

'I see you have the army on your side,' Blackstone said.

'*Some* units in the army are on my side,' Vladimir replied, 'but there are others – more numerous – which would gladly see me dead. Still, though I walk a tightrope every day, I have not fallen off it yet.'

'I take it that Captain Dobroskok is one of those soldiers who supports you,' Blackstone said.

'What makes you think that?'

'Something about the way you moved just then.'

'Explain yourself.'

'The men who rescued me on the train from St Petersburg were wearing masks, but I'd be willing to swear that one of them was you.' Blackstone laughed. 'Why were you doing your own rough work, Vladimir? Because you don't have enough men under your command who you can rely on? Or because there is a part of you which is still enough of the schoolboy to enjoy the rough and tumble?'

'The latter,' Vladimir admitted. 'But what has this to do with Captain Dobroskok?'

'The fact that you were on that train means you must have arrived in the village after his cordon was thrown up.

207

I've seen that cordon for myself. It was very impressive. You'd never have got through it without the Captain's co-operation.'

'True,' Vladimir agreed. He opened the door and stepped down from the train. 'I would like to promise you that we will never meet again,' he called back up to Blackstone. 'I am sure that is what *you* would like me to say. But with the world the way it is, we both know that is not a promise I can ever be sure I would be able to keep.'

One of the soldiers who was part of the waiting escort was holding out an opened military greatcoat. Vladimir stripped the provincial-official's jacket he had been wearing, and dropped it carelessly on to the ground. That done, he slipped on the greatcoat. As he walked the few remaining yards to the coach, he had already become a different man.

The train began to move off again. Blackstone lit a cigarette and wished that the next few minutes of his life simply did not have to happen.

Thirty-Two

'Thank goodness he's gone,' Agnes said, when she returned from the sleeping compartment.

'Why should you say that?' Blackstone wondered.

'Because he frightens me.'

'Did he frighten you when he was Peter the Revolutionary?'

Agnes sat down in the chair opposite Blackstone's. 'Yes, I think he did even then,' she said. 'But I pushed my fear aside, because I believed in what he was doing – or, at least, I believed in what he was *pretending* to do – and I wanted to find out more about it.'

'It's strange that you should have sympathies with a revolution,' Blackstone said.

'Is it? Why?'

'Because of your background. You were brought up in an Army cantonment, where the two cardinal virtues are faith in the established order and the discipline to do whatever is necessary to protect it.'

'And are we always to be governed by what happened to us in our childhood?'

Blackstone thought of his own childhood in the slums and the orphanage, and about how – even now – his first loyalty was to the decent people of the East End of London.

'Childhood is certainly not something that anyone can lightly discard,' he said.

'Well, I have,' Agnes said firmly. 'Trust me on that.' She reached across the gap between them and squeezed his uninjured arm. 'I'm so looking forward to being in England. I won't need any revolution once we're there.'

'Will it be so easy to give it up?'

'Yes, because I'll have you, and that's a full-time occupation for any woman.'

'When exactly was it that you decided you'd like to come back to England with me, Agnes?' Blackstone asked, deliberately forcing a light and teasing note into his voice.

'I think it was probably the first time I saw you,' Agnes replied, looking at him adoringly.

'I'm not so sure it was,' Blackstone said. 'I'm not even sure it was *your* decision at all.'

Agnes smiled. 'You mean that the way you swept me off my feet left me with very little choice in the matter?'

Blackstone shook his head. 'No. I mean that I think it was probably Vladimir's decision.'

Agnes tensed – not much, but enough for Blackstone to notice. 'Vladimir?' she said. 'Who's Vladimir?'

'The man who just left the train.'

'I didn't know his name was Vladimir.'

'No, you possibly didn't,' Blackstone agreed. 'But you know him under at least one of his many other different aliases.'

'What are you talking about?' Agnes demanded. 'I may have met him as Peter the Revolutionary, but as far as I was concerned, when he got on the train he was a complete stranger to me.'

'Then why did you tell him this carriage was not for ordinary members of the public?'

'Because it *isn't* for ordinary members of the public.' She smiled again. 'It's for very *special* people. People like us. People who are in love – and who are going back to England to share a new life together.'

'You're missing the point,' Blackstone said, refusing to be seduced. 'You say that, to your knowledge, you'd never met him before, and that from the way he was dressed you took him to be a minor official.'

'Yes, all that's true.'

'Yet when you spoke to him, it was in *English*. Why did you assume that this unknown minor official would even *speak* English?'

'So I made a mistake,' Agnes protested. 'My mind was confused. It's been a confusing few days.'

'The way you talked about Peter the Revolutionary, it seemed to me you'd known him for at least a couple of weeks,' Blackstone said. 'Is that right?'

'*About* two weeks,' Agnes replied, on the defensive now.

'He travelled down from St Petersburg on the same train that I did,' Blackstone said. 'He probably reached the village even *after* I reached the Big House. You've not known him for only two weeks, Agnes. He's been visiting the village for much longer than that – probably ever since you were appointed governess to the Count's children.'

'And why would he do that?'

'To see you, of course. By disguising himself as a muzhik, he could meet you without anyone who really mattered noticing it. The peasants would have seen you, of course, but they would only have found it amusing that a lady from the Big House would come into the village to debate with a revolutionary.'

'This is incredible, Sam. I can't believe I'm actually hearing you say it.'

'And even if the Count *had* found out,' Blackstone ploughed on relentlessly, 'he would only have assumed that you had mild revolutionary tendencies. He might have dismissed you from your post, of course, but that wouldn't have mattered. You could have been transferred somewhere else easily enough, and a replacement brought in. The only important thing was that the Count should never suspect what you'd really been doing in the house – because then he would have been suspicious of whoever was sent to replace you as well.'

'And what *was* I doing in the house?'

'The Count is not just any old provincial aristocrat. He's a personal friend of the Tsar's. That gives him influence. That gives him power. And that makes him dangerous to people like Vladimir.'

'You still haven't explained—'

'You were there to *spy* on the Count – to report back to Vladimir on what he said and thought, and how that might affect the future of the country.'

'You're talking as if I were a member of the *Okhrana*!' Agnes protested. 'Whatever could have given you that preposterous idea?'

'You went out of your way to convince me that the golden egg – by which, of course, we both mean the document – was still in the house,' Blackstone said. 'Why did you do that?'

'Why don't *you* tell *me*?'

'It was in case I decided to give up looking for it. Throughout the whole of the investigation you were very carefully guiding me. And for what purpose?'

'Because I wanted to *help* you, Sam!'

'Because *Vladimir* wanted you to help me. Because I was doing his work for him.'

'This is ridiculous,' Agnes said. 'If this Vladimir *did* have an agent in the house, then it certainly wasn't me.'

'When the robbery occurred, you and the children were visiting friends of the family,' Blackstone said.

'Exactly!' Agnes said, as if she'd scored a point. 'Why would I have left the house at that important juncture if I'd actually been working for Vladimir?'

'Because you didn't have any choice. You were the children's governess, and you couldn't refuse to go with them without making the Count suspicious. But later – because Vladimir really needed you – you were prepared to risk even that. Only four people were allowed to pass through the military cordon. Two English policemen, one Russian spy – and you! For the moment at least, you were more important than a Grand Duke.'

'Sam . . .' Agnes pleaded.

'And if I needed any more proof, there's always the fire.'

'The fire?'

'Vladimir started it so that whoever had hidden the document would panic and attempt to retrieve it. But in order for his plan to work, there had to be someone there to watch what the guests did. Vladimir was in his peasant disguise, so he couldn't do it himself. He simply had to have an agent.'

'One of the servants might—'

'The servants were all busy fighting the fire. The watcher had to be someone who wasn't involved in that. A woman who was *almost* a lady. You!'

'It's not true!' Agnes protested.

They could go on like this for ever, Blackstone thought – accusation and denial, denial and accusation – but he was weary of discussing the fire, and it was time to move on.

'It wasn't *real* blood I found on the sheets the night after we made love for the first time, was it?' he asked.

'How could you say that? How could you even *think* that?' Agnes asked. 'I sacrificed the most precious thing a woman owns. For *you*! And it means nothing to you!'

'You played the virgin well. You played almost *everything* well,' Blackstone told her. 'But once one illusion's gone, the rest quickly fall away as well. You once said we should always be honest with each other, Agnes. Why won't you be honest with me now?'

Agnes's shoulders slumped, as she finally gave in to the inevitable.

'It was real blood,' she said, 'but not blood which had flowed from between my legs.'

'Whose idea was it to pretend that you were a virgin?'

Agnes sighed. 'Vladimir's,' she admitted. 'He has always been a great source of good ideas.'

'It was meant to help disguise what you really were,' Blackstone said. 'To make me think of you as an innocent, vulnerable young woman, rather than a hardened agent of the *Okhrana*.'

'And since you are a decent man, it was also intended to make you feel responsible for me,' Agnes said listlessly. 'To make you lose any doubts that you trusted me, since I so obviously trusted you.'

'How did you become involved with Vladimir? Did he recruit you before you came to Russia?'

'No. I really was a just a governess at first. But then I met Vladimir, and he told me I was wasting my talents. He said that despite the fact I was a woman, my background had given me a military mind, and that he could use such a mind.'

'And what was in it for you? Money?'

'Money certainly came into it. I had no wish to grow old and penniless, and live out the remainder of my life on the charity of my last employer. But if money had been my only motivation, Vladimir would never have recruited me. To work for him, you have to believe.'

'In what?'

'In order. In discipline. Empires exist for a purpose, and however ineffective they are, they are infinitely better than what would replace them. Under the Tsar, millions go to bed hungry every night. But if he ever falls, they will have no beds at all – and will starve to death. And if the Russian Empire is swept away, what is to stop other empires following? What is to stop the British Empire – for which my father gave his life – crumbling into dust?'

213

'You admire Vladimir in almost the same way you once admired your father, don't you?' Blackstone asked.

'Of course I admire him! How could anyone who knows him *not* admire him?'

'And have you slept with him?' Blackstone asked, surprised to detect a note of anger in his voice.

Despite the situation she found herself in, Agnes laughed. 'All men are the same – even you,' she said. 'You don't ask if I ever loved him as I love you now, only whether I ever slept with him. But I'll answer your question anyway. No, I have not slept with him, though I would have done if he'd asked me to.'

'Why *didn't* he ask you to? Did he find you *so* unattractive?'

'Was that meant to hurt?' Agnes asked.

Yes, Blackstone thought, surprising himself for a second time in only a few minutes. Yes, it was.

'I'm sorry, I should never have said that,' he told her.

'I don't think Vladimir finds *any* woman attractive in a physical way,' Agnes said. 'Nor, in case you are wondering, any man, either. I used to think there was something physically wrong with him.'

'And now?'

'And now I think he does not dare to admit attraction. Russia needs him to be strong, and so he cannot allow himself any normal human failings.'

'Why did Vladimir have Major Carlton killed?' Blackstone asked, changing tack.

'How do you know he did?'

'I didn't,' Blackstone said. 'At least, not until you just refused to give me a flat denial. But the indications were already pointing towards him.'

'What indications?'

'The only person who might have been interested in seeing Major Carlton dead was the Duc de Saint-Cast, and he had no Cossacks at his command.'

'Cossacks, like most other commodities, can be had with money.'

'If they'd been working for the Duc, they'd have killed me, too. Of all the people involved in this affair, only Vladimir had an interest in me staying alive.'

'And me,' Agnes said.

'But only because that was what Vladimir wanted. If he'd deemed it necessary to have me killed, you'd have gone along with it readily enough. Isn't that the truth?'

Agnes sighed wistfully. 'Think what you want to think,' she said. 'After all that's happened, there's nothing I can do to alter that.'

'So why *was* Major Carlton killed?' Blackstone persisted.

'He said that he was related to the Count, which was true. And that his visit to the Big House was a purely social one, which was a lie.'

'The British Foreign Office asked him to arrange to be there at the same time as the Prince and the Tsar?'

'That's right. The Russians have professional spies. You are forced to rely on enthusiastic amateurs like the Major.'

'You still haven't said why he was killed.'

'Vladimir was afraid that his blundering about would endanger the whole operation. And from what I saw, he was right. Why did the Major take you out onto the steppe, Sam? To brief you on what he had discovered himself?'

'And to express his fears about a future European conflict,' Blackstone said.

'That is what Vladimir meant when he talked about amateurs,' Agnes said dismissively. 'Why could he not have briefed you behind the stables? Because that setting was not dramatic enough for him! And what kind of man would expose himself to the dangers of the steppe when there was no need to. A foolish one!'

'And a brave one.'

'Brave or foolish, he is still dead.'

Now she had decided to drop all pretence, Agnes appeared to be speaking as frankly and openly as anyone possibly could, yet Blackstone sensed that she was still holding something back.

'There was a second reason for killing Major Carlton, wasn't there?' he said, taking a stab in the dark.

'What makes you think that?' Agnes asked – the evasiveness in her tone showing him that he was right.

'Vladimir's the kind of man who feels that an action which achieves only one result is a wasted action,' Blackstone said. 'What was the other result he expected from killing Carlton?'

Agnes sighed again. 'He thought you would partly blame yourself for Major Carlton's death. He believed you would turn your remorse into energy, and that that energy would be directed towards the investigation.'

'He killed Major Carlton to give me an *incentive* to solve the case?' Blackstone asked, hardly able to believe what he was hearing.

'Yes. And it worked, didn't it?'

Of course it did, Blackstone realized with true horror. Of course it bloody well did!

'I was right when I said earlier that it was Vladimir's decision you should come back to England with me, wasn't I?' Blackstone asked.

'I *want* to go back with you, Sam, my darling,' Agnes said. 'I know you don't believe it now when I say that I love you, but you will in time – because I'll find ways to prove it to you.'

'Nevertheless, it was Vladimir's decision,' Blackstone said unyieldingly.

'Nevertheless, it was Vladimir's decision,' Agnes agreed with him.

'Why? So you could spy on me, as you did on the Count?'

'No!'

'Tell me the truth!'

'He asked me to report to him if I discovered anything interesting,' Agnes admitted.

'Of course he did!'

'But he did not have any high expectations that I *would* have anything to report. Espionage and diplomacy are not your life, as they are his. This is nothing more than an

216

excursion to you, Sam. When you return to your humdrum work in Scotland Yard, you'll be of no further use to Vladimir – because he has no interest in the doings of London pickpockets and bank robbers.'

'So what *is* in it for him? Why *does* he want you to go back to London with me?'

'You don't understand him,' Agnes said, as tears – which Blackstone was sure she was not faking – suddenly began to pour from her eyes. 'You don't understand any of us. What we do, or why we do it! What we think, or what we feel!'

'So explain it to me.'

'I am Vladimir's *gift* to you. He believes I could make you happy, and I know that I could. But let's forget Vladimir, Sam. Let's pretend he never existed, and we're starting afresh. Neither of us has to be anybody's gift. We could be a gift to *each other*!'

The train began to pull into yet another small station. Blackstone stood up and walked over to the window.

'It won't work,' he said.

'Why?' Agnes asked, almost hysterical now. 'Because of what I've been in the past? I can change, Sam. Away from the pull of Russia – away from all the politics and intrigue – I can become a completely new person.'

'Then *do* get away from the pull of Russia,' Blackstone suggested. '*Do* become a new person. But you can't become it with me.'

'Why? Because of your foolish pride? Because Vladimir found me before you did?'

'Because of what he's taken from me in the past. Because if I accept his gift now, he'll have a hold over me for ever – and I can't allow that.'

Agnes took a handkerchief out of her bag, and dried her eyes.

'You're quite right, of course,' she said. 'Vladimir is hard enough to resist even if you're not in his debt.'

'I'll protect you as far as London,' Blackstone promised. 'Once we're there, I'll give you what little money I have. From that point, you're on your own.'

The train had come to a halt. Agnes stood up and walked over to the door. 'Thank you for your kind offer, but it will not be necessary,' she said. 'If I am not to be with you, then I'll stay in Russia.'

Her hand reached for the door.

'At least stay on the train until we reach St Petersburg,' Blackstone suggested.

'I would prefer to get off here,' Agnes said, almost primly.

'But we're in the middle of nowhere. There probably isn't a hotel here, and God alone knows when the next train will come through.'

Agnes opened the door and stepped down on to the platform. 'Please don't worry about me, Sam,' she said. 'It will not be long before Vladimir hears about me and comes to find me.'

She smiled bravely, without a hint of tears in her eyes. But the moment she had turned her back on him, he could tell she'd started to sob again. As she hurried towards the stationmaster's office, the train began to pull away.